Praise for the novels of Jude Deveraux

"Deveraux spins an intriguing and unorthodox romance... An entertaining page-turner."
—*Kirkus Reviews* on *Met Her Match*

"*Met Her Match* is vintage Jude Deveraux from start to finish, a joy to read."
—*Fresh Fiction*

"Deveraux's charming novel has likable characters and life-affirming second chances galore."
—*Publishers Weekly* on *As You Wish*

"With three stories told two ways, this third book in Deveraux's Summerhouse series (*The Girl from Summer Hill*, 2016, etc.) is emotional, imaginative, and gloriously silly."
—*Kirkus Reviews* on *As You Wish*

"Jude Deveraux's writing is enchanting and exquisite."
—*BookPage*

"Deveraux's touch is gold."
—*Publishers Weekly*

"A steamy and delightfully outlandish retelling of a literary classic."
—*Kirkus Reviews* on *The Girl from Summer Hill*

"[A]n irresistibly delicious tale of love, passion, and the unknown."
—*Booklist* on *The Girl from Summer Hill*

"[A] sexy, lighthearted romp."
—*Kirkus Reviews* on *Ever After*

"Thoroughly enjoyable."
—*Publishers Weekly* (starred review) on *Ever After*

JUDE DEVERAUX

Met Her Match

mira

Recycling programs for this product may not exist in your area.

ISBN-13: 978-0-7783-3141-4

Met Her Match

First published in 2019. This edition published in 2021.

Copyright © 2019 by Deveraux Inc.

This edition published by arrangement with Harlequin Books S.A.

For questions and comments about the quality of this book, please contact us at CustomerService@Harlequin.com.

Mira
22 Adelaide St. West, 40th Floor
Toronto, Ontario M5H 4E3, Canada
www.Harlequin.com

Printed in Lithuania

MIX
Paper from
responsible sources
FSC® C021394

Met Her Match

Chapter 1

Lake Kissel
Summer Hill, Virginia

Terri Rayburn was looking out the glass front of her house at the lake. She liked the early morning calm, the few moments she had alone before she had to... Well, start solving problems. As the daughter of the owner of a resort, it was her job to fix everything. Arguments, leaky roofs, finding things, organizing people and events. Any and all of it was *her* job.

Her eyes widened. A man in swim shorts was coming out of the lake. That wasn't an unusual sight, but this one wasn't like the usual renter or cabin owner. This man was different.

The sun was just rising, sending light across his body and making shadows on his muscles. He looked like a well-toned football player. His face was turned to the side so she couldn't really see it, but she was sure she didn't know who he was.

She liked that his shorts were modest. Too many visitors to the lake thought it was fashionable to wear as little as they legally could.

His was the kind of body she liked. She'd never been attracted to men who were thin. She liked them big and muscular, a man who could pick up a rowboat and move it around. One who looked like he knew what a pickup truck was for. A man who could hold you and—

She shook her head to quiet her thoughts. It had been too long since she'd had a boyfriend!

When he walked toward one of her deck chairs and retrieved a towel thrown across the back, she came back to reality. As great as the vision of him was, he should *not* be there! He was on *her* property! Using *her* chair. Why couldn't the visitors learn to respect private property? And why couldn't her dad ever remember to tell them the rules? If she hadn't been away for the last two days, she would have made sure this new visitor understood that he couldn't go swimming wherever he wanted to. There were other cabin owners and renters to consider.

So now it was her job to explain to the man that even though the houses surrounded a lake and everyone here wanted to have fun, there were still rules to be followed.

She took a step toward the glass doors, then paused. The man was drying off now and the sunlight was hitting his back. He was very broad in the shoulders and small at the waist. Muscles moved about under his tanned skin. He looked like he spent a lot of time doing something that made muscles.

Okay, so no matter how good he looked, she was going to have to bawl him out. He had no right to be on her property. He needed to go back to wherever he was staying.

But as she watched him, her mind wandered to a different scenario. It was an unspoken rule that she, the manager's daughter, couldn't date any of the visitors at the lake, but usually that was easy. Skinny boys in Speedos; lecherous husbands who thought she was fair game; unmarried men who believed every woman wanted them. They were all there and Terri wasn't interested.

But this guy… She really liked the look of him! The size, the shape, even his skin color were all her favorites.

He tossed the towel over his shoulder and turned to face the sun. His face wasn't beautiful. Not like those high-cheeked models you saw everywhere. His was a man's face, strong jawed, coated in black whiskers, and he had short dark hair. No nonsense. Nothing pretentious. The only thing soft-looking about him was his lips. They appeared to be very kissable.

Terri closed her eyes for a moment, telling herself to cut it out. He was a visitor and it was her job to take care of him in a professional way. She was *not* to fantasize about pouncing on him!

She put her hand on the door latch. It was time to be the warden and tell him he had to go back to his own cabin and— "What in the world?" she said aloud.

The man walked across the terrace and slid open the door at the other end. She heard the whoosh of the door as he entered *her* house.

Terri instantly knew what had happened. Her father, Brody, was at the bottom of this! She had no doubt whatsoever that he was trying to matchmake and introduce her to this man. "Damn!" she muttered. As if she didn't have enough problems to take care of.

Turning on her heel, she stalked down the hallway. There were two bedrooms on that end of the long, narrow house, one very small and the other one larger. It had floor-to-ceiling glass on two sides.

The man was standing at the end of the bed in the larger room, his hands on the waistband of his wet shorts, about to peel them off. He looked startled to see her.

"You can't stay here," Terri said. His eyes were a beautiful shade of blue. He was older than she'd first thought. Midthirties, maybe. The hair on his chest formed a pattern from a centerline. He certainly wasn't a *boy*! She noted that he wore no wedding ring. *Not* that it mattered.

"I'm sorry," he said. "I was told the owner of the house was in Florida."

Nice voice. Really nice. Really, *really* nice. Terri's anger vanished. "Technically, that's true. My aunt owns the house, but I…" She straightened her shoulders. Why didn't she brush her hair when she woke up? Why did she always have to wear baggy, slouchy clothes?

"Are you Terri?" he asked.

"I am."

The man gave a nod of understanding. "This mistake is from my uncle. He mentioned that Terri might be staying in the house, but I thought that was the owner's name and that she spent most of her time in Florida." He gave Terri a quick glance up and down. "I'll be out of here in minutes." He walked to the closet, pulled out a canvas duffel bag and put it on the bed.

"Your uncle?"

"Kit Montgomery. Do you know him?"

"He and my dad are friends," Terri said. "Why would he put you in my house? There are lots of cabins available. My dad is a Realtor and he handles all that."

The man pulled some shirts from the closet and tossed them on the bed. "I've not met your father, but I know

Kit wants me to like Summer Hill since I'm going to be moving here. He said I should spend my first three weeks here at the lake instead of in town. I guess he didn't want to condemn me to staying in a house alone." He shoved some shoes into the bag, then looked at her. "I just want to say that this is a great house. I've been here two nights and I like the glass front, the water, all of it."

Terri knew that in the nearly two years that Kit Montgomery had been in town, he and her father had become great friends. "Thick as thieves," as the saying went. The first winter Kit lived in Summer Hill, he and Brody had spent a lot of time plotting together. At least that's how Terri thought of it. When Kit bought an old warehouse, remodeled it into a theater and put on a play in an attempt to win the woman he loved, Brody had been involved in every part of it. From buying the warehouse, to hiring construction workers, to casting the play, Brody had helped. When Kit got the girl, there had been several champagne corks popped.

As Terri watched the man pack, she considered the idea that Kit and her dad were again plotting—and this time, it was about her.

She looked at the man's bare back as he reached up to the top of the closet and thought that her dad had certainly had worse ideas than this one. "You want some breakfast?"

Turning, he smiled at her—and Terri felt herself softening. Oh yeah, there were a lot worse things than having this man as a…as a roommate.

"Only if I'm allowed to cook it," he said.

Terri smiled broadly. The men she'd known in her life couldn't work a can opener. But then, Terri wasn't much more advanced in that department. "Gladly. I hope you like Raisin Bran and I think the milk is still good."

"I went to the grocery," he said, then paused. He seemed to be waiting for something.

It took her a moment to understand. "Sure. Get dressed. I will too." She backed out of the room, hoping she sounded like this wasn't what she wore every day. Since she spent her life dealing with boats and motors and kids who thought "vacation" meant not bathing, she didn't try to be a fashion plate.

As soon as she was out of his sight, she ran past the kitchen and down the hall to her bedroom. In the closet by her bathroom were three plastic baskets stacked on top of each other and filled with dirty clothes. Why hadn't she done the laundry before she left!

Because two days ago, her father had given her the impression that if she didn't immediately go to Richmond and pick up the new life jackets, he might have a stroke.

"Have them FedExed," she'd said. She had three boats to see to, someone said a barbecue grill was down, a raccoon was getting into the garbage of number eighty-four, number eleven had a broken window and Moonlight Beach had used condoms scattered across it. She did not have time to go to Richmond!

But then Elaine twisted her ankle and couldn't drive and there were six boxes of dresses that needed to be picked up. She acted like adding to her already-packed dress shop immediately was the most important thing on earth.

Terri had glared at her dad and his girlfriend, Elaine. "You two haven't heard of delivery services? Get Anna to call—" She broke off at the sight of them. They wore identical pleading expressions.

So Terri drove to Richmond and when nothing was ready, she checked into a motel. While she waited, she saw a movie, went to a boat showroom, spent hours in a bookstore and generally enjoyed herself. She didn't get back until late last night.

That's why she hadn't done the laundry. She rummaged through drawers and pulled out a T-shirt and shorts. Not too tight; not too short. Just because a gorgeous man was in her kitchen, she wasn't going to tart herself up.

Okay, a bit of mascara, a comb through her hair. She looked in the mirror. She was always being told she looked like an "all-American girl." Right now she'd like to be a little more… Well, sultry. Exotic. Interesting.

She took a breath, dabbed on some lipstick and left her bedroom.

He was in the kitchen, his back to her, and looking down at two skillets on the gas stove. Terri hadn't been aware there was even one skillet in the cupboards. "What can I do to help?"

"Nothing," he said. "Just have a seat. You like eggs?"

"Sure. Anything." She sat down on a stool on the other side of the island. He wore a blue cotton shirt that looked like it had been washed many times, and jeans. On his left wrist was a black bracelet braided out of something. Horsehair, maybe?

He poured a mug of coffee, set it in front of her, then waited for her to taste it.

"Wow. You didn't get this from any store in Summer Hill."

With a smile, he turned back to the stove. "I brought beans with me. So what do you do around here?"

"You mean for work?" She waited for his nod. "Every-thing. If it breaks, someone calls me to fix it. I jump in the lake about twice a day to save some idiot who falls off a dock. Oh! Sorry. I mean I help the people who stay at Lake Kissel have a good time without visiting the emergency room."

"Or calling Dr. Jamie?" He put an omelet and toast in front of her.

"This looks great. Either Jamie or Dr. Kyle. Summer Hill now has *two* doctors. We've come up in the world. But you said you're going to live here so maybe you know about us." He was cooking eggs for himself but he was adding spices from little jars that were along the countertop. They hadn't been there before he arrived.

"Jamie is my first cousin. His dad and mine are brothers and I'm going to be working for Jamie's dad and an uncle."

"Doing what?"

He shrugged. "Money things."

She didn't think he sounded too enthusiastic about his coming job.

He picked up his plate of eggs and toast and walked toward her. "You mind if we move to…?" He nodded toward the dining table around the corner.

When she looked up at him, she knew he wanted to sit so he'd be facing the water. It's where she liked to be too. That they agreed made Terri smile—on the inside. She didn't want him to see it. Too early for that!

He sat at the head of the table, facing the view out to the lake, and Terri took the chair to his right.

"Who designed this house?" he asked.

"My dad's sister, Agnes. She drew it on the ground. Said she wanted to see the water from every room. She drew an octagon, with two rectangles jutting out the sides. She's a great cook so she wanted a long island where she

could serve guests. She used to invite lots of people here."
Terri looked around the place. She still missed her aunt
very much.

"But now she's in Florida?" His voice was encouraging, as though he wanted to hear more.

"Last year she had a small stroke, not debilitating, but
enough that Dad didn't want her living alone. I think he
meant for me to move in with her, but Aunt Aggie said I
needed my own life." Terri shrugged. "Anyway, she moved
to Florida to live with her late husband's widowed sister.
I think they have parties every day and drink margaritas
by the gallon."

He laughed. "Sounds good."

"Um, by the way, what's your name?"

"Sorry! Didn't I say? Nathaniel Taggert. Nate."

"Right. Like Dr. Jamie Taggert. I'm Terri Rayburn."
She held out her hand and they shook. He didn't have the
soft palm of a money person.

Nate pulled his hand away and looked back out the
glass front. "I get the impression that your dad has been
here since the beginning."

"He has. The Kissel family owned the lake and the surrounding land for over a hundred years. It's great farm-
land. There were a few cabins for the locals, but not many.
But the last generation, Bob Kissel and his wife, had no
children so they decided to make a community."

"And your dad helped?"

"Yes. It was one of those cosmic happenings. Dad came
to Summer Hill to visit an old army buddy and they were
planning to set up a construction company. One night at
dinner, Mr. and Mrs. Kissel were at a table next to them,
overheard it all, and they began to talk. By the end of the
meal, Dad and his friend had been hired." Terri smiled.

"It was a great match. The four of them got on well. And Aunt Aggie was widowed when I was little, so she came here to live and she handled the bookkeeping."

"And now your dad still runs the place. What about your mother?"

"She died when I was two." Terri didn't meet his eyes.

For a moment they sat in silence, both of them looking out at the lake, coffee mugs in hand. Maybe she was reading too much into it, but she felt comfortable around this man. Usually, she was running out the door to do whatever had to be done. Since she'd been away for nearly forty-eight hours, she had no doubt that her father's secretary, Anna, would have a long list of things for her to do.

But Terri didn't feel any urgency to leave to deal with raccoons and garbage and whatever gross stuff was littering one of their two beaches.

She took a breath. "There are about six cabins vacant right now and you could rent one of them." There were birds flying across the lake and the sun made beautiful shadows on the water.

"What do the cabins look like?"

"The usual. Two of them have porches along the front."

"But no glass-walled bedrooms?"

"Not a one. In the winter the sun is lower and it comes all the way across my floor."

"If I promise to be quiet and respectful and do all the cooking, could I rent the bedroom in this house? I'll pay double whatever you usually ask."

Terri was pleased at the idea, but she suppressed her smile. "I don't know… We have our yearly festival coming up and rents are pretty high."

"You have a month's worth of laundry that needs doing. I could help with that." When she looked startled, Nate gave a half smile. "Sorry. I looked around a bit, but not enough to figure out that the manager's sister wasn't living here but his daughter is. You think my uncle and your dad were up to something with this?"

"Oh yes. Definitely." Terri could feel her eyes growing warm with the thought of what the two matchmaking old men had in mind.

But Nate quickly looked away. "Maybe Kit wants me to help you with all the work around this place. Rescuing idiots, that kind of thing."

When Terri looked back toward the glass, she was smiling. "I'm sure that's it. Today I have to tell some Enders that they need to keep the lids on their garbage cans closed, and no, we will not shoot the raccoons." She looked back at him, at his shoulders straining against the soft cotton shirt. "You're big enough that if you told them, they might listen."

"You allow firearms here, do you?" He was frowning. "And who are 'Enders'?"

"Guns are not permitted. But then, perfectly sane people come here and they drink and party and cause as much trouble with a BB gun as someone with a twelve gauge. *Enders* is our name for people who come for the weekend. There are also Rounders and Players. Rounders are—"

"Let me guess. They stay year-round. So who or what are 'Players'?"

"They live elsewhere, but spend the summer here. Some are retired, but a lot of them are families with one person who earns the money. He or she is away during the week."

"And the ones left here like to play?"

"They do."

"You have activities for them?"

"There are some things for the kids, but the adults usually entertain themselves."

Nate looked at her, but Terri kept her gaze straight ahead. Explaining what the Players did was too embarrassing.

"Players. I get it."

Terri put her empty mug down. "Did you say something about three weeks?"

"Yes. That's when Stacy gets back. She has a booth at your festival and she wants me to get it ready for her. She shipped back a tent and I'm supposed to put it up."

Terri blinked at him. "Stacy?"

Standing, Nate collected the dirty dishes. "My fiancée, Stacy Hartman. She's in Italy now, but she'll be back in three weeks, so I wouldn't be here for very long." He turned away to go into the kitchen.

For a few moments Terri sat utterly still. How stupid could a person be? She'd thought the man was put into her house for... Well, for *her*.

She'd thought her father and his friend, Kit Montgomery, had been so concerned about her complete and total absence of a personal life that they'd sent her a gift. One tall, gorgeous man wrapped in a pair of wet swim shorts. It had seemed so obvious that they might as well have put a bow around his neck.

She buried her face in her hands. Stupid and naive. She was living in a fantasy world of glorious men appearing on her doorstep.

"Are you okay?" Nate asked.

She looked up. The sunlight was behind him, making a golden halo around his head. The damned shirt matched his damned eyes! The lake had never been as blue as this man's eyes were.

"I'm fine," she said. "I have a lot to do today and I'm late." She stood up. "I need to go. I just have to get my red notebook." She went to the couch to look for it, but when she turned around, he was so close she could feel the warmth of him. She did *not* look up into his eyes. Instead, she kept her head down and took three steps back. "Notebook. In office," she managed to say.

Turning, she hurried toward the front, slid the door open and ran out to the dock. Within seconds, she was in her pretty little wooden boat, had started the motor and was moving toward Club Circle.

When she looked back at her house, she saw Nate Taggert standing on the dock. Even from this distance she could see his puzzlement.

She truly hoped this man was unaware of what was going on.

Chapter 2

As Nate watched the young woman speed away in her nifty little boat as though she were leading a race at Monte Carlo, he grabbed his phone out of his pocket. As well as he knew anything on earth, he was sure Kit Montgomery had done this.

He called Kit's private number, the one only four people in the world knew. After years of being at the man's beck and call, Nate deserved access at all times.

Of course Kit didn't answer. Nate hadn't expected him to, but he was going to leave a voice mail the man wouldn't soon forget. "What are you up to?" Nate shouted, then lowered his voice as he walked back toward the house. "I know you did this, but *why*? You like Stacy. No, you *love* her. You introduced us, so why are you dangling another woman in front of me? Why did you—"

He broke off. There was no way in the world a man as stubborn and as sure that he was always right as Kit Montgomery was would listen to the message. Nate had seen Kit erase unheard voice mails from the President of the US. "Why should I listen? The bastard's always dead wrong," Kit had said.

Nate stopped in front of the house and calmed his breathing, slowed his heart rate. He'd learned how to do that the first year he worked for Kit. "If we go in there with your heart hammering in your oversize chest, they'll know we want this," Kit said.

"Doesn't our being here tell them that?" Nate had asked, and Kit responded by making Nate stand outside the door and wait—and miss all the action.

Now it was second nature to him to not show any trace of emotion. It had been very useful this morning when a tall, very pretty girl with a mass of brown hair tumbling about her head had walked into his bedroom. He'd been so deep in the thought of *What the hell am I going to do for three weeks?* that he hadn't heard her approach.

Nate had been in the house for two days but he'd spent most of the time with Jamie and his new wife.

Stacy's parents had said that he should stay with them, but they all knew no one wanted that. He'd told them he wanted to be at the lake so he could fish and rest and have a vacation. The truth was that he needed time to get over his anger at Stacy. The plan had been for them to be together for these weeks. But the day before he left DC, she'd told him that she'd won an internship in Italy with some big shot interior designer. "It's only for three weeks," she said over the phone. "I'll be back for Widi-wick and after that we can start planning our wedding. I'm dying to show you the office I set up for you. And I have a fabulous surprise from Dad."

"This is all the surprise I can handle," Nate had said gloomily. The thought of spending three weeks living in the same house as Stacy's parents was enough to make him jump on a military helicopter and go back to a war zone.

Of course Kit picked up on Nate's misery. You couldn't hide emotions from someone you'd spent years with and who'd taught you how to hide them in the first place. "I'll take care of it," Kit said in his best fatherly voice. "My friend Brody is the manager for all of Lake Kissel and his older sister owns a house there. She's in Florida and we all miss her. She was always cooking and making people feel at home. Terri might be there, but there are three bedrooms, so you'll be fine."

Nate leaned back against a tree. Why hadn't he been suspicious? He knew Kit had a silver tongue. He could twist anything around so it was true—but it also said exactly what he wanted it to. In this case, he'd made it sound as though Terri was Brody's sister and she was in Florida.

As Nate looked at the house, he felt sad at leaving it. Since he'd spent so much of the last twelve years living in tents, the glass-fronted house, with its indoor/outdoor feel, appealed to him.

He ran his hands over his face. He needed to man up to this. He couldn't possibly stay here. Terri was much, much too pretty. She looked like one of those girls who played baseball with the boys—and won. She probably used live bait on fishing hooks and—

Nate pushed away from the tree. He'd better end this now. Immediately. He knew she'd been attracted to him. And forgive him, but he'd felt the same about her. Her legs! They must be four feet long. Tanned. Strong.

Again, Nate calmed his breath. Quickly, he went through the house. When he grabbed his keys, he saw a red notebook that had fallen to the floor. He picked it up and hurried to his car. The passenger seat had one of his big green Dartmouth rugby shirts on it and there was a matching mug on the floor.

As he backed out of the drive, he hoped that when he told her he couldn't stay that she wouldn't get teary. He'd had girls do that. "I thought we had something between us," they'd said.

He and Terri had spent little time together, but he'd felt her interest in him. Seen her flirty looks.

And when he'd told her about Stacy, she'd nearly exploded. Jealousy?

As Nate pulled into the parking lot of the Lake Kissel clubhouse, he had a horrible thought. What if she and Stacy were friends? What if Terri told Stacy that they'd had a sort of flirtation? Spent some "meaningful" time together? But then, what could Terri say about their time together?

He got out of the car. *I'll be nice when I let her down*, he thought. *Gentle. It'll be easy, friendly. And once it's done, I'll run back to the house and get the hell* out *of it!*

Terri threw open the door to Anna's office, but the secretary didn't look up.

"Where is he?" Terri demanded.

Anna just slanted her head toward Brody's closed office door. She'd worked for father and daughter for fifteen years and she was used to their arguments. Although, since Elaine had arrived four years ago, the storms were quieter from Brody's side.

Terri stopped in front of the desk. "Remember that photo Della gave us of Stacy Hartman and the guy she's going to marry?"

"No," Anna said, and finally looked up. Terri's face

was red with anger. That wasn't unusual, but the fact that she had on makeup and her hair was combed was very unusual. "Della probably put it on the Shame Board."

One wall of the office had an eight-foot-long bulletin board where people pinned photos. It hadn't been the plan, but it had become a place to exhibit every embarrassing, nearly fatal, humiliating picture taken at the lake. If a girl turned too fast and her top popped open, you can bet a photo of it was on the board.

Terri only looked at it when she was trying to figure out things, like who stole flowers or fishing gear or any petty crime.

She scanned them all, then started lifting photos to see what was under them. She was annoyed to see six pictures of herself bending over. Butt shots of Terri seemed to be a favorite. "Someone should clean this thing up."

"Not my job," Anna said by rote. She'd learned that if she didn't refuse to do things she'd be like Terri and given responsibility for *all* of it.

"Ah ha!" Terri snatched a photo from beneath three others. She stared at it for a moment, then held it in front of Anna. "Know who this is?"

It was a picture taken at what looked to be a formal dinner. A young, very pretty blonde woman was leaning toward a large, handsome man wearing a tuxedo. He had his arm around her in a possessive way. "It's the mayor's daughter and some guy in a monkey suit. What a dress! I wonder where she buys her clothes."

"Not in Summer Hill, that's for sure. That man!" Terri tapped her finger on the picture. "He's living in *my* house. I woke up this morning and there he was."

"In your bedroom? Can I stay there tomorrow night and make a wish?"

With a look of disgust, Terri took the picture, pulled the door to her father's office open and slammed it behind her.

"I didn't do it," Brody said. He wasn't as tall as his daughter and the years had thickened his waist, but he was a good-looking man with salt-and-pepper hair. He and his daughter had the same eyes. They were a deep shade of brown that could go from softness to hardwood in seconds.

Right now Brody was uninterested in whatever his daughter was angry about. "Did you put the life jackets in the dock room?"

Terri was standing by the door. "You sent me to Richmond so you could move a man into my house."

Brody was going over a stack of invoices. "I think we need a new vendor for the ropes. This one is getting too expensive." He looked up at his daughter. "Yeah, so? Kit said the poor guy needed some peace and you needed some time off. He's only there for three days. So what's the problem? The old guy drooling in his soup?"

Terri tossed the photo onto his desk. "This look familiar?"

Brody picked it up and studied it. "He looks like Billy. That's still bothering you after all these years?"

Terri narrowed her eyes at him.

"Okay, don't look at me like that!" He looked back at the photo, knowing that he needed to cover his earlier mistake. Billy was *not* to be mentioned. "Isn't this Mayor Hartman's daughter? She has a booth this year, doesn't she? She's the cause of your anger? If so, where you gonna put her? Out on the Island?" It was his attempt at a joke. A booth set up on the little Island wouldn't get much foot traffic.

Terri didn't smile.

Brody sighed, put the photo down and leaned back in his chair, arms across his chest. "Okay, I'm sorry. Kit asked a favor of me. He wanted me to send you away so his old friend could stay there for three days. I offered another cabin, but Kit said Aggie's is the nicest. Anyway, you got a holiday and an old man had a place to stay. Now we're done. Could you go see about the mess on Moon?"

Terri put her finger on Nate in the photo. "*That* is the man staying in *my* house. And he's there for three *weeks*, not days. And he's going to marry Stacy Hartman."

Brody picked up the photo, looked at Nate and gave a smile. "That old devil, Kit," he muttered, then looked up at his daughter's angry face. "He was there when you woke up? So what'd you say? We have to stop meeting like this?"

"This is not funny."

"It is, actually. If this guy's engaged, why did Kit pair him up with you?"

"He's *your* friend, so you tell me!" Terri nearly shouted.

Brody was looking at the photo. "What's this guy's name?"

"Nathaniel Taggert."

"Ah. There's your answer. Kit mentioned him. They used to work together. Obviously, he wanted the boy to be around family, not stuck in a cabin by himself. I hope he doesn't expect you to cook for him." Brody looked alarmed. "You didn't cook anything, did you? He doesn't deserve—"

"I am not a babysitter," Terri said through her clenched teeth. "I know about this guy. Della told us about him."

Brody rolled his eyes. "Della Kissel tells us about everybody. The Gossip Queen. Since when did you ever listen to her?"

"Since the last time she said she was going to have you fired."

"She can't. The trust says—"

Terri clenched her fists. "I'm not getting into your fights with Della. She knows about this because she helped Stacy's mother sew the costumes for Kit's play and—"

"Wasn't that a *great* show? Of course after the first night, they had someone else playing Wickham and it wasn't as good, but—"

"Stop it!" Terri yelled. "You're trying to distract me from the subject. This guy is worthless! He's engaged to Stacy Hartman."

Brody looked confused. "I never knew you disliked her. You've never said anything bad about her. Did she…?"

Terri began to pace. "Stacy is perfect. Always has been. She's a flawless human being. I went to school with her from the first grade to the twelfth and I doubt if we ever exchanged even a dozen words. But why should we? Hers is the ruling family of Summer Hill, while mine is—" Terri glanced at her father. There were some places they didn't go no matter how angry they got. "Stacy Hartman is so wonderful even the principal consulted her."

"That's because he was friends with her father and—" Brody looked at his daughter's face. "Okay, so what's wrong with her?"

"If she likes this guy, then everything is wrong with *him*. Since he has to live up to her standards, that means he's rich. Ivy League school all the way. From the size of him, my guess is that he played that game… It's like American football but our teams have enough sense to wear padding."

"Rugby." Brody had dropped his arms and was looking at his daughter with interest. She was deeply and sincerely riled up about something. "I don't mean to be profoundly stupid here, but what exactly is your complaint about this guy?"

Terri stopped pacing. "I don't know. It's just everything, I guess. They're all alike. He's a money person. Probably moves Daddy's millions around. I wonder if he's ever been on a boat that didn't have a crew and a captain. I bet he'd squeal if he had to use live bait on a hook."

Brody was watching his daughter. Usually, the incompetence of the people around them made her laugh. At the end of a trying day, they'd sit in the big chairs at Aggie's house, beers in hand, look out over the water and laugh about it all.

But right now, there was something genuinely bothering her. He picked up the photo on his desk. Good-looking man, muscles straining against his clothes. Looked like he did flyes with boat motors. And Brody knew he was the only kind of man his daughter ever looked at twice.

Terri was saying how this guy probably only ate off china and silver—which may or may not be inside of Aunt Aggie's cabinets. Terri said she wasn't an overly domestic kind of female, so how did she know what was in there?

When Brody looked back at his daughter more carefully, he saw that she was wearing lipstick. Not like Elaine wore it so that a man couldn't keep his eyes off her lips, but there was some.

She likes him, Brody thought. Whatever happened this morning, his daughter *liked* this man. Then she'd found out he was engaged to cute, vivacious, everybody-loves-her Stacy Hartman. The mayor's daughter might be considered the Summer Hill Princess in the town, but at the lake—and in Brody's heart—Terri was the one who mattered.

On the desk were three listings for available cabins. Since Widiwick was just weeks away, he knew he'd rent all of them, but right now they were empty.

Terri was saying that Nate Taggert would probably

spend the whole three weeks drinking beer with his frat brothers who would fly in from Connecticut. When she turned away, Brody slipped the papers into his desk drawer.

She whirled around to face her father. "Put him in the Camlock place. He and his frat brothers can get drunk and trash it and there won't be much loss. But even if there is, I'm sure his daddy will pay for it all."

"It's been rented." Brody was hoping his eyes didn't show his lie. "Every cabin is taken."

"You're kidding."

"There was a flurry of activity while you were gone and I rented everything." He knew he was talking too fast. "Maybe this man can get his dad to *buy* him a place. I've got several that—"

"No! He's not staying here. The lake is just a diversion for him so he can see how the other half lives. I'm sure Stacy is grooming him to become mayor. If they have a cabin it will be in Italy. Or the South of France. Certainly not *here*." Terri sat down on a chair. "I'll just have to tell him that he can't stay at the lake."

"Or charge him rent."

"He said he'd pay double what I usually charge. As if I live in a boardinghouse!"

"Double, huh? How's your new car fund going? Is your roof still leaking? Did you fix those broken tiles in the front?"

Terri glared at her father.

Brody threw up his hands. "I understand. You can't—" His eyes widened. "Wait a minute! This guy didn't come on to you, did he? Did he make a pass at you?"

"Of course not. He cooked breakfast for me. We sat at the dining table and talked. He…" She trailed off.

"You don't think you could put up with him for just three weeks? The money would be useful. You know that I'd lend you some, but you said—"

"No! I mean, no to your giving me money. I earn my own way."

"You're only there at night." He was looking at her expectantly.

"Maybe," she said as she stood up. "*You* talk to him. I have a lot of work to do. You get Moon cleaned up?"

"Yeah, but it was, uh, littered again."

Terri grimaced. "We got them to clean up after their dogs, so why can't they clear up after themselves?"

Brody smiled. "Why don't you invent a different kind of pooper-scooper? One for what people leave behind on the beaches. You could go on that TV show and get somebody to invest in it. You'd make millions."

Terri gave a tiny smile. "Beach owners the world over would love me."

"Not difficult to do," Brody said.

"Thanks." She put her hand on the door. "Okay, I'll do it for the money. But you do the negotiating. I'm planning to stay away from him."

"I have a couch," he said.

"I may use it." Terri left the office, closing the door behind her.

Anna didn't look up. "Here," she said as she held out a list of things Terri had to do.

"Oh goody. What's in store for me to do today?"

"Same as always. Just because you were gone doesn't mean anyone else did your jobs. The Farleys are threatening to use a rifle if you—"

"Don't do anything about whatever their problem is,"

Terri finished. "Sure. I'll get on it." She was looking down the list. "Anything important?"

"I found your notebook." Anna nodded toward the little table by the wall.

Terri looked at it in puzzlement. She'd had it with her when she was in Richmond and she'd jotted down some boat prices. Since she'd gone straight home, how did the notebook get into Anna's office? "How did—"

"Yeah, I'll be there!" Anna yelled toward Brody's office, then stood up and looked at Terri. "Anything else you need from me or are you going to spend the day in here looking at pictures on the wall?"

"No, I—" She didn't say more because Anna went into Brody's office and closed the door behind her.

"What a weird day," Terri said.

By lunchtime, she didn't know if she was angry or ready to laugh. Everything on her list had already been done. The heavy grill that had fallen had been set upright. Bungee cords were holding down the lids to garbage cans. Two boat motors had been fixed. A glass repairman had been called for a window. Calling servicemen was something the residents never did for themselves. Why should they since Terri and her toolbox were at their beck and call? A child's bicycle had been found. Poison ivy vines had been pulled off a tree. Four boys were having a loud discussion about how rugby was a better sport than American football.

The answer that Terri heard to her every question was, "Nate." He fixed it; he said it; he suggested it; he showed them how. Mostly it was, "Nate did it." With his superhuman strength, he'd lifted the iron barbecue grill. With his extraordinary intelligence, he'd figured out how to lock the garbage can lids down. This was said as Terri stood there with bungee cords in her hand.

"He was great," said Mrs. Williams. Her husband only visited every other weekend. "Nate used my phone and called a local repairman. He should be here— Oh! There he is now. Isn't Nate just fabulous?" She ran toward the van pulling into her driveway.

"He can use a phone," Terri muttered. "Truly gifted man."

A little girl on a pink bicycle rode by and waved at Terri. "Nate found my bike," she called.

Terri put on a smile. "I bet it was on Timmy Gresson's porch because he wanted you to visit him," she said under her breath.

"Timmy had it," the girl called over her shoulder.

With an eye roll, Terri went back to her boat. There was one more thing on her list. The Coldmans needed their huge cabin cruiser on its long trailer put into the water. Mr. Coldman, an attorney, couldn't back up a trailer to save his life, so someone in the office—meaning Brody or Terri—had to back it up for him.

When she pulled up at the dock, the big boat was already in the water. Mrs. Coldman waved and called out, "Thanks for sending Nate to help us. Is he your boyfriend?"

"No," Terri shouted back. "He's not."

"Too bad. If I weren't already married I'd go after him." She laughed as though she was the only person to ever have said that cliché.

Terri managed to give a weak smile and a wave, then she turned her boat toward home. But when she got halfway across the water, a wicked little smile transformed her face. She went from anger to smirking. Turning around, she headed back to Club Circle.

Mr. Nathaniel Taggert wanted to play games, did he? Well, let the best woman win!

Chapter 3

Terri was sitting in the wooden chair in front of her house, sipping a beer and looking out over the dark water. It was nearly 9:00 p.m. when she heard the glass door behind her open. *Ah,* she thought, *wonder if he's tired.* She repressed a snicker.

She didn't take her eyes off the water as Nate plopped down in the chair next to hers. Even though she didn't look at him, she could smell him: sweat, grease, old oil, years of dust and grime.

She made an effort to hide her smile but only half succeeded. Without so much as a glance at him, she reached into the cooler beside her, withdrew an icy cold bottle of beer and handed it to him.

Nate drained it in one go, and she handed him another one. When it was half-empty, she passed a paper bag of burritos to him. He ate the first one in three bites.

"Smugness chokes a person," he said, his mouth full. "Too much of it and you die on the spot. And you can't be buried in hallowed ground."

Terri couldn't contain her laughter—and when she looked at him, it increased. There were cobwebs clinging to his shirt and in his hair. Not clean, new cobwebs, but the kind that were so filthy the spiders had abandoned them.

"Go on," he said. "I deserve it."

"If it helps, Dad said you did a great job. Better than I would have. And best of all, you didn't complain about having to do it. No siree bob, you cleaned that whole workshop all by your little self. Dad said you even cleaned under that old transmission. How'd you move it?"

Nate was on his third burrito. He didn't say anything, just held up his arm and flexed a bicep.

"Ooooh," Terri said. "Impressive."

He held out his hand and she gave him another beer. "So when'd you figure it out?"

"It was the notebook and Anna acting like she was downright eager to do anything my dad wanted. You heard it all?"

"Every word you yelled to your father went through my ears. Kind of like a verbal machine gun going off."

Terri felt guilty at what she'd said and opened her mouth to apologize.

"Don't," Nate said. "It was all true. Or used to be, anyway. My first two years in college I had a second major in beer drinking. I set records in my fraternity. I was world-class."

"Yeah?" Terri was smiling as she sipped her own beer. The lake was Y-shaped and her house was at the fork. With a bit of twisting and turning, they could see all of it. At one end a flashlight was moving along the path that ran beside the water. A rowboat with a light on the end was stealthily going southward. "So what made you stop drinking—or did you?" She nodded toward the empty bottles on the little table in front of them.

"This indulgence is a rarity. Brought on by having to clean out an eighteen-foot-long boat repair shop all by myself."

"And I thank you for it. It's been years since anyone could get farther inside than three feet. I hear the place is now so clean it could be used as a cafeteria."

"I just wanted to prove to you that I could actually *do* things."

"And I wanted to get out of having to clean that mess."

Nate held his bottle out to her and they clinked. "We both got what we wanted."

"So we did. What I want to know is what happened in your third year of college."

"Ah. That. The summer after the second year, I went home to Colorado and slept. Since I'd done little but party all year long, I was worn-out. I was on the couch, half-asleep, and when I opened my eyes, my dad was staring down at me. He said, 'We all make choices about what we want to do with our lives.' Then he stuck a finger in my belly—which was pretty soft."

"Then what?"

Nate shrugged as he wadded up the paper from the fourth burrito. "That was it. I took some summer courses at the University of Colorado, and when I went back to Dartmouth, I changed my major to business."

"All from one comment from your dad?"

"That's right."

"But a business major? Dad said you worked with Kit. Wasn't he some sort of diplomat?"

"Yeah," Nate said, and she heard the hesitation in his voice.

"Top secret? Can't tell me anything?"

Nate gave a half grin. "More or less. Uncle Kit is an expert on the Middle East and he wanted someone he could trust with him, so he asked me to join him, and I did."

"For how long?"

"Twelve years."

She turned in her chair to look at him. "Are you saying you spent twelve years traveling around the Middle East and now you're going to open a business office in little Summer Hill, Virginia?"

"I am."

Terri turned back toward the water. There were more flashlights now and three silent rowboats. "When you were in the Middle East with Kit, I guess you were working in glamorous embassies, and traveled in limos, and—" When he gave a snort of laughter, she looked at him.

"Kit grew up mostly in Egypt. He's as at home in a Berber tent as he is in an embassy. He fit right in."

"And you were with him." There was wonder in her voice. "I've never been out of the US. One time Aunt Aggie and I drove up to DC to see the cherry trees in bloom, and I've been to Fort Lauderdale twice to see her. We drove up to Boca Raton and that was nice." She reached down to pick up a white bag and handed it to Nate. "Fried apple pie from Sherry. She runs the kitchen at the Club."

"Thanks," he said as he bit into it.

They were silent for a moment. "This was nice of you." He motioned to the beer, the burrito bag and the pie. "I'd planned to eat some of your cereal, then shower and sleep. I have an idea you weren't too happy about what I did."

"You could say that. After everyone told me you'd done all my chores, I was pretty angry."

"More than the way you were with your dad?"

"About a hundred times worse."

"Remind me to never get on your bad side. Not again, anyway."

"I was halfway back to the house when it all hit me. I knew you had to have heard me with Dad, and..." She looked at him. "You sweet-talked Anna into giving you *my* list, didn't you? My guess is that you were there because you found my notebook and took it over."

"I did. It fell off the table by the front door. So you gave Anna another list. But there was only one thing on it: clean up the shop. Since I thought it was your job on your list, I kept expecting you to show up."

"Couldn't have even if I'd wanted to. The Roper family and all their possessions fell off the big dock. I had to save a dog, a five-year-old and three picnic baskets."

"A five-year-old, huh?" Nate said softly. "He okay?"

"We've learned to require kids under seven to wear life jackets. The child was floating along and smiling. He thought it was all part of his vacation. It was the parents who were screaming. I swear that hysteria causes more problems than the accidents."

Nate finished his pie and looked out at the water. "Can we talk about the coming three weeks? I'll pay—"

Terri's groan cut him off. "Now I really am sorry you heard what I said. I think I should apologize about Stacy."

"For saying she's perfect? She is. She's gracious and kind to everyone. Did you know that she helped Uncle Kit write the play they put on last summer? She was supposed to do all the sets and supervise the costumes, but she was with me so she couldn't. She— What the hell are all those lights?"

There were now over a dozen of them moving along the paths and through the water. "Dad and I call it The Dance of the Players."

"What does that mean?"

"You see," Terri said slowly, "when a man and a woman really love each other, they come together in a very special way that sometimes creates babies. It's—"

Nate was looking at her to cut it out. "You mean they're meeting for…for assignations?"

"If you mean sex, yes. Pretty much. I guess. I mean, I never look, but based on the evidence they leave on Moonlight Beach, I'd say yes, definitely for sex. I do know that sometimes the sand bothers the women in an…uh, intimate sort of way. Dr. Jamie might be able to tell you more about that."

Nate's face showed his shock.

"Husbands and wives are separated all summer," Terri said. "I imagine the ones who stay in the city are fooling around too."

"You seem very blasé about this."

"Grew up with it."

Nate was frowning. "What about you?"

"You mean, am I one of the Players?" Her smile disappeared. "Of course. When you're not here, I grab my big flashlight and run off to the cabin of whoever is available. I'm not in the least particular." She started to get up, but Nate put his hand on her arm.

"I apologize. Please don't leave. I need a bit more time to digest all this food before I can move. What have you decided about me?"

"Dad wants to adopt you so he can get free labor forever. How did you fix those boat motors so quickly?"

"Put gas in them." He was staring at her, waiting for her answer.

"If you pay rent, you don't have to work. Certainly not clean out entire buildings."

With a smile of satisfaction, Nate leaned back in his chair. "I like it here. Uncle Kit said I was part Montgomery because I like water so much."

"Don't Berbers live in deserts?"

"The desert is where you learn to truly appreciate water." He was quiet for a moment. "Terri, I'm sorry about the mix-up. My uncle hasn't answered any of the eight messages I left for him, but I think he put me here because he knows I need this. After Uncle Kit retired, I had a hard time working for the government. So hard, that I left."

Terri could hear the understatement in his voice and she waited for him to go on, but he didn't. "What about Stacy? Will she mind that you and I stay here alone? Just the two of us?"

"She's not the jealous type," Nate said quickly, then heaved himself out of the chair. "I can't stand the smell of myself any longer. You said your aunt used to invite people here. You mind if I have a few people over? I'll cook."

"I guess not," Terri said as she stood up, but she didn't meet his eyes.

He seemed to know what she was thinking. "But no silver or fine china. I promise."

She could hear the laughter in his voice. "Good because my tux is in the cleaners."

Nate grinned. "Rats! I brought my best ball gown and heels, and I really wanted to wear them."

"Mind if I borrow one of your high heels? I've always wanted to try kayaking."

Laughing, they picked up the cooler, the empty bottles and bags, and went into the house.

Chapter 4

Nate took a twenty-minute shower, but then it required that long to get clean. He smiled all the way through it. Terri had certainly won that round!

The truth was that he'd enjoyed himself. For the last year he'd been stuck at a desk. The only exercise he got was the artificial kind in a gym. He'd had years of following Kit around, bumming rides with soldiers on seaplanes, hiding in tents when they didn't want to be seen, on and on. It had nearly killed him, but he'd loved it.

But all that ended when Kit retired. Nate had been assigned to a desk and—

He broke off his thoughts when his phone rang. The ID said it was Stacy. Smiling, he answered it. "Hey, baby, I was just thinking about you."

"Miss me?" she asked.

"Totally. What about you?"

"I think about you every second. Did you get the boxes I sent?"

"What address did you use?"

"My parents'."

"Oh," Nate said. "Sorry, but no, I haven't seen them. I'll go tomorrow. Are you having a good time?"

"It's wonderful! Giovanni is brilliant. The way he sees color is something I can only hope to achieve. He puts shades of purple with strips of old gold and…" She took a breath. "You have to see it to believe it."

Nate was laughing. "I think I would have to."

"Dad said you're staying at the lake. Do you like it there?"

"Very much. I cleaned out an old shed today."

"I thought you were going to rest. Did you see the prototype for the business cards I emailed you?"

"Sorry," Nate said. "I didn't have time to open the attachment. What do you know about the people here at the lake?"

"Not much. It's a separate community from the town, but there's a lot of money there. I'm really hoping to get some new clients at the fair. I know Mr. Rayburn has sold several houses in the last year. I'd like to decorate them."

"I hear you went to school with his daughter."

"Terri?" Stacy said. "I did but I never knew her very well."

"Oh?" Nate asked.

Stacy hesitated. "She's a very pretty girl, isn't she?"

"I guess," Nate said. "Was there something bad between you two?"

"No." Stacy's voice had a coolness to it. "I wasn't a Mean Girl and I didn't ostracize her from my gang if that's the insinuation."

With a chuckle, Nate stretched out on the bed, phone close to his ear. "Never thought you could be anything but your perfect self. I'm just curious about this place, is all. Since you went off and left me here alone, the least you could do is tell me about it."

"Guilt!" There was laughter in her voice. "Poor Nate. Three weeks' vacation with nothing whatever to do so I should feel sorry for you."

"I guess I could ask someone else." His voice was sexy, teasing. "There was a woman named Jenkins who seemed to like me."

"Red hair from a drugstore box? Just so you know, there isn't anything on her body that's real and her husband owns some big company. He would make a formidable enemy."

"Are you *sure* you weren't a Mean Girl in high school?"

"Okay, you win. I take it you want to know about Terri. She and I weren't friends in high school because she was never there. She left the grounds as soon as class let out, and she was never in any extracurricular activities. She made okay grades but I don't think she spent much time studying. We all felt sorry for her because she had so much work to do."

"But I get the idea that something happened. Something traumatic."

"In the ninth grade, Terri was suspended from school."

"For what?"

"For injuring two boys."

"Two of them, huh?" Nate was grinning.

Stacy didn't join his humor. "The boys said she went crazy and picked up a rope from gym class. She swung it around and hit one of the boys in the ribs and he went down hard. I think she jumped the other one. For weeks, it was all the school could talk about."

"Was she a hero or was she ridiculed?" Nate was no longer smiling.

"Sorry, but Terri was the object of laughter. The boys were popular and Terri was always an outsider. The boys were taken to a hospital to be checked out."

"Terri was suspended but what happened to the boys?"

"Nothing. The principal—who was a great football fan, I might add—said their injuries might have damaged them for life and that fear was enough punishment."

"They didn't miss so much as a practice, did they?" Nate said. "I bet that at the next game they were back on the field being safely slammed into by two-hundred-pound teenagers and not by some skinny girl."

"I'm sure it was very unfair," Stacy said. "When I get back, maybe you and I can get to know the whole Rayburn family."

There was a tone in Stacy's voice that Nate had never heard before—and something told him that he should shut up about another woman. "So what's this Giovanni look like? He's not some hand-kissing Italian, is he?"

Stacy laughed. "Not at all, but the man who runs the company is a great flirt."

"I want to hear every word about everything. You aren't planning to make our bedroom pink, are you?"

While Stacy talked about fabrics and colors and furniture, Nate wondered what the boys had said that set off Terri's anger. For a girl to take on a couple of high school football players, it must have been something serious.

It was late when Nate hung up. He was smiling, feeling like he'd made up for putting his foot in it when he'd asked Stacy about Terri.

You didn't tell her you were living with Terri, an inner

voice said. Not *living* exactly, just sharing a house. Room-mates.

As he got up and put on a pair of pajama bottoms, he called Kit for the ninth time that day. As with all of them, it went to voice mail.

"I..." Nate began. "It's okay. Terri and I worked things out. For the next three weeks, we're going to be room-mates." He couldn't think of anything else to say so he hung up.

Moments later, his phone made the ding for a text mes-sage. It was from Kit. Ask Della about Leslie.

Nate dropped the phone onto the bed as if it had caught fire. "No!" he said aloud, his frown so deep his eyebrows were nearly touching.

"No, no, no." He'd had all the mysteries he wanted in his lifetime. Twelve years of them! Digging and research-ing and finding out who was doing what and why. That was Kit's love, not his.

All Nate wanted was peace. He wanted to marry the girl he was madly in love with, set up retirement plans for people and make some babies. Peace. No more midnight runs. No more *danger*.

As he climbed into bed, he punched the pillow. He'd thought Kit had put him in a house with a pretty young woman because of... What? Some temptation before Nate got married?

But it looked like it had to do with some damned mys-tery.

Nate calmed himself. He needed sleep. There was no telling what was planned for him to do tomorrow. He tried to think of good things. What was it Terri had said? That her father wanted to adopt him.

Beats Mr. Hartman, he thought. Stacy's father looked

at Nate like he might accidentally knock the china cabinet over.

As Nate dozed off, he remembered Terri's dad saying, *Della Kissel tells us about everybody. The Gossip Queen.* She had the same last name as the people who used to own the lake. Guess that meant she'd always lived there—which meant she'd heard and seen it all.

"Get out of my head, Kit Montgomery," Nate murmured for the millionth time in his life, then finally went to sleep.

The next morning, Terri heard Nate moving around in the kitchen and within minutes the divine smell of coffee filled her bedroom. Last night, when she'd heard his low voice on the phone, she told herself she should shut the door. But she didn't.

She lay in bed and listened to the sound—if not the words—of his voice. It had been years since a man had talked to her in that low, sexy rumble. It was intimacy that hinted at things to come.

The only time she'd had that closeness had ended so badly that she hadn't risked it again. Since then, there had been a couple of men who'd let her know they wanted something more permanent than just dating. But Terri had always backed away. She'd learned that a joke at a serious moment, running off to work or even a yawn could stop what he had been about to say.

As she listened—felt—Nate's voice, she told herself she was jealous. The Stacy Hartmans got it all. Cute, vivacious blondes with rich fathers seemed to own the world.

Yes, Terri thought, *that's good. Make yourself hate Stacy.*

But even as she thought it, she knew she was lying to

herself. Stacy had nothing whatever to do with this. Terri's problem was that she *liked* Nate Taggert. He made her
laugh; he challenged her. He could do things. He could…

She knew she had to stop thinking like that but it was
a long time before she could sleep.

Now it was morning and he was in her kitchen making breakfast. By the time she'd dressed—and put on a
small amount of makeup—she had herself under control. Maybe.

"Good morning," Nate said. He had on a rugby T-shirt,
cotton trousers and Top-Siders. The soles of the shoes pre-
vented slipping on slimy surfaces. "What's on for today?"

Terri sat down at the counter. "I could hire you out to
clean basements."

"No thanks. Do you wait to see what needs to be done
each day?"

"Pretty much." He put two plates of eggs and toast on
the counter. Hers was a bright yellow, but his had soft
spots of color from the spices he'd used. She switched the
plates. "Today you get the bland one."

"Wait!" Nate said. "You might not like that. You—"

Terri took a bite, and her eyes widened. "This is really
good. What is it?"

"I think they call it fusion cooking. I mix Western
scrambled eggs with Middle Eastern spices." He took his
plate to the stove and sprinkled some spice from the jars.
When he sat back down, he was smiling. "Most Western-
ers don't like it."

"I do. You did so much yesterday that you could take
today off. Go visit Stacy's parents." A grimace flashed
across his face so quickly that she wasn't sure she saw it.

"That reminds me," he said. "I have to go there today
and pick up some boxes Stacy sent. Why don't you go into

town with me? We could have lunch and I saw a florist shop near Jamie's office. I thought I'd send Hallie some flowers. She—" He broke off because the smile had left Terri's face. Abruptly, she got up and put her empty plate in the dishwasher. "Did I say something?"

When Terri turned to him, there was no humor in her face. "Summer Hill is a small town. If you walked through there with *me,* it wouldn't be ten minutes before Stacy and her parents were told that you and I are having an affair. Truth has nothing to do with gossip."

"Ah, right," he said. "Small towns. How could I forget? But what about here at the lake? No gossip?"

"Lots of it, but people in glass houses…"

"Can't throw stones. I guess you know too much for them to turn against you."

"That's about right."

Nate could see the way she was looking at the door, as if she meant to leave at any moment. He decided to change the subject. "I don't know if I'm off base in this or not, but yesterday it seemed that the kids were divided into separate groups."

Terri's smile came back. "The Cutters and the Socs. Oh. Sorry. That's from—"

"*Breaking Away* and *The Outsiders.*"

Terri was astonished. "Not many people know that."

"Being stuck somewhere and waiting for Kit allowed me to see way too many movies. I take it the kids in T-shirts are the Cutters, and the Socs are the kids in head-to-toe Ralph Lauren."

"Exactly. The Cutters are the offspring and siblings of people who work here. Sherry—who runs the kitchen—has two kids. The man who works the pizza stand has a daughter."

"Who looks after the kids?"

"We all do, but the oldest watch out for the youngest. And they know there are rules."

"And the Lauren kids?"

"Are content with owning the latest and the best. If you're thinking there's some kind of war between them, there isn't."

"Then you won't mind if I take a swing at getting the kids together?"

"Have at it." Terri looked at her watch. "I have to go. The fishermen will be going out so that means tackle will be falling overboard and I'll have to retrieve it." She stopped at the door and looked at him. "About earlier, I didn't mean to freak on you about going into town. It's just that the townies and the lake people don't mingle very well."

"Which one of you is the Cutters?"

"More like the Capulets and Montagues."

Nate didn't smile. "People ended up dead because of that war."

"No deaths yet, just some people who wish they were. I'll see you at Club Circle."

Nate watched her go to the dock and get into her wooden boat. He raised his hand and she waved back, then he went to the kitchen to clean up. She'd liked his eggs, liked the spiciness of them.

Stacy hated them. She liked American-style Italian food and French cuisine, but past that, she had no interest in other foods. But Terri—

He told himself to stop that. His mother had always said that when you love someone, you accept them as they are. You don't say, "I love you, now change everything about yourself."

He checked his cell phone, saw that he had some emails from his family and took the time to answer them. He told them he was doing well, and yes, he was holding up in Stacy's absence. As he was about to leave, he tried to resist, but he couldn't help looking again at the text Kit had sent. Ask Della about Leslie.

Even though Nate wanted nothing to do with Kit's mysteries, he remembered some of the gossip he'd been told yesterday. Several people had stopped by the shop while he was cleaning it and one of the people they'd talked about was Della Kissel. She was the youngest daughter of the family who had once owned the lake and the surrounding land. Word was that she was a very nosy little woman who snooped into everything about everyone. Something that was interesting was that no one had said she was a liar. She just seemed to listen and observe and repeat. Endlessly repeat.

As Nate got into his car, he stopped. Was it his imagination that Terri had frozen at the mention of a flower shop? Of course not, he told himself. He'd spent too many years working with people who had secrets on top of secrets—and more buried beneath them.

By the time he got to Club Circle he was smiling—but he lost it when he saw three kids sitting on a bench in the shade doing nothing but swinging their legs. To his left were four older, Lauren-clad boys with a brand-new boat and motor, and it looked like they had no idea what to do with it.

Nate stood there for a moment, looking from one group to the other. For the most part, the people who had stopped by the shop were retired men who desperately wanted to tell Nate that they used to "be somebody."

An idea began to take shape in his mind. But first, he

wanted to do something about the idle kids. In the trunk of his car was some sports equipment, mainly balls for soccer and rugby. In front of the big clubhouse was an area of lawn, well kept and lush. It was *not* meant to be a sports field.

Too bad, Nate thought as he kicked a soccer ball into the middle of the field. When all the kids stopped moving and stared at him, Nate began to smile.

"Come on!" Terri yelled at Nate. It was early afternoon and she was standing up in her boat, wearing her yellow slicker, a waterproof hat pulled down over her face. The rain was starting to hit hard.

Nate was on the dock, three soccer balls in his arms, and blinking against the rain.

Terri waved her arms at him to get in the boat.

Nate motioned toward the parking lot and his car, but Terri shook her head. When Nate still stood there, water beginning to run off his nose, she pointed to her open mouth, then rubbed her stomach. He pretended that he didn't know what she meant.

"Food!" she yelled.

With a half grin, Nate nodded in understanding, dropped, then kicked the balls under the overhang of a building.

"Funny!" she said as he got into the boat and she took off.

The rain was coming down harder and Nate was getting drenched, but he held his face up to it and wiped his hands over his head. He was using it as a shower.

"Get down!" Terri shouted.

When it came to shouted warnings, Nate was well

trained. Instantly, he flattened out, his chest on the wooden seats.

Terri bent and the next second they went under a steel fence that stretched from one piece of land to another. She slowed the motor as they entered a narrow spit of water. On both sides were stairs leading to houses that could barely be seen through the pounding rain.

As soon as she reached the dock, Nate got out and did a perfect cleat hitch to tie the boat in place.

Terri followed him and they ran up the stairs.

At the top was a house, all cedar and glass. Terri ran to a small porch, pulled a ring of keys from her pocket and unlocked the door.

Inside, they stood in a puddle as she removed her slicker and hat. Nate was so wet he made her laugh. "Stay there and I'll get you a towel." She went down a hall.

Nate remained by the door, but he could see through to the front with its big glass windows looking out at the water. The rain was beating down hard, making a misty fog that seemed to enclose them.

The interior of the house was too "designed" for his taste. The part of the living room he could see had white couches and chairs, with white pillows that glistened like they were made of silk. It wasn't the kind of room where you could drink beer and eat nachos with your friends while you watched a football game.

"Here." Terri held out a stack of clothing and towels. "These belong to Greg, who owns the house. He's about a hundred pounds overweight so they should fit you."

"Was that a slam?"

"Just a fact." She was smiling. "Don't take a step off the welcome mat. These floors are… I don't know what they are, but I make sure they stay dry."

She was still holding the stack as Nate began to peel off his wet shirt. When his hard, flat stomach was exposed, she just stared.

"Give me a hand, will you?" He was tangled in the wet cloth and it was stuck.

She tossed the dry clothes to the floor, then reached up and pulled. When the neckline caught on his ears, they both worked on it and finally got the shirt off. Terri handed him the towel, then stood there watching him dry off.

For a moment, their eyes met—and she could feel her face turn red. "Lunch," she murmured and pointed to the room just off the entrance. "Kitchen." She scurried away.

Around the corner from him, she opened the freezer door. "Pizza okay? Miranda leaves a variety in here for me. Do you have any preference?" When she closed the freezer door she could see Nate's reflection in the shiny surface.

He had his back to her and he was peeling off his wet trousers. They landed on the mat. Then came his boxers. He stood up straight and was drying himself, lifting his legs to do his thighs.

Terri could feel herself beginning to sweat. He had a truly magnificent body! Shoulders the width of half an oar, then down to a small waist. The curve of his behind was tight and high, topping thighs that were like tree trunks.

When he started to turn in her direction, she nearly leaped toward the sink.

"Just so the food has flavor," Nate said as he pulled on the dry clothes. "Why does someone leave food for you here when you live just a few feet away?" Nate was standing behind her. "Are you okay? You're shaking."

"Just got cold from the rain, I guess."

He put his hands on her shoulders and turned her toward the living room. "Go sit down and I'll stick a pizza or two in the oven. What about wine?"

"Can't. I have to work later."

Nate nodded toward the windows. "This isn't going to stop anytime soon. Let's have lunch and you can tell me all about this place."

"Love to," she said as she sat down on a white chair. She didn't dare put her shoes on the ottoman for fear of getting it dirty. She could hear him in the kitchen. "The Kissels—"

"No," Nate said. "I want to know about you and the present. It was good to finally meet your dad."

Terri laughed. "He loves you. Really. He asked me how much you'd charge to work here full-time. He and Uncle Frank—"

"And he is?"

"The sheriff. Remember I told you that Dad first came to Summer Hill to visit an army buddy?"

"And they were going into business together." Nate handed her a glass of cold white wine. "There's red if you want it."

Terri hesitated, but she took it. "This is good, thanks." She was watching Nate as he looked from one white piece of furniture to another.

"I'm afraid to sit down."

"You have Greg's clothes on, so I think you're safe."

"Good point." He sat on the couch, but didn't lean back and he kept his drink on the all-glass coffee table. "Is the sheriff the buddy?"

"No. That was Jake." Her voice lowered. "He and Dad were great partners and worked well together. We were all shocked when he suddenly died just as I graduated from college."

"Ah." Nate seemed to be searching her eyes. "What plans of your own did his death force you to give up?"

Terri shook her head in wonder at his keen perception. "All of it. Everything. I was going to go through Europe with some girlfriends. Europe on two cents a day, that sort of thing. We were going to have wild affairs and..." She shrugged. "Dad needed me, so I returned. What about you? How'd you get involved with Kit?"

Nate ignored her subject-changing question. "How's the sheriff connected to your dad's partner?"

"Frank Cannon was Uncle Jake's bad boy little brother. He was always getting into trouble. When I was a kid I thought Uncle Frank was wonderfully exciting. But Dad and Uncle Jake were always threatening to murder him if he didn't straighten up. Finally, Uncle Jake said that since Frank knew so much about criminals, he should try to catch them. For once Uncle Frank listened and now he's the sheriff of Summer Hill."

"How did he—"

"Oh no, you don't. It's your turn. Tell me about your years with Kit Montgomery."

Nate started to speak but the timer went off for the pizzas and he got up. "Shall we go to the dining room?"

"They have a rug in there that costs more than I made last year."

They looked at each other and when a flash of lightning lit the room, they smiled. "I'll get the towels," Terri said and ran down the hall.

By silent agreement, they had decided to eat while sitting by the windows and looking out. They'd have to move some furniture and they'd have to cover the white upholstery in case food was dropped, but they could enjoy the storm.

When Terri returned with an armload of towels, Nate had moved two chairs in front of the big window. Terri covered the pristine surfaces while he sliced the first pizza.

Minutes later, they were seated in front of the window. The lights were off so there was only the hazy gray of the rain. They set their wineglasses on the sill, their plates on their laps.

"So tell me all," Terri said. "Start when you went back to Dartmouth and majored in something besides beer. What I want to know is why you chose business. From what I've seen, you're not a person who sits still."

"Was that a compliment? I'm the guy you have to babysit. Remember? I squeal at live bait. I only eat off fine china. Never been on a boat that didn't have a crew. I—"

"But I was right on most of it. Are you going to tell me about Kit or just whine that I misjudged little ol' you? And by the way, I got the rugby smack on."

Nate grinned. "You got a lot of it right. I majored in business because I have a natural aptitude for it. Ask me to add, subtract, multiply something."

"Okay—2,782 times 671."

"Mmm, 1,866,722."

"I'm impressed. I guess. If you're right."

"I am," he said, his mouth full. "How many houses do you look after and do they all leave food for you?"

"I look after many of them, but only about eighteen or twenty at a time. A lot of people leave things for me. It's an enticement. A bribe to get me to spend time in their house. Empty houses get into trouble. A couple of years ago some of the kids who work here during the summer got hold of the keys and began using the cabins for...uh, parties."

"That ol' sex thing again, huh?"

"That's right. If you're so good at math, what made you run away with Kit?"

He looked out the window for a moment. "I think it was my mother introducing me to a very pretty girl." He looked at her. "You ever have one of those moments when you can see the world with crystal clarity?"

"Yeah. At Uncle Jake's funeral. When I saw my father crying and saying he couldn't run this place alone, I knew what I had to do."

Nodding, Nate looked back out the window. "That's exactly how I felt. I could see my future. I looked into that girl's eyes and I saw everything. I would go into business with my uncles, and in a couple of years I'd marry the girl standing in front of me. I could see three kids—it was like I even knew their names." He took a breath. "I panicked. I don't know why. It wasn't as though what I envisioned was awful. It just seemed like the end. I threw some clothes in a bag and flew to Maine to be with my Montgomery cousins. They always seem to be sure of what they want to do in life, so I hoped some of it would rub off on me." Nate was silent as he looked at the rain.

"I take it that being there didn't help you to decide."

"No." Nate gave a low chuckle. "But then, Uncle Kit arrived. All of us—kids and adults alike—were in awe of him. For all that he was part of the family, none of us knew much about him. We used to make up things, like how he was the prototype for James Bond, that sort of thing."

"I can believe that," Terri said. "Does he *ever* slump?"

"No, never. No matter how tired he is or how defeated, he carries himself in a way that makes people follow him, believe in him." There was awe in Nate's voice.

He picked up another slice of pizza. "I'd been there

about a week when one day we were in the big living room of the old Montgomery house watching some football game and arguing over who should win. But I was standing against a wall, my mind full of the question of what I was going to do with my life. Kit came in, looked around and stopped at me. He said, 'Come with me.' I followed him outside and…" Nate shrugged. "He asked if I'd like to work for him. Even now, I'm astonished that I didn't hesitate for a second. I said yes. The next day we took off in a government helicopter."

"And you stayed with him for twelve years."

"Yes. Technically, I worked for the CIA, but actually, I was Kit's…"

"Assistant?"

"Yeah, right. I was his whatever he needed. Bodyguard, human calendar, the buffer between his temper and people who wanted to remove his head. We went everywhere. We stayed in five-star hotels and in tents full of scorpions."

"I can tell that you hated every minute of it." Terri was smiling.

Nate's eyes took on a faraway look. "I liked the people. We met some so rich they thought they were gods—and others who were so poor they were starving."

"And you got along with all of them," Terri said.

"More or less. But I had to learn how. Kit has a ferocious temper and he hates stupidity. And trust me, we saw a lot of that!"

"But then, Kit retired. Why didn't you stay on?"

Nate took his time answering. "I've never said this before, but Kit hurt my feelings. Injured my ego. He'd never mentioned retiring. We were in the desert, sitting by a campfire, and he told me he was going to retire and go to Summer Hill, Virginia, to get the woman he loved.

In all our years together, I'd never heard of the town or the woman. I knew his ex-wife, but their relationship was more rage than love."

He took a deep drink of his wine. "One thing about Kit is that when he makes up his mind, he doesn't change it. Just six weeks later, he was out of the service and I was left behind."

"How did you do without him?"

Nate laughed. "Since most of the things he and I did were…how do I say this?…off the radar, my record was very tame. No one knew what to do with me, but since I had a business degree, I was given a desk job." He grimaced. "I was put to the task of dealing with big financial accounts."

"So you were back where you started."

"It was like my years of following my uncle around the world had never happened. They all thought I'd been Kit's secretary. They'd dump papers on my desk and give a couple of taps and say, 'Need it by Thursday.' At one point I ripped my shirt open and showed the scars of three bullet wounds that I got when Kit decided to get involved in a tribal war. But my official record said that when that happened, I was on recreational leave. I'd actually been in a hospital fighting for my life. Kit's blasted secrecy had been carried through into my record."

"And then you met Stacy."

"Yes. Kit met her in Summer Hill and got her to go to DC. He wanted her to meet his son." A muscle in Nate's jaw began to clench. "You know how it is. Blood is thicker than water. I walked into firing rifles in front of that man, but when it came to introducing pretty girls, he only wanted his son. But Rowan was fed up with his dad playing matchmaker, so he invited me to go to dinner with them."

"And you and Stacy fell for each other."

"It wasn't difficult since Rowan was on his cell most of the meal. I knew that first night that Stacy was exactly what I'd missed out on. I was thirty-three years old and every cousin my age, every guy I went to school with, was married and had at least one kid."

"And even Kit had left you for a girl."

Nate grinned. "Right. I left the service. I didn't look back. I had to endure lectures about ruining my record, about losing my pension, all of it. But I'd made up my mind."

"Like Kit," Terri said.

"I guess so. But it was really Stacy who made me decide. She's pretty and educated and talented and…" He shrugged. "You know her so you understand."

"So that's what you're going to do with your life? Marry Stacy, have kids and open a financial office in Summer Hill?"

"You make it sound boring, but that's exactly what I'm going to do. My uncles, Mike and Kane, are geniuses with money, and I'm going to start a branch management firm. I'm going to help people prepare for retirement, that sort of thing."

"That sounds like an excellent plan. Well thought out and sensible."

Nate looked at her, trying to see if she was being sarcastic or not, but he couldn't tell.

She smiled at him. "If you don't like that work, Dad will give you a job at the lake. In fact, I'm sure he'd let you run the whole place. He and Elaine could go travel and see the world."

Nate was watching her as she kept her eyes straight ahead, but he couldn't tell if she was serious or joking. He decided to go the lighter way. "Would I have to get my real estate license?"

Terri grinned. "Oh yeah. That's a big part of the job. Showing houses to clients and hearing them complain that everything is wet. You get to explain that lakes are liquid." She turned to him. "Is Stacy a water person?"

"I don't know. I never asked her. We lived in an apartment in DC and she liked it. She used the pool a few times."

"That's good for you," she said. "I wish you all the best the world has to offer." The words came out with more feeling than she meant to expose. She could feel Nate looking at her.

"What about you?" he asked. "You have a plan for your life?"

"Oh sure." There was laughter in her voice. "Someday I'll take over for Dad, my hair will turn gray and I'll be seventy and showing lawyers and trophy wives how to bait hooks. And cleaning up beaches of naughty bits."

Nate didn't laugh but kept looking at her profile.

Terri turned toward him, but she didn't meet his eyes. "You finished? I need to get back to work."

It was still raining hard. Nate got up, empty plate and glass in hand. "What do we do next?"

She stood up. "I need to check on the cabins. You can... You're a guest here. Go enjoy yourself. I'm sure there are people in the clubhouse."

"I could have an exciting game of pinochle."

"Are you kidding? The Player wives are into strip poker."

"Hedonistic place, isn't it?"

"Not on my part," she said, then started to correct herself. She didn't want to sound like some lonely heart. "At least not when the Turner Twins aren't here." She had the satisfaction of seeing Nate blink. As she headed for the kitchen, she turned so he wouldn't see her smile.

"I'll go with you," he said as he washed their dishes and left them on the stainless steel rack to drain.

"Checking cabins is no fun." She couldn't suppress the hope in her voice. "It's dull work. And this rain isn't going to stop."

"When you're on a camel in the desert and the sun is trying to sizzle your brain, you dream of rain like this."

She narrowed her eyes at him. "You're scared that if you don't go with me, Dad will ask you to do something awful, and you're afraid of the women playing strip poker. You're using your travels to make me take you with me, aren't you?"

"Pretty much. Actually, that's exactly right. Please? I won't be any bother. I'll carry your umbrella, and who are the Turner Twins?"

Terri made a face as though she was contemplating his request. "I don't carry an umbrella and they're double boyfriends. They'll be here for Widiwick."

"I've been meaning to ask what that means."

"You get a wish."

"Like right now I wish the very kind and caring and really beautiful Terri Rayburn would let me go with her and not leave me alone with a bunch of half-naked women? That kind of wish?" Her eyes widened at his words. "I think I'm an imbecile. Give me a ride back to the clubhouse, will you?"

Terri laughed. "On the behalf of my former schoolmate, Stacy Hartman, you're going with me. Do you *always* get your way?"

"Mostly." Nate was grinning. "So where do we go first?"

"The Mortons leave homemade cookies in the freezer for me."

"Yeah? Any game birds anywhere? I invited some people over for Saturday next and I thought I'd stuff a few quail or maybe Cornish hens and grill them."

She drew in her breath. "How many people did you invite?" There was horror in her voice.

He went to the front door and opened a coat closet. "Think Gary would mind if I borrow his rain gear?"

"It's Greg, and how many people?"

"Just three adults and three kids." He put on rain gear and held Terri's coat for her. "You see, I have this plan. I've found some very interesting retired people here. If there's one thing I've learned from my travels, it's that old people and young ones belong together. I saw a kid was playing with a toy airplane so I want him to meet—"

"Hugh Evans," Terri said. "Former pilot."

"Yes. Sound like a good idea?"

"A great one." Terri was very serious. "But if the word *party* is spread around, everyone at the lake will show up."

Nate opened the door. "We've got over a week to plan. How about if we cook something Egyptian? You can help. Or is what your dad said about your cooking true?"

Terri still wasn't smiling. "We need to stop this evil word from spreading."

"What word?"

"*Party.* That's all these people do. And I'm sure they're dying to meet you." She could tell that she wasn't scaring him off.

"As you so wisely ascertained, I was in a fraternity. Think I should order some kegs?"

"How about the Clydesdales pulling a loaded beer wagon?"

Nate grinned so wide it looked like his face might crack open. "I like it already. Mind if we go where the cookies are first? I need sustenance."

"You just ate a whole pizza."

"What can I say? I'm a growing boy."

Terri smacked her hand against his hard stomach. "*This* is what's going to grow." She'd meant it as a teasing gesture, but the feel of his flesh under her hand made her hesitate. Hand still in place, she looked up into his eyes. The laughter was gone and he was staring at her in puzzlement.

He gave a quick frown, then ran outside into the rain. When he was several feet away, he turned back and he'd regained his laughter. "Come on! I'm hungry!"

Terri locked the door, then ran after Nate and got into her boat with him.

Chapter 5

"What's going on with our girl?" Sheriff Frank asked as he entered Brody's office. He didn't bother with preliminary greetings. They'd known each other too long, been through too much together, to do anything other than say what they meant. "I hear she's living with some guy. Cousin of Dr. Jamie."

Brody was looking through a file cabinet. "They're roommates, that's all. They've been working together."

"Oh." Frank plopped down in a chair. He was a short, muscular man in a brown uniform. His badge picked up the light and reflected it. "Della told me about him."

Brody groaned. "And you listened to her?"

"Little old lady snoops are law enforcement's best friends, and she keeps me well-informed. I guess you know that Dr. Kyle put her in the hospital in Richmond for some tests."

"She's not even here, but she's telling you about Nate?"

Brody put some files on his desk and sat down to look at them.

"She did, and she told me about the entire hospital staff. I think maybe what goes on there is worse than what's on TV. Everybody jumping into bed with each other. It's a wonder they have time to hand out all those lovely pills."

Brody's head shot up. "You aren't...?"

"Back on the drugs?" Frank said good-naturedly. "Yeah. I stole six orange bottles while I was there. I had a real happy night."

Brody gave him a look to cut it out and returned to the papers.

Frank was frowning. "What's made you so mad? You haven't had any break-ins, have you?"

When Brody looked up, his eyes were bleak. "Does my daughter's heart being stolen count?"

"You can't keep her all to yourself forever," Frank said in a patronizing voice. "Someday Terri's going to meet a nice young man and get married and give us grandkids."

Brody grimaced. "Too bad you didn't *listen* to Della's gossip. I want to show you something." He went out the door, through Anna's office, to the outside.

It was a beautiful day and there were several kids playing soccer on the lawn. They were being coached by a man with a limp and sparse gray hair.

"I've seen him before," Frank said.

"How about photos in *Life* magazine? He coached the US soccer team in the Olympics."

"Does he live here?"

"He's spent ten summers here, but no one asked him what he did before he retired."

"So who...? Ah," Frank said. "This guy Nate asked?"

"He did. I swear that in the week Nate Taggert has been

here he's learned more about the residents than I know after a lifetime here."

"I can believe that," Frank said. "But then, it was always Leslie who was the social one. She—" He stopped at the look Brody gave him. "Sorry. The forbidden subject. It's just that she made friends. You and Terri are clones in being workhorses. So this guy helps around here and you said he's stealing our Terri's heart? What's the problem? He's old and ugly?"

"There he is, so what do you think?" Brody nodded toward the dock.

A big, good-looking young man put his hands on the waist of a heavy-set woman and easily swung her out of the boat onto the dock. She was smiling up at him like he was a rescuing knight.

"He's built like Billy," Frank said under his breath, then turned to Brody. "What's the problem?"

"Nate's engaged to Lew Hartman's daughter."

"Wonder why Della didn't tell me that? But Stacy is a nice girl. She—"

Brody gave him a hard look, then walked away, Frank right behind him.

"This isn't good, is it?" Frank said when they were inside Brody's office. "How many boyfriends has our Terri had since she dumped Billy?"

"None that we know of. But then, any boy she looks at, you run through the system to see if he's ever had so much as a parking ticket."

"Give me the stats on this guy so I can find out about him."

Brody gave a snort. "Since he worked for Kit Montgomery, you'd have to have the security clearance of the Secretary of Defense to find out about him."

When Frank heard a laugh that he'd been hearing since Terri was a toddler, he went to the window to look out. He'd never been married and had no children, so Terri was as close as he was going to get to his own child. In his eyes, she was beautiful and smart and deserving of all the good in the world. Just his unbiased opinion.

She was standing beside the big guy and watching the kids play soccer. They weren't touching but were as close as two people could be without contact. Every once in a while, she glanced up at him with sparkling eyes full of laughter.

From what Frank could see, Terri was wearing her feelings in the open—and that made him frown. She was usually cautious around men. Over the years, he and Brody had shared laughter when they saw the young men come on to Terri. They tried every line ever created. They tried to impress her with tricks on water skis, on motorboats, with the size of Daddy's cruiser.

None of them had succeeded. Frank and Brody had watched as Terri dumped pails of bait over their heads. She'd pushed four Enders off a dock. Mostly, she just froze them with a look and walked away.

But this guy… Frank had only seen Terri look at a boy like this once before—and that had been a long time ago.

Brody was standing beside him.

"You said they're living together?" Frank asked softly.

"Yeah, but Terri says nothing is happening."

"If circumstances were different, I'd wish she'd go after him. Put on a red dress and high heels and give cute little Stacy Hartman a run. May the best girl win the prize."

"And what happens if she wins him?" Brody asked as he went back to his desk. "People add the breakup to my daughter's résumé? The Hartman family is well liked in

Summer Hill. Stacy is practically the town's princess, while Terri is…is…" He couldn't finish the sentence.

"I know." Frank was still looking out the window. In the few minutes he'd been watching, Nate had never so much as glanced at Terri. He was beginning to think her interest was one-sided.

But just as Frank was about to look away, he saw Terri turn toward the kids, and Nate gazed down at her. Frank could see the caring in the man's eyes. Caring, lust, even a kind of hunger was there. The man's expression was so intense that it made him draw in his breath. "How long have they known each other?"

"Just over a week," Brody said. "Sometimes, that's all it takes."

Neither of them said so, but they knew that six hours after Brody met Leslie, he'd said he'd found the woman he was going to marry.

"And how bad is it from his side?" Frank was hoping that he was wrong about what he'd seen.

Brody said that one day he saw Nate jump off the dock, fully clothed, after he'd wrestled with Terri on the soccer field as they fought for the ball. "The boy needed to cool off. I'm not sure he knows how much pain he's in."

"So maybe he'll break off his engagement and…" Frank didn't finish because both men knew what would happen. Terri already had two strikes against her. Add another one and she'd have to leave town. "The gossip here would be more than she could bear," Frank said softly. "Terri would have to move to some big city where people don't know each other. Then she'd be far away from…from *us*." Frank collapsed onto a chair. "This is a problem."

"Yeah," Brody said. "A really *big* problem."

* * *

Nate and Terri were closing the hooks on the life jackets of a couple of little boys. The kids' parents were putting their gear into a rented boat, and Terri was giving them directions to Moonlight Beach.

"Moonlight?" the seven-year-old asked. "Doesn't the sun shine there?"

This unintentional double entendre made his dad laugh and his wife elbowed him.

Nate and Terri exchanged looks. People on holiday! He nodded to something behind her back. "I think that man is trying to get your attention."

Turning, she saw her father and Uncle Frank standing by the clubhouse.

"I take it he's the sheriff?"

"Yeah," Terri said, standing up. "I'm sure he's here to find out all about you. Uh-oh."

As Nate watched, the sheriff bunched his fingertips, kissed them, then flung his arm out. It was a gesture Nate had seen many times in Italy, but rarely at home. "I think he's glad to see you."

"No," Terri said with a sigh as the boys ran to their parents. "I mean, yes, he is, but he means that I have to fix the kisses." Looking at the sheriff, she raised a hand in question and he held up three fingers. "Damn it!" She looked at Nate. "I have a job that will take me about an hour and a half. I'll meet you back here." She headed to her boat.

Nate was right behind her. "So whose kisses do you have to fix? Are they French or regular?"

Terri laughed. "Neither. Unfortunately. It's all three signs. I have to go get my car and drive around the lake to—"

"*You* can drive a car? I thought maybe you had webbed feet since you live on water. And I'm going with you."

She'd already learned that no amount of persuasion kept Nate Taggert from doing whatever he wanted to do. He was like some great unmovable bear. When he said he was going to do something, he *did* it. "Not all of us are rich girls with fancy BMWs. I have a car in my garage."

"I saw it." His tone implied that the ancient vehicle didn't deserve to be called an automobile.

She didn't answer, but when she turned to her boat, she was smiling. Since she'd met Nate he'd become... What was he actually? Friend? Companion? Coworker? "Soul mate," she whispered.

"What did you say?" Nate asked as he got into her boat and started the motor. Gradually, they had assigned themselves jobs and duties. Who did the laundry? Terri. Who cooked? Nate. Who went to the grocery? Together. Who controlled the remote? Nate. But then, Terri liked to read so she didn't mind. Who lost things? Who found things? Who drove? Even who handled the banking? That was Nate.

On the fourth day, her father had tried to have a serious talk with her. "You're getting too attached to him. How about if I move in with you and Nate stays in my apartment?"

"We're doing fine," Terri said. "I enjoy his company. He's easy to live with. Did you order the extra beer for the party?"

"You two are never more than inches apart."

"So? We're friends."

"When you see him say 'I do' to Stacy Hartman, are you going to smile and be happy for them?"

"Of course. Dad, it's okay. Really, it is. I admit that I am attracted to him, but Nate has absolutely none of that boy-girl interest in me. He's utterly and completely faithful to Stacy Hartman in body and mind." She knew her father wasn't convinced, but she wasn't going to give up an excellent workmate for her dad's worries.

Terri was in the boat with Nate and they were heading to their house. No, she corrected herself, to *her* house. Well, technically, it belonged to Aunt Aggie, but it seemed like it was theirs.

She and Nate were already so used to each other that they didn't speak as they ran into the house and went to opposite ends. Bathroom break, then a quick run to the kitchen. Terri beat him to the fridge to get a couple of oranges and bottles of water. She knew he was *always* hungry. When Nate got there, he grabbed a handful of paper towels.

They were out the front door in minutes, then stopped. His silver-blue BMW was in the driveway. Her fifteen-year-old car was inside the closed garage.

"Which vehicle should we take?" Nate asked as though it were a real decision to be made.

She ignored his question. "Why'd you change shirts?"

"I thought maybe we'd have lunch in town."

"In what state?"

"Colorado," he answered as he opened the door to his car and got into the driver's side.

In a familiar way, Terri sat beside him, spread paper towels on her lap and began peeling the oranges. "There's a roadside stand nearby. Great tacos."

"Nope. Sit-down restaurant in Summer Hill. Look, the whole town has seen us together. What's wrong with a man and a woman being friends? Didn't I see a bookstore somewhere? With the way you go through murder mysteries, I'm sure you need new ones."

She held up an orange slice, he opened his mouth and

she put it inside. "I could use a few. Cale Anderson has a new one out."

"Did you know that she's Jamie's mother?"

"No!"

"Which way?"

"Any way Cale Anderson wants to go, I'm with her. Her last one about PTSD made me cry. Is she really his mother? Do you think I could meet her someday?"

"Yes, of course. And Jamie can tell you where his mom got her inspiration for that book. But right now I don't know where we're going so I don't know which way to turn."

"Either way. We have to go around the whole lake. Uncle Frank said all three signs have been kissed."

He turned right. "And we're back to the kissing. What's that all about?"

"I'll have to show you."

"I look forward to it." He drove on the road that encircled the lake. The area had four entrance-exits, but otherwise the lake was a community unto itself.

"Here!" Terri said. "Pull over onto the gravel."

As soon as he stopped, she got out. Behind the huge sign that welcomed people to Lake Kissel was a small metal storage unit that Terri went to.

Nate got out of the car and stood in the shade of a big oak tree eating orange slices and wondering what Terri was doing. When she came out of the shed with a canvas bag slung over her shoulder, and struggling with a ten-foot ladder, he ran to help. "What are you doing?"

"Set it up there, then step back and look at the sign."

He opened the ladder, braced it, then walked to the edge of the road. Someone had put graffiti on the billboard. But it wasn't the usual kind. The *L* of Kissel had been painted

over with white to match the background, and a big red
S was in its place. The sign now read Welcome to Lake
Kisses. He couldn't help laughing.

"If you think it's so funny, you get to fix it." Terri was
holding up a long piece of red vinyl and two spray cans.

"You want me to block out kisses?" He sounded hor-
rified. "But kisses are one of the greatest things ever invented. They're—"

"Just do it," she said. "Or I will. I hope I don't wobble
on the ladder." She'd learned that his sense of... What?
Chivalry? Protection? Male chauvinist pigginess? Whatever it was, she knew he wouldn't like her climbing up
the ladder.

A steel platform had been installed at the bottom of the
sign to make it easy to change. When she handed him the
strip of vinyl, he held it. "What is this?"

"An *L*. I had a hundred of them made to match the
signs. You paint over the *S*, spray glue on the back of the
L, then stick it in place. Changes *kisses* back to *Kissel*."

"You're kidding."

"Not at all. Dad and I have been doing it for years.
When I was in high school, I caught some kids in the act
of vandalizing the boards. I tried to get Uncle Frank to
put them in jail, but he wouldn't. He just made the kids
repair the damage, but they had so much fun doing it, it
wasn't a punishment."

"It is to me," Nate grumbled as he went up the ladder.
"It's a desecration."

Stepping back, Terri directed him. When the wind
caught the white paint so it sprayed on him, Nate unbut-
toned his shirt, removed it and tossed it to the ground.

Smiling at the sight of his beautiful bare upper half,
Terri stretched out under the oak tree, head on her arm and

ate the rest of the orange slices. She watched Nate struggle with changing the kisses. The paint blew back in his face, then the glue got on him. The top of the *L* stuck to the bottom, then to his hands. The same things had happened to her the first few times and she got angry at her honorary uncles, Jake and Frank, for laughing at her. But now she had to admit that watching Nate was a bit like seeing a comedy routine.

A blue Fiat full of very pretty young women came by, slowed to a roll, and they began whistling at the shirtless Nate.

"I like kisses better," one of the blondes shouted out the window.

"I'm in cabin number seventy-one. I'm there alone on Tuesday nights," a brunette yelled.

"Hey, Terri! Did you import him just for us?"

"I do love a hairy chest. It's so *male*!"

Laughing, they sped away.

Nate looked down at Terri on the ground. "That was a friendly group."

She stood up and dusted herself off. "If those girls got you alone, you wouldn't live through it." As he came down the ladder, she squinted up at the board. "That's the worst job I've ever seen. You got paint on the *L* and you pasted it up crooked. It looks like Lake Kisse, then a slanted hyphen."

"I was probably sending some subliminal message. I like kisses better."

She was standing in front of him, her eyes on his bare chest. "You got paint on you."

"It'll come off." He was silently watching her as she raised her hand to his chest. She meant to brush away the paint, but it didn't come off. It was stuck to his hair and skin.

Nate didn't move as Terri ran her hand up onto his shoulder. Her hand was so warm, so—

"Hey!" came a male voice. "Terri is *mine!*"

They had been so absorbed in her touching Nate's bare skin that they hadn't heard the Mercedes SUV stop on the road.

As though coming out of a trance, Terri dropped her hand and turned toward the car. Inside were two gorgeous, identical young men with dark hair and eyes, and those cheekbones that clothes designers so loved.

"Terri, my love, couldn't you wait for me?" the one driving called out.

The other one leaned across. "Are we on for the Widiwick dance? You'll be my date like last year?"

Terri picked up Nate's shirt off the ground. "Don't flatter yourselves. Hayley and that lot just arrived. Go pester them."

"So who's the tank?" He was nodding toward Nate. "Can it talk?"

"Talk and break bones," Nate said in a menacing growl. "Why don't you two pretty boys find the other girls and go play?"

Terri looked at Nate in surprise. Was his anger for real?

"Looks like we have some competition this year. You're on, old man."

Laughing, they drove away.

"Who are they?" Nate asked.

"Turner Twins." She was staring at him. "You wouldn't really hurt them, would you?"

Nate laughed. "Maybe a little." He took his shirt from

her. "Do you really date those morons?" He started back to the car.

"No, but I've thought about it. And by the way, one is in law school, and the other one is on his way to being a doctor."

"An ambulance chaser and a quack. Just what the world needs more of."

Laughing, Terri got in the car beside him.

It took nearly two hours to change all three signs. On the second one, Terri climbed up to the platform and showed Nate how to do it. Everything was accompanied by laughter and the teasing they'd so easily fallen into.

By the time they finished, it was midafternoon and Nate said he was dying of hunger. Again, Terri suggested tacos, but Nate insisted on Summer Hill. Neither of them seemed to think of eating separately.

As soon as they reached the first house in town, a pretty white clapboard with a deep porch, Nate was aware of the way Terri gripped the seat. In the years he'd spent with Kit, he'd learned that subtle body movements told as much as—and sometimes more than—words did. In this case, Terri's words had been light, sounding as though she found the town of Summer Hill too boring to even visit.

But as he watched from the side of his eye, never full on, he got the impression that Terri was... Well, afraid of something.

Even as he thought about what he was going to do, he regretted it. Damn you to hell and back, Kit Montgomery, he thought as he parallel parked on the street. Kit had created in Nate an insatiable need to *know*.

"The only decent restaurant is down there," Terri said. "Are you parking here because you don't get enough exercise at the lake?"

Smiling at her joke, he got out, went around and opened the door for her. He knew she hadn't waited for him but she was picking up the orange peels where they'd fallen onto the floor. He liked that she cleaned up after herself, and sometimes after him. He liked—

Actually, so far there wasn't anything he didn't like about Terri Rayburn. He imagined a lifetime of friendship between them. He told himself that friendship was why he was doing what he was. He'd seen her reaction to the mention of the flower shop and he meant to find out what caused it. "I need to go in here," he said as soon as she was out of the car. He watched her intently, the same way he studied people when Kit dropped a bombshell on them. Later, Kit would ask Nate what he'd read on the faces of the people.

When Nate nodded toward the flower shop, Garden Day, about half the blood drained out of Terri's face.

"I'll meet you at the bookstore," she said. "It's over—"

"I know where it is. I want you to help me pick out flowers for Jamie's wife. I need to thank her for putting up with me for those first days. What do you think I should get for her?"

"I've never met her so I have no idea. Ask…them. They'll know."

Nate blinked at the underlying venom in her voice. It looked like someone in the flower shop had been part of something bad in Terri's life. He didn't want to force her to relive whatever it was. "Okay, let's go to lunch. I'll do this later." He knew he shouldn't do it in a gossipy little town, but he slipped his arm through hers.

Before Nate could take a step, a pickup truck stopped beside them. Inside was a large man, older than Terri, who looked as though he might have once been in shape, but now he had a belly and the beginning of a double chin.

"Hey, Rayburn!" he said, his voice taunting. "Good to see you finally got the courage to come into town." He looked at Nate with a smirk. "Looks like you hooked another one." With that, he sped off down the road.

Nate was truly aghast. "What was that about?" When he saw the truck halt at a stop sign, he took a step toward it. "I think I'll have a talk with him."

"It's nothing." Surprising him, Terri clamped down on Nate's arm, threw open the door to the flower shop and tugged at him to go inside.

It took him a moment to adjust to the dim light, and besides, he was frowning deeply after the jerk in the truck. Even so, he could feel how Terri had stiffened beside him. Her fingers were digging into his forearm so hard it was almost painful.

It was a pretty shop and it smelled good. There were shelves of flower arrangements, a big wall refrigerator to the right. Before them was a counter and a register, a curtain behind it.

When the curtain moved, Terri's hand gripped even harder. He was certainly glad her nails were short!

A girl, high school age, a cell phone in her hand, came out from the back—and Terri let go of his arm in what seemed to be relief.

"Can I help you?" the girl asked as though she didn't really mean it.

"We need flowers for Dr. Jamie's wife," Terri said.

Instantly the girl's eyes brightened. "I think Dr. Jamie would like roses. Or maybe sunflowers. My mom makes me go to Dr. Kyle, but Dr. Jamie is always there. Maybe next year I can go to him."

Terri had gone from looking scared to smiling. "This is Nate. He's Dr. Jamie's first cousin."

The girl's eyes widened. She glanced up and down Nate as though appraising him. "You do look like him, but you're older."

Glaring over the girl's head, Nate narrowed his eyes at Terri. He'd get her back for this! "I am very old," he said solemnly. "And I'm nothing more than a boat jockey, not a doctor like Jamie is. Did you know that he's a military hero?"

"Is he?"

The girl started to ask questions, but Nate sidestepped and went to Terri, who was looking at the flowers on the far side. "For that, you have to cook dinner tonight," he said under his breath.

"And where do you plan to eat?"

"Good point. I'll think of another punishment."

"How about a trip into Summer Hill? That should be repayment enough. What about these flowers? They look good. I think I better go before—" She broke off.

"Before what?"

He saw Terri's head come up and her body become as rigid as steel. As though she knew someone was watching her, she turned around slowly.

The girl was gone, and standing behind them was a woman about Terri's age, with dark blond hair. Everything about her was thin: hair, eyes, shoulders, arms. But it wasn't a fashionable thinness. Unless Nate missed his guess, this girl had grown up without enough to eat.

She was staring at Terri as though she needed something from her. Nate couldn't identify what her eyes were pleading for. Pity? Sympathy? No. He thought it looked like she wanted forgiveness.

For a moment Terri just stared, then she mumbled, "I'll meet you at the bookstore." In the space of a breath, she was out the door, and he saw her hurrying down the street.

Nate turned back to the young woman. He wanted to ask her questions, but he didn't know where to begin.

With Terri gone, her expression changed to business-like. "What can I help you with?"

"These," Nate said, and picked up a vase full of yellow and blue flowers.

"Certainly." She took the vase and put it on the counter. "Do you want them delivered or will you take them?"

"I'll take them." Nate was looking out the front window. Terri was nowhere to be seen. He looked at the woman who had her back to him as she wrapped the flowers in yellow tissue paper. He was a stranger in town so he knew better than to directly ask her what was going on. "Mind if I ask you a personal question?"

He saw her narrow shoulders rise as though she was about to fend off a blow. "Of course not." She didn't turn around.

"Just as we came in here, a guy in a pickup stopped and made some unpleasant remarks to Terri. What was that about?"

When she turned around, she was smiling, showing perfect teeth that he was willing to bet had all been capped. Needed because of an accident? Or a childhood without a dentist?

"Red truck? Hasn't shaved in a week? Dirty baseball cap?"

"You must have seen him." Nate knew his tone was flirtatious, but he didn't want her to refuse to answer.

"That's Hector. When Terri was a kid, she knocked him down. He says she injured his spine so badly that he missed out on a career as a pro football player. Truth is that it was booze and drugs and lack of talent that did it. But it's easier for him to blame someone else."

Nate was frowning. "He said Terri had 'another one.'"

Just as Terri had done earlier, the woman's face seemed to lose color. "She used to date a guy named Billy Thorndyke. He was big, like you. Everyone in town thought they were going to…" She didn't finish her sentence as she pushed the flowers across the counter toward him.

As Nate handed her a credit card, she put up her hand.

"No, thanks. You're a friend of Terri's so there's no charge. Listen, Mr.—"

"Nate Taggert."

"Take care of her. Terri Rayburn is a very good person."

He nodded, his mind trying to piece together what he'd been seeing and hearing. "Actually, could you please send these to Dr. Jamie's house for his wife? Tell her thanks and love from Nate. I changed my mind. I think I'll take Terri out for tacos."

"Good," she said, and went back to smiling. "I'm Kris Lennon. Anything you need for Terri, just tell me. Night or day, I'll be there." She wrote on the back of a business card and handed it to him. "This is my cell number. Call anytime."

"Sure. Okay," Nate said, and left the store. Outside, he looked up and down the street. It was such a pretty little town, and so peaceful that it looked as though nothing bad could ever have happened there.

But it had. And whatever it was, Terri seemed to be on the receiving end of it.

Nate pulled out his phone and sent a text message to Jamie.

Could you get Aunt Cale to send some autographed books
to Terri at the lake? Do you know what happened between
her and Kris at the flower shop?

The reply came back right away.

No idea. Della Kissel is the town gossip. I'll have Mom
overnight books. I hear the entire lake is invited to a party
at your house.

You two coming?

Nope. I'm staying home and frying bananas for my pregnant wife. How's Stacy?

Fine, Nate wrote back, then put the phone back in his
pocket. When it buzzed again, he didn't answer it, but he
reminded himself that he needed to call Stacy tonight. He
went across the road to the bookstore.

Chapter 6

Terri was dreaming about Nate. They were in her boat, the one her father'd had built for her. She and Nate rode in silence but when they looked at each other, they smiled as if they were sharing some secret.

They went to one of the houses Terri looked after. It was a beauty, rented out last summer to an actor who ended up in jail. As she and Nate went inside, she began telling him the story of the actor and the local play, but Nate suddenly turned. His eyes were dark. Hot. Wanting her. Telling her it was time.

Terri drew in her breath. In the next second, Nate pulled her into his arms and—

"Are you gonna get out of bed or laze around all day?" Nate said from the doorway.

Reluctantly, Terri opened her eyes halfway. Her bedroom curtains were closed, but she could see that it wasn't full daylight yet. She turned onto her stomach. "Go away."

"Today's the party and you said you were going to help

cook, so we need to get started. And there's a pile of trash in the lake. I can see it from the front windows. It has to be cleaned up."

"Udah."

"What?" When he walked to her bed, he could barely see the top of her head.

Terri pulled the cover down a bit. "It's where the old dock was. Things catch on the poles. Could you please leave? I was having a great dream."

"About those skinny boys?"

"Yes. All about them," she said.

Nate sat down on the side of the bed. "I may have invited too many people for tonight. Or rather, this afternoon. The kids asked if they could come and I couldn't say no, so I really do need to start cooking."

"Order pizza," Terri mumbled.

"I promised them a Bedouin feast."

Terri turned over and pulled the cover down to her neck to stare at him. "You promised to cook some foreign banquet for what appears to be the whole lake?"

"Not *all* of them are coming. Who lives in the big house on the hill?"

"Stanley Cresnor."

"Yeah? He's one of my uncles' clients. I had no idea he was here."

"Or you would have invited him?"

"Ah. Sarcasm," Nate said. "Now that's my Terri. Come on and get up and help me get this show underway."

Terri yawned, then stretched. And when she looked back at him, he was staring at her. For the flash of a second, the hot eyes she'd seen in her dream were his.

"Where is everyone?" came a familiar voice down the hall.

"Go out the door," Terri hissed.

It took only three long steps and Nate disappeared out Terri's bedroom door.

"In here, Dad," Terri called as she got out of bed and pulled on her jeans. She had on a bra and T-shirt before her dad got to her bedroom. "What are you doing here so early?"

Brody was looking around the room and at the bed. "Where's Nate?"

"I have no idea." Terri's voice was a model of innocence.

Brody opened the curtains to let the early morning light in and he let out a sigh of relief. "There he is. Where's he going?"

Terri went to stand by her father and saw Nate in her boat going toward the east shore. "Probably to the old dock. You can see that it has something on it."

"Yesterday some kids overturned a couple of boats. I told them to clean up, but they're not afraid of me like they are you, so they didn't get it all."

They stood side by side as they watched Nate maneuver the little boat near the big white objects. He tugged but they didn't move.

"Cut the lines," Terri said aloud.

"There are probably a thousand ropes caught on those old posts. He's going to do it the right way."

Nate stood up in the boat, pulled his shirt off, then eased over the side into the water.

"He can't do that!" Terri started out the door. "I need to warn him about how deep the lake is there."

Brody caught her arm. "I think your young man can take care of himself. Look! He's come back up and he's putting things in the boat. That's great. That place needs a cleaning. I've been meaning to do it for years."

When her father turned away, Terri saw the pain on his face. The night of the storm that took the big dock down was the night her mother went away. After that, there had been a couple of years when Brody had been grieving so deeply that he could barely function. His partner, Jake, had done most of the work around the place but that didn't include replacing an old dock.

"I have a truckload of food and booze that Nate had me get," Brody said. "Where do I put it?"

Terri was glad to change the subject. After yesterday in town she'd had all the reminders of the past that she could stand. She slid the door open. "I'll help you unload in a minute, but I'm going to watch to make sure Nate doesn't do anything stupid."

"Good idea," he said, and they went to the chairs outside. Nate dived underwater, then came back up with some pieces of garbage and tossed them into the boat.

Terri waved at him to let him know they were keeping guard, then sat down beside her father.

"You know, don't you, that you're getting in over your head with this guy?" Brody said.

"I do. I didn't but I do now. What's that saying about it being better to have loved and lost?"

"Than not to have loved at all. Yeah, I heard it, but as one who lost I'm not sure the pain is worth it." Brody's words were gloomy, but then he grinned at his daughter. "Except for you. I wouldn't have you if I hadn't loved. So how's he getting along with his fiancée? The girl he's going to *marry*."

Terri did not want to talk about that! Her dad had said his piece and no more needed to be said. "I hear Della got a release from the hospital just so she could come to the party. Are you going to ask her out?"

Della Kissel was at least fifteen years older than Brody, but she'd had a crush on him since the first day she saw him.

"I've had enough teasing about that from Frank, so don't you start. Did you know that he agreed to bring chicken and beef for the party? And I think he's planning to help cook."

Terri looked at her father sharply. "What's he up to?"

"I have no idea. But you know Frank—he always has a reason for whatever he does."

"He's not going to bring up the past again, is he?" Terri asked softly. "That thing about finding out his version of the truth? We know what happened." Nate had nearly filled the boat with rubbish that had been trapped under the lake's surface.

"I think I made it pretty clear to Frank the last time he started asking questions that I wanted him to stop. He swore that he would. But now he seems to want something from Nate."

"What's your guess?"

Brody got up and walked the few feet to the edge of the water and motioned to Nate that that was enough. Nate held up his hand, index finger raised. He had one more dive to make.

Brody turned back to his daughter. "I think Frank wants Nate to take over his job. Frank's behaved himself for years now and I think he wants to retire and spend his days fishing. Or doing anything besides getting up at 2:00 a.m. because of a complaint about noisy neighbors."

"It's not going to happen. Nate's going to work with money. He said Stacy already has an office for him."

Brody looked at his daughter. "It's on the ground floor of the Thorndyke house."

"Oh." Terri didn't return her father's stare as she watched Nate lift himself into her boat. He motioned that he was going back to the clubhouse to sort out the rubbish for recycling, then he'd be back. She nodded and waved, then looked at her father. "Let's go unload your truck. And don't tell Nate any of this about a job. Let him make up his own mind."

"You mean let him see that if an active guy like him has to sit at a desk all day he'll go insane?"

Terri couldn't suppress her grin. "Exactly. Have you seen the office?"

"No, but Frank has. He said it's got chairs with shiny steel arms. And there's Native American artwork on the walls."

"Because Nate grew up in Colorado." Terri took a breath. "That's a nice house. Maybe he and Stacy will live on the top floors."

"Yeah, maybe. Come on! Let's get to work before we depress ourselves."

Smiling, they started walking through the house. "That's us. More identical than the Turner Twins. By the way, Nate met them."

"How was that?"

"Quite gratifyingly awful. They were all jealous of one another."

"They should be. That reminds me. Elaine wants to bring a few clothes up here this afternoon. She thought you might like something new to wear."

"As opposed to my usual five-year-old T-shirts?"

"I suggested red and sparkly. Maybe low cut."

"Dad!" She was shocked.

"I'm on Team Terri. So shoot me. Elaine talked about skinny jeans and high heels."

"Absolutely not!" Terri said, then smiled. "Not too high anyway. She say anything about makeup?"

"She has a case the size of a footlocker filled with nothing but little pots and bottles."

"That's about exactly how much I'm going to need after years of sun and water." Smiling, Terri slipped her arm through her father's and they went outside to his truck.

Terri took her father's advice and chose a pair of tight pants and a red silk blouse. She and Elaine were in her bedroom and the bed was covered with clothes. Since Elaine had come to the lake, she'd been as close to a mother as Terri had ever had.

Elaine had been widowed two years before she arrived at the lake. She'd been driving from New York to Atlanta, where she planned to buy into her friend's dress shop. Elaine had always been involved in the fashion industry, and she was looking forward to being her own boss. She'd pulled off the highway to have lunch by a sign that said Lake Kisses.

That day Brody, Frank and Terri had been sitting at one of the tables in front of the pizza stand. They were going over some plans for enlarging the pavilion so they could host a farmer's market.

"You'll get more townies in here with this," Frank said, but when Brody didn't answer, they looked at him. Terri was startled to see that her father had taken on the appearance of some predatory animal. His eyes were intense!

Terri just stared at him, but Frank chuckled. In the next second they turned to see a woman at the counter. She was forty-ish and kept herself in shape: tall, slim, short dark hair. She wore tailored black linen trousers, a white blouse and gold earrings.

As though he were in a trance, Brody got up and went to her.

Frank, wearing a smirk that twisted his whole face to one side, got out his wallet. He put a twenty-dollar bill on the table.

Terri was still gaping at her father. She'd never seen him look like that or go after any visitor. In fact, he did his best to get away from them.

"Twenty bucks says she doesn't leave here," Frank said.

She looked at him. "What are you talking about?"

"Her. The chick in city clothes. She didn't go to the office so she's not here to rent. I know she doesn't own, so she's probably meaning to keep going."

"She could be somebody's guest." Terri watched as her father smiled at the woman and began talking while his eyes seemed to travel up and down her.

"Nope," Frank said. "I've only seen your father look at one other woman like that and he married her."

"You're crazy! Dad doesn't—" She stopped talking because her father slipped his arm through the woman's and they walked toward his office.

Frank put the bill back in his wallet. "You owe me twenty bucks." He got up.

"I didn't agree to your dumb bet." She was staring at her father as he ushered the woman into his office. She looked back at Frank. "But... I mean..."

Frank grinned. "Your dad used to be one of the Players. In fact he probably started them on their paths to eternal damnation."

"My father would never—"

"You better face it, kiddo, your daddy may seem to be

alone, but Brody Rayburn isn't celibate. See you later and you can introduce me to your new stepmom."

"She isn't going to be—" Terri broke off because she was shouting and people were staring. Frank waved his hand but he didn't look back.

It had turned out almost exactly as Frank had said it would. By the next morning, Brody had talked Elaine into opening a dress shop right outside his office. He'd put her in a store that had mostly sold sunscreen and ugly towels. Two weeks later, Brody tore down the wall into the boat storage next to it to give Elaine more room. He'd had to deal with some anger when people had to take their boats out of storage, but he didn't hesitate.

When the women around the lake saw a showing of Elaine's clothes set up in the clubhouse, they volunteered to help build the new store.

From that first day four years ago, Elaine and Brody had been a pair. Everyone except Frank had expected Terri to be jealous, but she hadn't been. She loved the woman almost as much as her dad did.

"You're sure about this?" Terri asked, looking at herself in the mirror over the dresser. They had the curtains drawn because the house and grounds were beginning to fill up with people.

"You look beautiful," Elaine said. "The Turner boys are going to be falling all over themselves at the sight of you."

"Oh. Them."

Behind her, Elaine smiled. "You shouldn't dismiss those two. They're handsome and rich and a lot of fun. They—"

"Can't do anything." Terri turned away from the mirror. She looked at the clothes on the bed with longing. It had been years since she'd worn pretty clothes. She used to take hours to get dressed and now she spent the day without so much as brushing her hair.

"You're right," Elaine said. "The Turner Twins can't get the kids together, can't throw a party for everyone, won't clean up lakes and old boathouses. They aren't liked by everyone they meet. They aren't a Pied Piper come to life."

Terri sat down on the bed and picked up the sleeve of a blouse with pearls along the cuff. "No one is like Nate."

"Oh, honey." Elaine sat down beside Terri and put her arms around her. "Don't fall in love with a man who's already taken. That's the way to get your heart broken. Just wait. Give him time to decide what he wants to do."

"The mayor's daughter or the girl at the lake? Not a difficult decision to make."

Elaine leaned back to look at her. "I don't know this Stacy Hartman, but I do know you, and you're as good as any young woman on this planet."

"Yeah, I guess," Terri said. When a ball bounced against the glass doors, she sat up. "I'm okay. Maybe I should go out with one of the Twins. Nate says one's an ambulance chaser and the other one is a quack."

Elaine laughed. "I think I agree with him." She waved her hand around. "How are you with all of this?" She meant the people who were inside and out of the house.

Terri got up. "I love it. You know how bad Dad and I are at socializing."

"Don't get me started. Getting him to leave the lake to go to a movie takes a week of nagging."

"That's an idea. Maybe we should open a—"

"Movie theater here? Absolutely not. You two need to learn that a world away from this lake exists. So you don't mind your house being overrun?"

"Nate will take care of it. This morning he was saying

that he and I would have to do the cooking, but he found a chef. Did you know that Mr. Parnelli used to cook for a five-star restaurant?"

"I didn't," Elaine said as she got up. "But I think your Nate knows more about the people here than I do. Everyone has met him."

"You like him too."

"Of course I do," Elaine said. "He carried in all the boxes of clothes you got in Richmond, then helped me unpack them. He liked that blouse you have on."

Terri quit fiddling with the collar in a way that said *If Nate likes it, so do I.*

Elaine pulled the curtains open. Outside the sun sparkled off the water. There were many smiling faces of people who were already there, even though it was early afternoon.

As she began gathering the clothes, Elaine saw Terri looking to one side. Nate was by the water, his phone to his ear, and he was frowning. Looked like he was arguing with someone. *Hope it's* her, Elaine thought.

With Terri's back to her, Elaine hung the blouse with the pearl-encrusted sleeves in her closet. She'd already ordered a dress for Terri for the Widiwick dance—and she truly hoped it got torn to shreds in passion.

Chapter 7

When Terri entered the living room, she had the great satisfaction of seeing Nate's eyes widen at the sight of her. He'd been laughing with three of the retirees, men Uncle Frank called would-be-Players. "They would if they could." It was a private joke he shared with Terri and her father.

She acted as though she hadn't seen Nate's appreciative look and went to the kitchen, her heels tapping on the stone floor. The long counter that her aunt used to fill with her homey desserts and casseroles was now covered with bowls and platters full of beautifully arranged food. Behind the counter was a retiree, Mr. Parnelli, in a white apron. He was flanked by two of the weekend widows, who were busy chopping and mixing, and from the look of the big stove, setting things on fire.

"Looks good, doesn't it?" Nate said from beside her.

She didn't turn to look at him. "I had no idea what

these people could do." The three of them were working together as though they'd always done it.

"Mr. Parnelli was a top chef and the ladies worked in various positions in restaurants before they married."

"Then they married money and now dedicate their lives to whatever their husbands want." She was smiling as she turned toward him. A couple of kids ran past them and jostled into Nate so that he took a step forward. His nose almost hit Terri's.

Instantly, he stepped back. "You got taller."

"It's the heels. I almost forgot how to walk in them."

"It's interesting that you do know how."

She started to reply, but over his shoulder she saw Della Kissel enter. She was a small, older woman, her face wrinkled from a lifetime of sun. Everyone in town said she had vision an eagle would envy—and at least four eyes so she saw everything.

Terri took Nate's hand and pulled him around the corner, then stopped and glanced back toward the kitchen. "Della Kissel just arrived and I have to protect you. You're fresh meat to her. If she sees you, she'll imprison you and interrogate you throughout the night."

"Yeah?" His voice was suggestive. "What's she look like?"

She sniffed his breath. "How much have you had to drink?"

"Two beers. Maybe three. Everybody is asking questions about me. I think they want to see my résumé."

"That's good. Maybe you can get some clients for your money business."

He was leaning against the wall. "I thought I had a job cleaning up rubbish from under the lake. Why was that dock taken down and how deep is it there?"

"When Dad and Uncle Jake put in Club Circle, the dock was too far away. It came down in a storm and no one rebuilt it. No one's measured the depth, but Mr. Kissel said he'd lost a couple of cows down there."

"It wasn't a cow I saw under the water."

Terri was peering around the corner. "Della is searching for you."

"Sure it's not you she wants?"

"As she loves to tell people, she used to change my diapers. There isn't much of anything that she doesn't know about me. Uh-oh. She's coming this way." Again Terri took Nate's hand, led him past the bathroom into her bedroom and shut the door.

Nate immediately stretched out on the bed. "People sure show up early for parties here."

Terri glanced out the window. "If I could, I'd turn on a neon sign saying *I told you so*. These people have nothing else to do except party. And since Mr. Do-Gooder you went around asking what everyone used to do, they now want to show off. In *my* house."

Nate gave a one-sided grin. "You don't sound like you hate it."

Terri flopped down on the other side of the bed and looked up at the ceiling. "It's been nice."

"What has?"

They'd always had a lighthearted teasing between them, but she grew serious. "What you've done here has been good for all of us. Dad and I tend to be so focused on getting the work done that we forget to have fun. Aunt Aggie used to have parties, but she invited her favorites and…" Terri turned to look at him. "You include everyone in what you do and everybody here likes you."

Instead of the smile she expected, Nate frowned. "Don't

sell yourself short. What you do to run this place is extraordinary. You're like a tribal chief keeping everyone in line. I'm just the clown."

She looked back up at the ceiling. "You're more than that. You work a lot too. You—"

"Hey!" He cut her off, as though he wanted to stop this serious talk. "Are you hungry?"

"Not especially, but I'd put money on it that you are. I'm sure Della would love to have lunch with you."

Nate got off the bed. "It's 3:00 p.m. and I haven't eaten since breakfast. I've been listening to stories of how great each man used to be. It seems that today we whippersnappers don't know what real work is. This was said while I was pulling some black strings off my arms. Got them while diving for trash."

"You shouldn't have gone shirtless." She stood up.

"If a pretty girl is watching me, I tend to strip off. Can't let all those bench presses go to waste. Why don't we—"

There was a knock at the door. "Terri? Are you in there?"

"That's Della," Terri whispered.

"I can't find that nice young man who is engaged to *marry* Stacy Hartman," Della said through the door. "He isn't alone in your bedroom with *you*, is he?"

"Subtle," Nate whispered, then slid open the door to the outside. "Follow me."

Terri practically ran past him.

Outside, there were two men attending the big barbecue grill that had magically appeared at Terri's house. It was covered with sizzling meat. When Nate grabbed sausages and bread, Terri opened a cooler and took out three small bowls of food. She had no idea what they contained.

"Here," Elaine said from behind her, and handed her

a big pink tote bag. "I put a jug of lemonade inside. Take your time. This party hasn't officially started yet."

Terri knew she should protest that she and Nate weren't running off to some love tryst, as Elaine seemed to be implying. They were escaping Della's nosy questions. But Terri just smiled. "Thanks."

Minutes later, she was running toward her boat, Nate close behind her.

And not far behind him was Della Kissel calling to Terri.

"Go!" Nate said and Terri stepped up her pace.

They practically leaped into the boat. Nate untied it while Terri started the engine. She took off so fast that Nate nearly flew out the back, but he just laughed.

Terri headed toward Club Circle, where all the shops and public buildings were, but then she made an abrupt turnaround and headed back toward her house. She thought Nate would ask what she was doing, but he didn't. She stayed close to the east shore, went into a little cove, then came back out near one of the three bridges. It was a place Nate had not seen before.

Terri cut the engine to low, then slowly went near the south side of a piece of land surrounded by water that was known as the Island.

Nate jumped into the shallow water to pull the boat onto shore. There was a stake where he could tie it.

"Damn!" Terri said as she looked at the water. She had on tight jeans and the absurdity of high heels.

Nate walked through the water and held out his arms. He didn't need to tell her to jump.

Terri decided to forego the girlie protest of "I'm too heavy" and "I could take off my shoes and wade in" etc.

In a very practiced gesture, she stepped up to the side and fell backward.

Nate caught her without so much as a grunt and carried her to the sand. "You've done that before, haven't you?"

She did *not* say "a hundred times" as those words would require explanation. "Maybe. Della is going to torture both of us."

Nate noted that she didn't answer his question.

"You can put me down now."

"Not until we get somewhere we can sit and eat."

"Ah yes, food. Your number one concern. Did you get me out just to save time?"

He didn't reply.

She loved the feeling of his big body against hers, and she wanted to lean her head against his chest. If she did, she'd be able to feel the warmth of him, hear his heartbeat. For a moment she'd be able to imagine that this was real and that he belonged to her.

Abruptly, he dropped her legs to stand her on the ground. "I'll get the food."

Half an hour later, they'd eaten the food they'd brought. Nate congratulated her on having so wisely chosen two delicious salads and a whole bowl full of brownies. They laughed over how they had blindly snatched and run.

But through it all, she kept feeling that he had something serious he wanted to say to her. Please, she thought, don't let it be questions about the gossip she was sure he'd heard by now.

When they finished their meal, Nate stretched out on the grass in some dappled sunlight, while Terri sat a few feet away. "I got bawled out by Stacy," he said.

"Oh? Any reason?" It wasn't easy to keep the hope out of her voice.

"For imposing on you."

"Because you make so much noise in the morning? And because you hog the remote and you seem to think that televisions are made only for watching sports? Or is it that you put so much chili pepper on that chicken yesterday that I could barely eat it? And you—" She broke off because he was smiling broadly.

"She doesn't know about those horrible things."

Terri drew in her breath. "Are you saying that you haven't told her that you're living with me?"

"I'm just renting. We're not *living* together." He turned his face to the sun, enjoying the warmth. "Stacy was quite…uh, vexed with me for inviting people to your house. She wanted to know if I'd asked your permission and I said I had." He turned toward Terri. "I did, didn't I?"

"You asked if a 'few friends' might come over. And you ignored my warning about the whole lake showing up." She was teasing him.

"If you want them to leave, I'll kick them out." He started to get up.

"No!"

Smiling, Nate lay back down. "I told Stace I didn't think you were upset, but I promised to make sure."

"And that's why we're here?" Terri realized that she'd had a bit of hope that it was for another reason. She knew he was staring at her, but she didn't dare look at him. He was much too good at reading what was inside people's minds for her to meet his eyes. "So what else did Stacy say?"

"She reminded me that I have brunch at her parents' house tomorrow at eleven."

That idea made her laugh and she turned to look at him. "That sounds exciting. I bet they'll be overjoyed when you show up in a rugby T-shirt and grab your food with your hands."

Nate didn't smile. "Her parents hate me."

Terri gave a snort of disbelief.

"I'm serious. They can't stand me. Her dad thinks I'm going to knock over the furniture."

"Bull in a china shop?"

"Exactly."

Terri stretched out a few feet from him. Her feet were bare and the grass felt good on her toes. Nate sounded truly upset by this. "I doubt if they actually dislike you. It's just that you're not Bob and your parents aren't the Aldersons. Why don't you get your mom and dad to come to Summer Hill and court the Hartmans? Or maybe your money uncles could befriend them. Then they might forgive you about Bob and—"

Nate sat up. "I have no idea what you're talking about." He sounded shocked. "Who is Bob? I've never heard of the Aldersons."

"Oh dear." Terri stood up and reached for her heels. "I think we better go back. Della will be telling everyone that you and I are here doing the naughty. We need to cut the gossip off before it begins."

"Sit!" Nate ordered.

She obeyed. "Wow. Do you know that you sounded just like Kit? Did I ever tell you that he once stopped three boatloads of people with just his voice?"

"I know all about Kit Montgomery. What I don't know about is Bob and company."

"I don't think it's my place to tell," Terri said primly. "Stacy is the woman you're going to marry and she—" She couldn't endure Nate's intense glare. She swallowed.

"Robert—Bob—Alderson was Stacy's boyfriend all through high school."

"High school," Nate said.

"And college. Look, I really think—"

"So when did they break up?"

"I don't know!" Terri's voice was rising. "As you've seen, Summer Hill and the lake are separate. I went to school in town but we keep socialization in our own territory."

"When was the last time you saw Stacy and this Bob together?"

Terri gave a sigh of defeat. "Last spring, Stacy came here to talk to Dad about Widiwick, and Bob was with her. Not long after that Della told us that Stacy was in DC and was having an affair with someone Kit knew. Soon after that she told us about the engagement. I'm sure Stacy broke up with Bob before she met you."

Nate was frowning. "And his parents?"

"They're best friends with Stacy's parents." She stood up. "I think we should go back."

Nate didn't move. "So it's not *me* they hate, it's just that I'm not someone else."

"I guess so. This is something you should talk to Stacy about."

"What's Bob look like?"

"Your height but thin. He played basketball in high school."

"What's he do now?"

"I don't know." Terri was getting tired of this. "I'm a lake person, not one of the Summer Hill elite. I eat food wrapped in paper, not off two-hundred-dollar plates." She turned away. "I'm going back to the boat."

Nate caught up with her. "I didn't mean to make you

angry or to pry into town secrets. I'm just trying to figure out why her parents dislike me so much."

She could see the puzzlement—and some hurt—on his face and she relented. "They'll be fine once they get to know you. It's just that the Hartmans and Aldersons have been friends for years. Lew's first wife died, but when he remarried, his new wife fit right in. And when she had Stacy, everyone said she'd grow up to marry the Aldersons' son."

"You said you didn't know much about what went on in Summer Hill."

Terri could feel her temper rising. Enough already! "I couldn't very well miss the head cheerleader and the star basketball player all over each other all through high school, now could I? Oh! Sorry. I didn't mean that."

But Nate was staring out at the water. "I'm beginning to understand. Poor guy."

"You mean Bob?"

"Sure. He lost Stacy. He must be miserable. Let's go back."

Terri was blinking at him. "Yeah. Sure. Uh… I left my…" She couldn't think what to say but ran back into the seclusion of the woods. What she wanted to do was scream so loud she'd knock the leaves off the trees. Instead, she made her hands into fists and stamped her feet until she'd stirred up a cloud of dirt. "Poor Bob," she mimicked quietly. "He lost Stacy. Lost the most wonderful, fascinating, beautiful, intelligent, interesting—"

"Come on!" Nate yelled. "There won't be any beer left."

"Princess Stacy will conjure some with her Wand of Perfection," Terri muttered.

"Are you all right?" Nate was standing a few feet away from her.

"Ah, here it is." She picked up a pebble off the ground and slipped it into her pocket. "Can't lose *that*!" She walked past him with her nose in the air.

Behind her, Nate was smiling.

When Frank got to the party, it was already in full swing—and that's what he wanted. He was taking a risk that Brody would throw him out because he was carrying his guitar.

The sight of it did cause Brody to groan, but it didn't make him angry. That was a step forward! Terri began to ask questions. When Frank told her that her father used to sing in a band, she was shocked. "I never knew. You never told me," she sputtered.

Frank noted that Nate Taggert was hovering behind her, as he always seemed to be. Since Nate had arrived, all Frank had heard about was this young man. He worked; he had ideas; he settled problems.

And Terri adored him. The two of them were never apart.

Since Nate's arrival, Frank had been hoping that the presence of this man would change things at the lake. That he'd change Brody and his daughter. That he'd... Frank had his own ideas about what he hoped the man could do, but he didn't voice them even to himself.

At the sight of Frank's guitar, it took just minutes before a couple of old-timers raced off in their electric golf carts. An hour later, thanks to Nate, a sound system was set up outside Terri's house. When the music started blaring across the water, if there was anyone at the lake who wasn't there already, they showed up.

Brody sang. His voice was rusty from years of disuse, but he did well. Two of the old codgers could really make the strings on a guitar move, and the women! Lord but they could dance! Down and dirty as if they were sixteen again. When someone yelled, "Long live Woodstock!" there was a roar of agreement.

Through it all, Frank kept his eyes on Terri. What he wanted most in the world was for her to find happiness. She'd been working since she could pick up a fishing pole. She'd been twelve when she first saved the life of a tourist. The guy was drunk, fell off the dock, went under and didn't come up—and only Terri had seen him. She ran down the dock and kept running off the end into the water, legs still churning. Brody was screaming at her to stop but when she didn't, he went in after her.

When Terri came up, she had the drunk by the collar and Brody pulled him in. Later he bawled her out and hugged her, then yelled some more, then hugged her more. But it had no effect on Terri.

All through elementary school, high school and into college, Terri had never let up on her workload and her responsibilities.

There was a time during high school when they thought Terri was going to do something besides take care of other people. There'd been a young man. To everyone's disappointment, it hadn't worked out.

Since then, as far as they knew, there'd been no other men.

But now there was this Nate Taggert. He and Terri laughed together, danced, passed a beer back and forth.

Throughout the night, the many guests asked questions. Where was this? Was it time for that? Where's the bathroom? Thousands of questions. What Frank liked was that as many questions were directed at Nate as they were at Terri. It was as though people already saw Nate as belonging at the lake. Maybe even saw him as belonging to Terri. Saw them as a couple.

At the first break the band took, Frank stepped away. He wanted to move around and see what was going on.

The first thing he noticed was that Nate was spending time with little Della Kissel. Damned if he wasn't *flirting* with her!

What's he up to? Frank wondered. He and Kit Montgomery had had some long talks about his work in the diplomatic services. Kit was a great storyteller. "If it hadn't been for Nate I would have wrung that bastard's neck," was something Kit had said more than once. He told how Nate was calm even in the midst of gunfire. And Nate was "so damned likable that people believed he was on their side," Kit said.

Frank had wanted to see Nate with Terri, but as he watched the young man get drink after drink for that gossipy little woman, Frank became more interested in them.

He wants something from her, Frank thought, and he couldn't suppress a grin. Brody kept saying that Nate was deeply in love with Stacy Hartman, but what would Della have to say about Stacy? As far as Frank knew, no one had a bad thing to say about her.

Now, Terri... There were a lot of lies told about her. And many secrets were being kept.

If Nate was plying Della with drink to find out something, did that mean he was interested in Terri?

That hope made Frank play the next set with such enthusiasm that people stopped dancing and cheered him. The oldies weren't the only ones who were good on the strings.

When Della began weaving from too much to drink, Nate volunteered to drive her home, and helped her into his car. Her house was small and ordinary, the grounds around it neatly kept. Inside, it was packed with furniture that was part antique, part just old, and floor-to-ceiling shelves full of ornaments. It looked like Della's hobby was haunting auction houses and estate sales. It was all clean and tidy, but the close-knit clutter of it made Nate's skin crawl.

She was hardly in the door before she turned to him. "So what is it you want me to tell you?"

He was pleased that she knew why they were there. "I want to know about Billy Thorndyke."

"Billy?" Della gave a sly smile. "Shouldn't you be asking about Bob Alderson?"

"I know about him. Who I don't know about is Thorndyke."

"You're like me, aren't you? You want to know everything about everyone."

"We all rationalize what we do," Nate said under his breath.

"What was that?"

"Nothing. Tell me about Thorndyke."

"Is it him or Terri you want to know about?" Again, that sly look came back.

"I guess I'll go back to the party," Nate said. "I'm sure you'll be all right here alone." He didn't get one step closer to the door before Della called him back.

"I think I'm going to need some help tonight," she said. "When you get to be in your fifties as I am, life is harder for you."

Before he turned back toward her, Nate rolled his eyes. She hadn't seen fifty in a decade.

"I'll just slip into something more comfortable."

When she stepped behind an old-fashioned screen, Nate walked around the room, looking at what was on

the shelves. He'd learned that silence often made people
talk. And it was only wanting to know that made him stay
there. When he saw some items that he knew were valuable, he was almost distracted from his purpose.

"Billy was a big guy, like you, and that's Terri's type,"
she said from behind the screen. "The only other man I've
ever seen her with was an NFL football player who came
here for a couple of weeks. You know, I think I should
warn you that you'd better be careful. If Terri decides she
wants you, she may put on a tight dress and try to take you
away from dear little Stacy Hartman. I guess you know
that her father is the mayor."

"Yes, I know that."

"But maybe Terri won't try anything. She's a nice girl
now, but she used to be just like her mother."

"Her mother?" Nate had heard nothing about the
mother except that she'd died when Terri was two.

"Oh yes. She had a job in a store in Summer Hill, and
when she met Brody, she went after him. She put on a tiny
bikini and her short shorts and Brody never had a chance.
Leslie always got what she wanted."

At the name "Leslie," Nate's eyes widened. It was the
name Kit had texted to him. Nate waited for her to con-
tinue.

"Everybody here at the lake hoped Terri wouldn't turn
out to be like her mother. But she did. In high school Terri
was a real *femme fatale*—if you know what I mean." Della
stepped out from behind the screen. She had on a negligee that looked to be about thirty pounds of pink silk and
white lace. She could have played a courtesan from the
1890s. As she sat down on an overstuffed blue couch, she
fluttered her lashes at Nate.

"Terri?" he encouraged as he took a chair a few feet away.

An involuntary sigh of exhaustion escaped her, but her love of gossip made her go on. "Terri began wearing makeup when she was quite young. You wouldn't know it to look at her now, but she can be a real knockout. Put her in a slinky dress and wow! Back then she wore a lot of things that were tight and revealing. But then, she only had her dad, and Brody was overwhelmed with everything. He had no idea how to handle a beautiful teenage daughter. If he'd just had a wife… Or if he'd allowed me to help him, I could have…" She trailed off.

Nate could see that the drink was catching up with her and she wouldn't stay awake much longer. He wanted to get her back on track. "Billy Thorndyke?"

"Oh, poor, poor Billy. He had no resistance against Leslie's daughter. He was so in love with Terri—and truthfully, we thought she was with him." Della leaned toward Nate. "You have to understand that Billy Thorndyke was from a *very* good family in Summer Hill. They'd been in the town from when it was settled, so it was a huge step *up* for Terri Rayburn. Not that there's a class system in this country, but…"

"I understand." Only years of training in diplomacy enabled Nate to keep what he felt off his face.

"Terri and Billy went together for over a year. Their… What do the kids call it? One of those initial things. PD… Public…"

"PDA? Public display of affection?"

"That's right. Those two were always all over each other. Groping. Fondling. And Terri kept wearing less and less clothing. I tried to talk to Brody about her, but he wouldn't listen. He was downright rude!"

"What a shame," Nate said. "And there you were trying to help."

"That's exactly what I thought! And I turned out to be right because Terri dumped Billy. *She* dumped *him*. Flat. Just like that. One day they were all over each other and the next she wouldn't speak to him. I tried to get Brody to tell me what was going on, but he said he didn't know and that it was none of my business. I've always cared about him and his child so how was it *not* my business?"

"I bet you didn't let his words stop you."

Della gave a girlish laugh. "Certainly not! Poor Billy was heartbroken. We saw him pleading with Terri to listen to him. Begging! It was humiliating. But Terri would walk away. To see one of Virginia's finest young men debase himself like that was more than most of us could stand. I mean, Brody is a tip-top man, but Terri is Leslie's daughter. How did she dare hurt the Thorndyke son?"

All Nate could do was swallow and nod. If he spoke he might tell the vindictive little woman what he thought of her.

"Anyway, about a month later, the Thorndyke family moved. It was like on some murder mystery show. They didn't tell anyone they were planning to go. They just packed up and left in the middle of the night—and they never returned. They hired someone to oversee the packing of their furniture, and sold the house to someone in the family. In the years since, they've never returned to visit all the people they know and love. We heard that Billy's father took a job in Oregon. But what kind of state is that? Who lives there?"

Della took a breath. "All because Terri dropped dear Billy. He was the type of boy who was destined for great things but he didn't do any of them. The world never heard of him. He still lives in Oregon, and I think he works for his father." She looked at Nate as though she was about to cry. "How could Terri have done that to such a lovely young man?"

Only years of training enabled Nate to keep from lashing out at the dreadful little woman. "Did you try to find the answer to your question?"

"Oh yes. I asked everyone what they knew, but not even Brody had an answer to explain what his daughter had done." Della's eyes were bleary as she again leaned toward Nate. "I tried to tell him that I could have helped. If Terri had been *my* child, things would have been very different."

Nate had to grit his teeth to keep from replying to that scary thought. "What happened with Terri's mother?"

Della was struggling to keep her eyes open. "No one told you? She ran away with another man and left her young husband and two-year-old daughter behind." She paused to let this revelation sink in. "That child was left alone and she cried for hours. I think a lot of her problems now stem from that horrible night. She may think she doesn't remember it, but she does."

"And Brody?" Nate asked softly.

"He never recovered from his wife leaving him. I told him we'd all seen it coming. The way Leslie used to swish around this place in her skimpy dresses made men go crazy for her. Just as I predicted, she ran away with one of them." Della gave a sleepy, one-sided smile. "You want me to tell you a secret?"

"Very much."

"I tried to tell Jake—you know, Brody's partner—this when it happened, but he wouldn't listen. He threatened me that if I told anyone he'd... I don't want to remember what he said but I've kept quiet all these years."

"What did you tell Jake?"

"I believe that Leslie ran away with the man staying in cabin twenty-six. He was a very handsome man. Not as good-looking as Brody, but he had the advantage that he was rich. The man told me he was there because his wife was visiting her college girlfriends. He said she didn't like water, so it was his chance to stay at a lake. I never believed him. I saw the way he looked at Leslie. And I saw her talking to him. *Twice!*"

"You certainly keep an eye on people, don't you?"

"I do my best." She fell back against the sofa, too tired to keep her eyes open. "Today no one wants to hear about what I see. Now they have the internet and reality shows. I ask kids why they'd want to watch what's going on with strangers when the same things are happening right here." She suppressed a yawn, but didn't open her eyes. "Have you seen the lights that move around the lake at night?"

"I have," he said softly.

"The stories I could tell you about who visits whom! Those women have babies nine months after a visit to Lake Kisses." She gave a little laugh. "I tell people that we're as good as a fertility clinic. They… They…" She was drifting off. "People think I can't keep secrets but I do. I haven't told the mayor that you're living with Terri. That counts, doesn't it?"

"Yeah," Nate mumbled, and he saw that she had at last fallen asleep.

It took Nate several moments to recover from the anger he'd kept inside as he'd heard what the woman said. Whatever the truth was behind a high school breakup, Della Kissel had magnified it into something horrible—and years later she was making sure the flames kept burning. Bad things had happened to the Rayburn family, but instead of comfort and support, they'd had to deal with

Della's snide innuendos and her endless prying into painful wounds.

As Nate stood up and looked down at the little woman, he shook his head. What in the world had caused her to become so miserable that she wanted to take everyone down with her?

He left her on the couch. She was small so it fit her and the huge silk garment would keep her warm.

Outside, he felt as though he'd left a den of poison, as though an evil smoke was curling through the place, seeping into every crevice, into every pore of his skin.

He drove back to Terri's house and got out of the car. The doors and windows were open and there was music and laughter, but he didn't go inside. He leaned against his car and breathed deeply of the cool night air. If there weren't a houseful of people, he'd strip off and go swimming in the lake. Maybe the water would help to clean the inside of his mind.

"I see you've met Della."

Nate wasn't surprised to see Frank Cannon stepping out of the dark. He didn't have on his sheriff's uniform, just jeans, and a T-shirt that said he'd been conceived at Woodstock. "I did."

"I saw you plying her with drink, then volunteering to drive her home. No one willingly spends time with her unless they want to know something. So what was your question? About Stacy or Terri?"

"I wanted to know about Billy Thorndyke."

"Ah. Right. How our Terri dumped the golden boy?"

Nate could hear anger in Frank's voice. He'd seen that the man loved Terri, so it was understandable. "I don't get it," Nate said. "A high school breakup is blamed for 'ruining' some kid's life? And a girl's shove to a footballer 'ruined' his life? Why is Terri being blamed for these things that are blown way out of proportion?"

"Leslie," Frank answered. "It all comes from her."

"If Della is to be believed, she was the Slut of Summer Hill." It was dark, but from the light of the house, Nate could see anger flash in Frank's eyes.

"She wasn't," he managed to say. "Della Kissel wanted Brody, but Leslie got him." He took a few breaths to calm down. "You heard Della's jealous version of the story, so anytime you want to hear the truth, come to me. I have files."

"I'm not a mystery solver," Nate said. "I'm going to marry a lovely young woman, open a branch of my family's investment firm and start a family. That's all."

"I understand," Frank said. "And that goal led you to get Della drunk, take her home and ask her a lot of questions. But I can assure you that the truth of Leslie Rayburn is much more interesting than what Della Kissel tells. Not that I know it all. My contacts are too limited to find out much. But one thing I did discover is that Leslie didn't exist before she arrived in Summer Hill."

"I don't—"

"I know!" Frank put up his hand. "You don't want to be involved. You had all that with Kit. He told us enough about his life that I know what you two did. Now you're what? Thirty-five? Six? You want to retire and make babies. I want to retire and fish and read cowboy stories. We all have our dreams. But in the end, we do what we *can*." He took a few steps toward the house but turned back. "Let me give you some advice. Don't mention Leslie to either Brody or Terri. And Billy is taboo to her. You start opening your mouth and you'll find yourself thrown out of the house, out of the friendship, and no longer welcome at the lake. You got that?"

"Yeah, I do," Nate said.

"Hope you have a happy life, kid. That new office of yours sure is slick. Summer Hill ain't never seen nothin' like it. It's New York in Virginia—with some Texas thrown in." With his laughter drifting into the dark, Frank went into the house.

Chapter 8

Terri didn't want to be awake. She wanted to snuggle back under the covers and stay there. It was Sunday and it must be very early because she didn't hear a single motor on the lake.

She got up, went to the bathroom, then, yawning, started to get back into bed. The clock said it was ten fifteen, but that couldn't be right. She never slept late. Besides, Nate was supposed to be at the Hartmans' at eleven. He must have already gone. Odd that she didn't hear him.

She was nearly back to sleep when she realized that he hadn't left. There was no way he could have slipped out of the house quietly enough that she hadn't heard him. By the end of the party he'd been grilling food. If he hadn't taken a shower last night, he needed one this morning, which meant that he had to get up *now*!

She threw back the covers and, barefoot, ran past the kitchen and down the hall to Nate's room.

He hadn't drawn his curtains so no light came in. Nate

was still in bed, on his stomach, and the blanket across his waist bared his broad, naked back.

For a moment, all she could do was stare. How very much she'd like to touch him! She'd like to pull off her clothes and get on top of him. Feel the warmth of him, the heat, her bare breasts against his nude skin. She'd like to kiss his neck, then move down his spine.

Turning, she took a step out of the room. She couldn't do this to herself. She had to get control. Maybe if she got dressed and went out in her boat, she could calm down.

But what about Nate? If he slept through the brunch, they'd ask questions—which could lead to finding out where he lived.

"Oh hell!" she muttered. When she was back in his room, she did her best not to look at Nate's bare skin. She grabbed a pillow and threw it at the back of his head. "Get up! You're going to be late."

Turning away from him, she went to his closet and slid the door open. "I bet you haven't even thought about what you're going to wear." She spoke so loudly that she was close to shouting. "It's supposed to be hot today so maybe you can get away with no jacket." She pulled out a white short-sleeved shirt and held it out. "No. Too informal. You'd look like a salesman."

She pulled out a light blue long-sleeved cotton shirt. "This one will do." As she tossed it on the end of the bed, she looked at him.

He'd rolled over and put a pillow behind his head, but his eyes weren't fully open. His naked chest was exposed. She threw another pillow at him, but he caught it before it hit his face.

"Late for what?" he mumbled.

"Brunch. Remember that? At the mayor's house?"

With a groan, Nate shook his head. "I think I broke a toe last night. Or maybe it was an ankle."

Terri was going through hangers of Nate's trousers and stopped at a black pair with a crisp crease down the front. "Nothing on you is broken and you can't get out of this. You have to take a shower. You smell like beer and smoke."

That made Nate give a snort of laughter and he threw back the cover. The only thing he had on was a pair of blue boxers.

Terri watched him walk into the bathroom. Legs! Was every part of him big and strong and hard? It wasn't until Nate disappeared around the doorway that she let out her breath.

"There are no towels in here."

"Look under the sink."

"I used all of them last night when the Wilson kid got sick. Elaine put them in the washer and later I stuck them in the dryer." Nate looked around the door. "Could you get me a couple? Please?" He went back into the bathroom and turned on the shower.

Terri took off running down the hall. She and Nate had had to adjust to each other's laundry. She'd learned to search his pockets. "You washed this paper and I can't read it," he'd complained. "It's the model number off that broken pump that's under cabin sixty-two. Now I'll have to slide back under there in that filth to read it again." Her request was that he not put her bras in the dryer. "They're expensive and the dryer destroys the elastic. Just sling them over the shower door."

She got two towels out of the dryer, hurried back down the hall and got clean underwear out of his chest of drawers. She'd put them in there the day before.

The bathroom door was ajar and, keeping her eyes off the shower, she put her load on the counter. She paused by the door, her face turned away from him. "So what did you want to know from Della? The dirt on Bob Alderson? Your competition?"

"Does everyone think I was after something from her?"

That question startled her enough that she turned around. *Ah*. Nate naked behind a piece of frosted glass. She could see the silhouette of him. He was shampooing his hair. But it was so short that maybe he was using bar soap. It seemed odd that there was something she didn't know about him. "Who else asked you? Wait. I bet it was Uncle Frank. I saw him watching you flirt with Della. Anyway, what did you find out?"

"I wasn't flirting."

She saw him pause under the water as he rinsed his body. His strong, hard body. She *had* to get out of the room! But Nate's voice made her stop. "What have you heard that's bad about this guy Alderson?"

Terri was silent as she watched him. He was making her body ache.

"Are you still there?"

Terri saw him lean forward as though he meant to look out. Quickly, she sidestepped and left the room, then hurried to the closet to rummage through his few pieces of clothing.

When Nate came into the bedroom, he had a towel around his waist. It wasn't a Dad towel that fastened high above the belly button. No, it was way down low on his hips. She did her best not to look at him—and she began talking fast. "Pick me up at five and we'll go get something to eat and I'll tell you about Widiwick. Tomorrow is what Dad calls the Day of Demons."

"Is that what they were talking about when they said D Day? I thought that was about WWII."

"No. It's about tomorrow. The sellers come to put up booths and tents. It's chaos and tears and fights and too many accidents. Either Dr. Kyle or Jamie will be here."

"If it's a war, Jamie will show up. But what's this about? I thought it was a festival."

"I'll tell you everything later, but we have to be back at six thirty for Dad's meeting." Her voice was rising. Nate was just feet from her and wearing only a towel! "You can't wear one of your T-shirts to a meal with the mayor's family. And no jeans! Here, these will look nice." Stepping around the bed, she held up the black trousers, blocking her view of him. "I can't decide if you should wear a towel or not." Instantly, she realized what she'd said. "I meant a tie." When he was silent, she looked at him. He was staring at her in an odd way, almost as though he was angry at her.

"You need to put some clothes on." His voice was a deep-throated growl.

Terri looked down at herself. She had on an oversize T-shirt and underpants. While the top half of her was covered, nearly all of her legs were bare. "Sorry. I ran down here." Across a chair was a pair of his gray sweatpants and she quickly pulled them on. They were huge on her and she had to tighten the drawstring to keep them up. "Better?"

Nate didn't smile. "Some, but I wish I didn't have a memory." Shaking his head as though to clear it, he dropped his towel to the floor. All he had on were clean boxers.

"Hey!" Terri said, frowning. "If I'm to cover up, why isn't it the same for you?"

With a shrug, Nate picked up his trousers. "You want me to explain the inequality of the world to you? Can't do it." Trousers on, he reached for the shirt she'd laid out for him.

Terri was holding two black belts, one very dressy, one with visible lacing. "Hmmm. Since it's a brunch, maybe the less formal belt will do."

Nate was standing in front of her with his hand extended.

She handed him the less formal belt and he began slipping it through the loops. "I want you to take this brunch seriously. You must mind your manners, eat nothing with your hands and do *not* ask for a beer. Drink whatever they give you. If they offer you a cocktail, ask for something civilized, like a…a…gin and tonic. That's good."

He was standing close to her and rolling up the sleeves of his shirt. "Anything else, Mom?"

"Mom?" Terri's eyes widened. "That's a good idea. You should have taken the new Cale Anderson book with you as a gift. I'd give them my copy, but it has my name in it. It was really nice of your aunt to send it. She—"

Smiling, Nate put his hands on her shoulders and spoke calmly. "Everything will be fine. I've been to three state dinners at the White House. No one complained about my table manners."

"I know. It's just that you've been here for a while and lake people are a bad influence. Ask anyone in Summer Hill." She stepped away from him.

When Nate's smile left him, she thought that for all his bravado, he seemed genuinely worried about the meeting. But it was just brunch with his future in-laws. How bad could it be?

He glanced at the bedside clock. "I'm going to be late."

They walked to the front door and when Nate turned to

leave, he hesitated, then glanced up at the house as though memorizing it. "I don't know why, but I feel like a kid leaving home for the first time. I wish I'd said no to this, but…" He took a breath. "I guess I should go."

"Gift!" Terri said. "You should take a gift. Stay here."

She ran to the kitchen, grabbed two bottles of wine left over from the party, then ran back to him. "I'm sure Stacy would have put them in pretty bags with ribbons on them."

He grinned. "I would have taken a six-pack."

"Or a pan full of chicken bits so hot Mayor Hartman would have had a heart attack."

For a moment they laughed together, then Nate straightened his shoulders. "Okay, I have to go. I'll see you later."

To the astonishment of both of them, Nate gave her a quick kiss on the lips. It wasn't a kiss of passion, but one like a married couple would exchange. Familiar, easy, practiced. Only it wasn't.

They both stepped back, startled, eyes wide.

"I, uh…" Nate said.

Terri recovered first. "It's okay. We're both nervous. Go! I'm sure Mayor Hartman is a stickler for punctuality."

"All right." Nate was backing toward his car, looking at her as though puzzled by something.

"And quit kissing people!" Terri said. "Don't greet Mayor Hartman with a kiss on the lips. Or Mrs. Hartman. Forget all the years you've spent in countries where they kiss everyone. No lip kissing!"

Her joke pulled Nate back to the present. "I hear they have a cook." He opened the door of his car.

"Kissing her is fine. Just not the mayor."

Smiling, Nate nodded as he started the engine and backed out.

Terri went inside, closed the door and leaned on it. Nate

kissed her. It's all that was in her mind. It wasn't the kind of kiss she'd like to have had, one where they were both so overcome with passion that they couldn't stop. Tongues and lips and clothes flying off. Nope, not that kind of kiss at all. It was more…

Friendship, she thought and pushed away from the door. "I get friendship and Stacy gets the passion. Stacy gets the *man*." As she looked out the front glass at the lake, she imagined Nate at brunch. No doubt he'd use his White House manners and win the Hartmans over. How could they not like him? Everyone at the lake adored Nate. Last night at the party, he'd been the hit of the evening. It may have been Terri's house, but everyone asked Nate about where things were and what they could do—and he'd answered them all.

Yes, the Hartmans would fall in love with Nate. *And then what?* she thought. When he got back would he tell her that he was moving out? He'd probably say, "I'd forgotten how much I deeply and truly love Stacy Hartman and I'm going to go stay with her parents. They make me feel closer to the woman I love with all my heart and soul." Or something like that. Knowing Nate, she'd see him putting his bags in his car and he'd call out "See you around, kid" as he drove away.

She went into the kitchen. The cooks had cleaned up after themselves, and people had picked up rubbish, but the place could still use a good scrub. She started to get cleaning supplies out, but then she thought, *Screw it*! She was going to go to Club Circle and see what other people were doing. Right now she did *not* want to be alone.

As Nate drove away, he didn't let himself think about what had just happened with Terri. It had been an accident. Caused by his ridiculous worry about spending time with Stacy's parents.

He'd tried not to let the fact that they'd never liked him bother him, but it did. Maybe it was the novelty of it that got him. All his life he'd been *liked* by people.

As a child he'd been the one chosen first for teams—and he'd used his popularity to help underdogs. He used to say that he'd only be on a team if some scrawny, nerdy kid could be with him. Helping people had always made Nate feel… Well, powerful. Needed.

During all the years with Kit, it had been Nate who calmed nerves. When Kit yelled, "Come!" people followed. But after they were there, it was Nate who took care of them. He solved problems and settled arguments. Kit could never be bothered with where people could get food and water.

The fact that Stacy's parents had taken one look at Nate and curled their upper lips in distaste had jolted him. In the two weeks they'd spent visiting in DC, Nate had done everything he could to please them. He called in favors and got Mr. and Mrs. Hartman—there'd been no invitation to call them by less formal names—into museums after hours, backstage at plays. Mr. Hartman had a long meeting with the Virginia senator.

But none of it had made a difference. On the last night, at dinner at an elegant restaurant, Mrs. Hartman had picked up her salad fork and nodded to Nate. It took him a moment to understand that she was showing him the correct fork to use. After all his work over an exhausting two weeks, their opinion of him as a lower-class, uneducated Neanderthal had not changed.

As he pulled into the driveway and turned off the engine, he didn't get out. He just sat there, dreading what was to come.

He didn't like their house. It was probably built in the 1940s, but had been greatly added onto over the years. It was now two stories, with a roof that jutted out supported by two tall columns.

Stacy had seen Nate's face the first time he saw the house. "Isn't it dreadful? But Dad grew up wanting the Stanton house and when he couldn't get it, he tried to make his parents' house as Stantony as possible."

Whatever the reason, Nate truly disliked everything about it—especially the location. Right in town, stores on both sides of it. It was too public for his taste, but Llewellyn Hartman was the mayor of Summer Hill and he took the idea of being available to the citizens—his subjects—very seriously.

Nate put on his best diplomatic face, got out of his car, went to the door and rang the bell.

Mrs. Hartman greeted him. Like Stacy, she was a small woman, all pink and blonde, with porcelain skin that had always been protected from sun and weather. She gave a bit of a smile but it wasn't real. She even aimed a kiss at his cheek but her lips didn't touch him.

"We have other guests." Her tone implied that Nate needed to be warned. Or what? He'd misbehave?

Nate followed her into the living room that he knew had been decorated by Stacy. She'd done her best to give it what she called "the Kennedy vibe." Fabrics that looked worn, almost careless. Cottons, not silk. "Rich but not flaunting it," she'd said.

Standing to one side of the room were two men and a woman. One was Llewellyn Hartman, a short man who probably weighed the same as he did in high school. He kept his shoulders back in an almost military stance, although Nate knew the man had never been in service.

Next to him was a taller man, about the same age, with a look of prosperity about him. Close by the men was a woman, also taller, slim, wearing half a dozen pieces of gold jewelry. Mrs. Hartman went to stand beside them.

All four of them were staring at Nate in silence. He'd been in some tough social situations before, but this could possibly be the worst. Did he introduce himself? Or should he knock over a crystal vase and reinforce what they seemed to think of him?

"Hello," came a voice from behind him.

Turning, Nate saw a tall, thin young man, good-looking in a polished sort of way, his hand outstretched in welcome.

"I'm Bob Alderson and these silent rocks are my parents. In case you haven't guessed, everyone is furious with you for having stolen the girl they wanted for me."

"Really, Bob," the taller woman said. "Do you have to be so crass?"

Nate shook the man's hand, gratefully.

Bob put his hand on Nate's shoulder, and said, "Don't let them get you down. It was mutual with Stace and me, but they won't believe that." Bob grinned at the two sets of parents. "I'm starving. Let's eat!"

They went into the dining room, and as Nate knew it would be, the table was set formally. When Nate had worked in DC, he'd sublet an apartment from a cousin who was temporarily working in Milan. It was a big place, all the furniture was upholstered in white. The tables, big and little, had glass tops. Stacy had loved it so much that he'd never had the heart to tell her that he hated it.

Every night when he got home from a job he detested,

he'd been greeted by Stacy dressed as sweetly as a 1950s housewife. She'd made him an exquisite dinner of salad and some low-calorie protein and lots of steamed vegetables. He never told her that on days when he hit the gym, he ate a foot-long sub with some hot and spicy filling before he went home to her cute little dinner.

Meals with Stacy weren't like the ones he'd shared with Terri. The rain outside, feet propped up, big slices of pizza, beer—and revealing confidences.

"Nathaniel," Mrs. Hartman said, "you seem to be amused by something. Care to share it with us?"

He looked up. The Aldersons were across from him, their eyes accusatory. The Hartmans were at opposite ends of the table. Bob was beside him. Nate couldn't come up with a reply.

"Carol," Bob said to Mrs. Hartman, "I bet Nate is thinking about how sublime this frittata is. You have outdone yourself."

Mrs. Hartman blushed with pleasure. "Oh, Bob, you've always been so charming."

The implication was plain. By comparison, Nate was a thug.

"I hear you've been staying at the lake," Mr. Alderson said to Nate. "They are quite different people, aren't they?"

"I like it," Nate managed to say. "I enjoy my time there and I do my best to help out."

"Doing what? Baiting hooks for weekend widows?" Mr. Alderson's voice was smug—and filled with dirty innuendo.

"I think that—" Nate began, and there was anger in his words.

"How's Terri?" Bob's voice was loud, drowning out

whatever Nate had been about to say. "I always liked her in high school. We tried to get her on some of the sports teams but she always ran home to work. I haven't seen her for a while. How is she?"

"Great." Nate gave his first genuine smile since he'd arrived. "She and her dad run the place. Actually, Terri does most of the work. If there's a problem, she fixes it. Everything from keeping raccoons out of the garbage to saving the lives of people who fall into the lake. Last night we had a party at her house and nearly everyone at the lake came. Brody was singing and Frank played a guitar, then some of the old-timers showed up with instruments and it turned into rock and roll heaven. We…"

Everyone but Bob was looking at Nate in horror.

"That sounds like a party at the lake." Lew Hartman's voice showed his disgust. "I'm glad the sheriff was there in case it got too rowdy."

Mrs. Alderson was staring at Nate. "Terri Rayburn is a very pretty girl, but she broke Billy Thorndyke's heart. We thought maybe Billy was destined to be President someday, but after Terri dropped him, he lost his spirit."

Nate kept his head down. If he let himself go, he might tell the woman what he thought of her. *I must be a diplomat!* he thought. He looked across at Mrs. Alderson and did his best to take the anger out of his eyes. "You seem like someone who knows things. Can you explain Kris Lennon's strange behavior to me?"

The question seemed to knock the woman off balance. "Lennon? I don't know anyone by that name. Where…?"

"Crystal Wilkins," Mrs. Hartman said.

"Oh yes, of course. I'd forgotten about her. And Abby and Rodney. Oh my, but that was a long time ago."

Within seconds, the four adults started talking over each other as they remembered the Wilkins family.

Bob glanced at Nate and gave a discreet thumbs-up. The subject had been changed, and a new story was being told.

"Years ago, four pretty girls from the East Coast went to Lake Kissel for a month. But Abby Lennon met a Summer Hill boy, Rodney Wilkins," Mrs. Alderson said, and smiled at Mrs. Hartman. "We went to school with him. Remember how gorgeous he was?" She paused for a moment. "Nearly six feet tall, black hair, blue eyes. Rode a Harley at sixteen. When he walked down the hall, every female stopped to look."

"Of course, he wasn't the right sort," Mr. Alderson added.

"No," Mrs. Alderson said. "Roddy was pure, primal sex appeal!"

"Mother!" Bob said in mock protest.

"Anyway," Mrs. Hartman said, "Abby came to visit the year after graduation and she and Roddy fell for each other. They eloped and she stayed in Summer Hill."

"And Roddy became a deputy sheriff," Mr. Hartman said. "He was good at his job. Fair and honest."

"We all liked him," Mr. Alderson added. "One night I had too much to drink but I still drove home. Roddy stopped me and—" He shrugged. "He could have put me in jail but he didn't. My life might have been different if it weren't for him driving me home that night."

"Abby and he were a happy couple and they had a baby, Crystal, and..." Mrs. Alderson trailed off.

"When Crystal was three or four, Roddy was in a car accident," Mr. Alderson said. "It wasn't his fault. The drunk driver walked away unscathed, but Roddy was badly hurt."

They all looked at Mr. Hartman. "Roddy's face was torn up and the left side of his body smashed. For the rest of his life he was always in pain and..."

"And always angry," Mr. Alderson said.

Mrs. Alderson leaned forward. "We think he was abusive to Abby and the child, but they would never say so. She became the support of the family and..." She looked at the others.

"It was bad," Mr. Hartman said. "The church tried to help, but Roddy wouldn't accept charity."

Everyone grew quiet at the memory.

"But now the daughter owns a flower shop," Nate said.

"Yes, she does," Mr. Hartman said. "Poor Roddy died just as Crystal was about to graduate from high school. He could no longer ride a motorcycle but one night he tried to."

"Ran headlong into a tree," Mr. Alderson said. "Dr. Everett said his alcohol level was through the roof."

"The day after the funeral," Mrs. Alderson said, "Crystal and her mother left town. We didn't see or hear from them until two years ago. Mother and daughter came back to Summer Hill, bought the flower shop and have done a splendid job of running it. They've become a true asset to this town."

"Like Billy Thorndyke," Nate said softly.

"Billy?" Mr. Hartman asked. "What does he have to do with the Roddy Wilkins family?"

"Nothing that I know of," Nate said. "It's just that the stories are the same. At about the same time, the Wilkins family and the Thorndykes abruptly left town."

Instantly, expressions of distaste were back on the faces

of the four older adults. Their spines went rigid and they looked at Nate with glaring stares.

"I can assure you," Mrs. Alderson said, "that there is no connection between the two families. The Thorndykes were our friends. Why young Billy was so infatuated with Terri Rayburn from the lake, no one could understand— but a Wilkins? Certainly *not*!"

Mr. Alderson put his hand over his wife's. "I seem to remember that Abby was friends with Leslie Rayburn."

"Sometimes," Nate began, his voice low and hard, "people—"

"Hey!" Bob said as he abruptly stood up. "I think I should take Nate to see his office. Anyone object to our leaving?"

No one moved but their expressions said it all. *Please take him away* was written on their faces.

When they were outside, Bob said he'd come with his parents so they'd better take Nate's car. "Unless you want to walk. Your office is very close."

"Of course it is," Nate muttered. "Let's use my car." He drove as Bob directed him. They went down a side street and pulled into the drive of a big Victorian house. Nate was glad to see that it wasn't too gaudy. With the mood he was in, if the house had been painted a dozen shades of purple he might not stop.

He and Bob got out of the car. There were tall shade trees around the house and a gentle breeze swayed the leaves. The pleasantness of it was calming Nate.

"I want to apologize for my parents," Bob said. "You won't believe it, but they're very nice people. It's just that they love Stacy so much. Her mom and mine have been best friends since before Stace was born."

"And they wanted their kids to marry."

"Right," Bob said.

"What about you?" Nate's eyes zeroed in on Bob's.

"I love Stacy and we really tried to make it work. We wanted to please our parents, but…" He shrugged. "It was boring. We knew everything about each other. I sat beside her in the first grade so I know she hates peanut butter. I was there when Elliot Pierce hit her with a stick and she kicked him back, so I know why they still dislike each other. I helped her glue fabric swatches in her notebooks. I cried with her when Daisy died."

Nate was trying to keep his expression neutral. He didn't know any of these things about Stacy. Twice he'd bought her chocolate-covered peanut butter cups. She'd eaten a few but she'd never said she didn't like them. And what notebooks? "Daisy?" he asked.

"Her cat. She *loves* cats!"

"Oh, right." When Nate said he liked dogs, not cats, Stacy hadn't registered an opinion one way or the other.

"I just want to say that it was a mutual breakup. One night after we went to a movie together we didn't have a word to say because we knew what the other one thought. There was no reason to talk. When we got in the car, Stacy said, 'Let's break up.' I said, 'That's the best idea I've heard in years.' We were both very happy."

Bob gave Nate a look of apology. "Sorry for this, but Stacy and I were too cowardly to tell the parents. We just kind of avoided the whole subject."

"Then she met Kit."

"She did," Bob said. "She worked on that play with him and he sent her to DC to meet his son—not his workhorse of an assistant."

"And she returned with me." Nate wasn't good at hiding

his bitterness over that. Kit sent a princess to his prince of a son.

"And as you saw, the parents haven't recovered. But don't worry. Stacy will straighten them out."

That idea bothered him. He'd helped solve international skirmishes but it would be his wife-to-be who'd handle four disappointed parents?

"You ready to see your office?"

Nate looked up at the house with its deep porch. "Who owns this place?"

"I don't know. Someone in the Thorndyke family, but it's all done by mail."

"Could it be Billy Thorndyke?"

Bob grinned. "The boy dumped by the beauteous Terri? Speaking of whom, the scuttlebutt is that you two are more than friends."

"Not true," Nate said, but he looked away. "After you."

Bob took a key from his pocket, unlocked the big front door, and they went inside.

Within seconds, Nate knew he hated the place. There were two large rooms plus a kitchen, a bath and a pretty garden room in the back. Stacy had done a brilliant job of decorating. She'd used the apartment in DC as her starting point, and mixed modern furniture with pieces from the Southwestern US. On a big pine door was a brass plaque: Nathaniel Taggert. Inside was a desk of heavy oak, with Western carvings down the sides. It was something that someone from Colorado would be assumed to like.

The framed paintings and drawings were of ranch scenes. There was even a glass-fronted box containing different kinds of barbed wire. The rugs were Navajo.

"Look like your home state?" Bob asked.

"Sort of." Nate didn't add that it was a tourist's version

of Colorado. He looked out the window of what would be his office and saw a shaded front yard and the street. There was a sidewalk where a woman was walking her dog.

This is it, he thought. *This is where I'll be spending most of the rest of my life.* Behind the desk was a huge chair done in artfully aged brown leather. "I'll be a Colorado cattle baron in Virginia."

"What was that?" Bob asked.

"Nothing." He turned back to the man. "So what do you do?"

"I have a law degree but so far I haven't used it. I'm going into politics so I'm trying to build my résumé. I'm going to Africa to do some teaching." He paused. "I think I ought to tell you something."

"What's that?"

"Stacy's father bought the old Stanton house for your wedding gift."

Nate looked at him in question.

"You know that big white house in the center of town? The one with the fountain in front of it?"

For a moment Nate was blank, then his eyes widened. "You don't mean that derelict old place with the columns, do you?"

"The very one. Stacy and her dad love that house."

"Stanton," Nate whispered as he began to remember. "Her parents' house was remodeled to look like it."

"Yeah," Bob said. "When Lew was a young and ambitious lawyer, he wanted the biggest house smack in town, where he could see and be seen. But the owners wouldn't sell, so he made his house as much like it as possible. He laughs about it now. So anyway, he finally bought the big old house, and he's going to give it to you and Stace. She will *love* making it back into the showpiece it once was.

You'll have to live in construction for a couple of years, but someday you'll have a grand staircase to walk down. Stacy will wear one of her Dior gowns and— Are you all right? You look like you're going to be sick."

"I, uh, I need to go to the doctor." Nate's voice was barely audible. "I mean Jamie. My cousin. I need to see him. Now."

"Sure," Bob said. "I'll walk back to Lew's place." He put the key on the corner of the desk. "This is yours now." He started for the door, but turned back. "Nate, I don't really know you, but I do know Stacy. She's mad about you. You're all she could talk about the last time she was here. The elegant dinners, your apartment, your glamorous nights out. She kept saying that you were her dream man, that it was as though she'd made you up, that you were too perfect to be real. She's so happy you're going to come here to live and open an office. She can't bear to leave her parents, and now that her brother has moved to LA, she's tied even tighter here."

When Nate was silent, Bob said goodbye and left the house.

Nate waited a while then he went outside, locked the front door and sent a text to Jamie.

Meet me in the gym. 2 minutes.

He turned off his phone and went to his car.

Chapter 9

Jamie watched Nate lower the Olympic bar, the multiple forty-five-pound plates making it bow. He'd been quiet since his cousin arrived, but then, it hadn't taken much to see that Nate needed to talk.

Yesterday, Della Kissel had come to Jamie's office. She was Kyle's patient but she'd demanded a second opinion, which in Summer Hill meant seeing Dr. Jamie. He'd been told by Kyle that her tests in Richmond showed that there was nothing wrong with her. "The woman will live to be a thousand," Dr. Kyle had said. "Unless someone gets sick of her gossiping and offs her."

Della had wanted to be alone with Jamie so she could tell him about Nate and Terri. "I promised Brody I wouldn't say anything to anyone, but you're a relative so I think you should know. Did you know that your cousin is engaged to that lovely Stacy Hartman? Did you know that her father is the mayor? Have you heard that she dropped dear Bob Alderson for your cousin? It was the scandal of the year! Why would she want a bear of a man like Nathaniel Taggert when she could have an elegant gentleman like Bob? Although I must say that when Nathaniel was at my house with me in my nightclothes it was quite, quite intimate—if you know what I mean. Does your cousin make passes at *all* women?"

Jamie put his stethoscope away. Della's heart rate was rising with each question. "No," he said, smiling. "He only comes on to the very pretty ones."

That had pleased her so much that he was able to get her to talk about people other than his cousin.

The visit had warned Jamie that something was going on with Nate. But then his wife, Hallie, had figured that out. The first two days Nate had been in Summer Hill he'd practically lived with them, but then Terri Rayburn returned to town and they'd not seen him since.

Nate did another dead lift. Sumo style, legs wide, one hand outward, the other back. He moved slowly, never jerking the weight, the knurled bar scraping his shins. Like all dedicated lifters, his shins were scarred from years of dragging a heavy bar up over them.

Jamie, sitting on a bench, wiping sweat off his face, was waiting. There were rigid, unbreakable rules in a gym. Don't drop the weights. Put what you use away—don't leave it for someone else. Grunting at machines was for girls. Only free weights made a man exert to the max. Don't talk to someone who's lifting.

He and Nate were at the gym at Tattwell, a restored plantation just outside Summer Hill that was owned by a distant relative. The wide doors were open and the breeze kept the air cool.

"It's just that I feel like my life is being taken over," Nate said. "Where I live and work. *How* I live. It's all being decided for me. I'm beginning to feel that it's a play that's already been written and I've been cast in the role."

"Did you and Stacy talk about this before you got here?"

"I thought we did." Nate ran a towel over his face and neck, then picked up a fifty-pound dumbbell and started doing preacher curls. He was so angry he did twelve reps. For a lifter, if he could do a full twelve, that meant the weight was too light. He picked up a fifty-five-pound dumbbell. "I needed to get away from where Kit dumped me in the middle of a bunch of desk jockeys with all their blasted paperwork. I thought I was going to go insane. Then Stacy was there and she wanted to live in this little town and—" He broke off to do eight reps. Slow, using as much force to lower the weight as to lift it.

"Summer Hill. Where Kit had moved."

Nate gave Jamie a hard look. "Don't start playing psychologist on me. Kit being here is a coincidence."

Jamie wasn't about to challenge Nate when there was so much anger in his eyes. "I'd be a psychiatrist. Medical degree, remember?"

Nate didn't smile, but did another eight reps. When he finished, he looked at Jamie. "I love the girl but I'm not liking the life that's been planned out for me. And I can't stand her parents."

Nate seemed to be in danger of not saying another word, so Jamie decided to encourage him. *Misery does love company!* "Whatever you have to say about in-laws, I can top it. You should meet Hallie's sister! She's a tall, skinny, shapeless blonde who truly believes that every man in the world wants her. She manipulates her poor husband like he's her toy—and the guy seems to love it. When she's around Hallie, I have to watch her every minute in case she decides to do or say something hateful. Right now she's jealous because Hallie is expecting and she isn't. She thought that because I'm a doctor I could give her a shot of some miracle drug and tomorrow she'd be knocked up. Vain girl!"

Nate put down the single dumbbell and picked up a set of forty-pounders and Jamie knew he was going to do flyes. That Nate wasn't sticking to a single body part and working it to exhaustion was a sign of how upset he was. They'd been taught by their fathers, and they knew to structure their workouts around a body part. Back, chest, legs. But today Nate was all over the place. He was doing squats and bench presses in the same day. Not what they'd been taught!

Jamie stood up to spot Nate on the incline bench with the flyes. If an arm gave way—a common occurrence—the dumbbell could come down on a face. Or a pec muscle could be pulled away from his chest. With Nate's anger and as heavy as he was lifting today, all manner of bad could happen.

"At least you wouldn't be living around the corner from them. Mayor Hartman is giving Stacy and me the old Stanton house as a wedding present."

That so shocked Jamie that he almost let Nate's arms go out too far on his next rep. The house was an eyesore, but worse, it was at the crossroads of town. "You'd never be able to step out of your house without people seeing you. You wouldn't like it there."

"I know, but Bob said Stacy loves the house. Did you know that she was nearly engaged to Bob Alderson?"

Jamie wasn't going to tell him that Della Kissel had filled his ear. "I've heard rumors."

Nate put the weights on the floor and sat up on the

bench. "Stacy never told me a word about him." He stretched out on another bench, this time under a bar loaded with forty-five-pound plates.

At least he's sticking with chest for two exercises, Jamie thought but didn't say. "So what's it like living at the lake? I hear you're friends with the manager's daughter." Jamie watched as Nate's whole body changed. His face relaxed so much he almost smiled. "What's she like?"

When Nate did a mere five reps with the heavy bar, Jamie thought that just the mention of the name had softened Nate so much that he couldn't do a full set.

Nate sat up. "You know Cameron Diaz's legs?"

"Oh yeah."

"Terri's are better. She runs around the house in big shirts and shorts so little you can't see them. Sometimes she just has on blue lacy underthings and.., And during the day she has on cutoffs that..."

Jamie turned away to hide a smile. "Anything else you like about her? Other than physical, that is?"

"She doesn't let me sleep."

"You mean she… In your bed?"

"No, no, not that," Nate said. "I mean I have to be awake and listening and thinking all the time. She zings out jibes at me that are like shots from a BB gun. I have to dodge them or send them back with equal force." Nate was smiling. "She's interesting and funny and smart. And she works! She runs the whole lake. Her father sits in his office most of the time or wanders off with Elaine or—" Nate stopped talking.

"She sounds like a handful, but if you two are sharing a house, that must be difficult."

"I don't know how to explain it, but we're like two wheels working at the same speed. Within twenty-four hours of meeting, we each had our own tasks to do." He gave a half grin. "Her bras and my pockets."

"Bras, huh?"

Nate stood up. "It's not like that. It's all platonic. We're like brother and sister."

Jamie didn't dare make a reply to that. Nate's essay on female legs didn't sound very brotherly. He spoke softly, thoughtfully. "What are you going to do?"

"Do? What do you mean?"

"I mean about Stacy. You don't like her parents or where she wants to live. Are you two still engaged?"

The anger returned to Nate. "Of course we are. I'm in love with Stacy and I plan to marry her. We're going to do the whole forever thing."

Jamie didn't comment, but then he didn't need to. Loyalty was a trait his family prided themselves on. "Didn't you and Stacy live together in DC?"

Nate began to disassemble the bar, even though he'd only done one set. "More or less. She stayed over one night and didn't leave. It was never official, but yeah, we did."

"How were you together?"

Nate shrugged. "It was in DC so I had to do things for Kit. He got us invitations to those dinners with four forks. Stacy loved every one of them."

"What does she eat?"

"I don't know. Bird food. The greener the better. I lost eight pounds in the first two weeks after she moved in. I had to sneak out to a steak house before going home to have dinner with her."

"What does Terri like to eat?"

Nate laughed. "Anything. She's not a health food nut. One day it was pouring down rain and we went into one of the cabins and threw some pizzas in the oven. She works so much that she burns up calories. Anyway, we sat there for a couple of hours and I, uh, I ended up telling her my life story."

"How you ran off with a Montgomery and your own family hardly saw or heard from you for years?"

"Yeah. All of it."

Jamie picked up some dumbbells and racked them. "What are you going to do when Stacy gets back?"

"One thing for sure is that we have to talk. I hate the office she made for me and I hate the house she wants us to live in."

"Where do you want to live?"

"I'm thinking about buying a cabin at the lake and remodeling it. Have you ever seen Terri's house?"

"No, I haven't. Tell me about it."

"The whole front of it is glass. It doesn't make me feel closed in. There are people around but I never feel exposed. You should have come to the party we had. We just left the doors open and people came and went as they wanted to."

"Is that the kind of party you and Stacy had in DC?" Jamie's voice was quiet, and very serious.

Nate turned to him in anger. "What are you hinting at?"

"Absolutely nothing. I think you should go home with me and stay for dinner. Hallie's better at talking than I am and she can—"

"What time is it?"

"Quarter to five. Why?"

"I have to go," Nate said. "Can you…?" He waved his arm at the gym.

"Sure, I'll clean up. You have an appointment?"

"Yeah. I'm meeting Terri at five and we're going to sort out Widiwick. She's going to tell me—"

Jamie didn't hear the rest of it because Nate was already in his car and speeding away. He hadn't showered or changed out of his sweaty shorts and tank top. He'd been so anxious to get to a girl who was like a sister to him that he'd forgotten everything else. "Poor Stacy," Jamie said, then began racking the weights.

Chapter 10

As soon as Terri saw Nate inside his car, she knew he was in a bad mood. Since she'd never known him to be late, she was waiting for him when he pulled into the drive. His brows were drawn into a single line and turned down so much that he looked like an emoji.

This could be interesting, she thought. *Wonder how he deals with anger?* The fact that a visit to his future in-laws had caused his bad temper made her feel good. When she remembered seeing Nate laughing and drinking beer with her friends and relatives, she had to suppress a smile.

She went to the passenger side of the car, but Nate got out. He had on a tank top and big shorts that reached to his knees. And heavens! but he was pumped. Muscles bulged out on him like he was a toy action figure.

Only he was real and he was sweaty. Glistening. Glossy with it. The curve of his muscles highlighted by sweat made her put her hand on the car to steady herself.

"Here!" he said in a growl as he tossed a towel at her. "I didn't have time to shower."

"Oh? I didn't notice." She did her best to sound sarcastic and not as though she was being consumed with lust. *Bet the hood of the car would be very warm against my bare backside*, she thought.

Nate turned his back to her and peeled off his shirt, exposing about three acres of hot, damp skin.

Terri put both hands on the car. Otherwise, her knees were going to collapse.

He turned his head toward her. "Can you wipe down my back?"

Could she...? *Only your back?* she wanted to say. Not any front bits? She said nothing as she picked up the towel and walked around the car. She stumbled only once.

Nate bent forward so she could wipe his back.

Control! she thought. Act like every cell in your body isn't tingling. Act like you do *not* want to jump on him, knock him to the ground and tear at him with your teeth and tongue.

She swallowed. "So what's got you so riled up?"

"Nothing," he snapped.

Ah, she thought. *One of those.* A man who had to be coaxed into telling what his problem was. Billy had been like that.

As she ran the towel over him, her hands slowed. And then her left hand slid off the towel onto his skin. She wiped with the right, and followed on bare skin with her left. Her hand on his moist skin. She moved from his shoulder down to his spine, to his waist. The furrow that ran down his backbone was deep enough to run a boat in. A boat that contained just her.

"Are you done?"

Abruptly, Terri stepped back. "If you weren't so fat it wouldn't take so long."

Nate gave a grunt—then proceeded to slide his shorts off.

Not thighs, she thought. *Chest, back, arms, okay, but not* thighs! "Do you mind?"

He looked at her in surprise, as though unaware of what he was doing. He opened the back door of his car and stepped behind it, using it as a screen. "Didn't mean to shock your delicate sensibilities. I didn't want to be late to meet you, so I ran over here straight from the gym."

Terri was holding the towel, damp with his sweat. She wanted to bury her face in it. Instead, she held it at arm's length between thumb and forefinger. "So I noticed."

Nate gave her a look over the top of the door as though he knew the truth. "Where do you want to eat?"

"Depends on what you want."

"A sixteen-ounce T-bone and a potato the size of my foot. Plus a gallon of liquid."

"I know a place."

In minutes, Nate was dressed in jeans and a T-shirt and he got in behind the steering wheel. As Terri sat beside him, he wiped his face with the towel.

"I could get you a clean one."

"Don't need it."

Terri didn't reply to that, but told him where to turn to get to the local steak house. He drove in silence, a muscle working in his jaw, his eyes glaring at the road.

"So tell me about this wicked thing."

At first, she didn't know what he meant. "Right. Widi-wick." When she glanced at him, she could see that he wasn't paying attention to her. But then, she didn't dare say what was in her mind. He looked so good she wanted to rip his clothes off. Run her tongue— She took a breath. "We paint our naked bodies green and purple and run from house to house setting off firecrackers." His angry expression didn't change. "Turn here." She pointed to the left but Nate went right. "This isn't the way. You need to turn around."

Nate pulled into the big gravel parking lot of a two-story building with a rough wooden front. There was a sign across the front. Kale House.

"This isn't the steak restaurant," Terri said. "This is new and I think it's—"

"Then we'll eat something else here." He got out of the car and waited for her.

Inside the restaurant, it was like stepping back into the 1970s. Tables with red-and-white-checked cloths, Chianti bottles with multicolored candle wax running down them. Peace symbols everywhere. The three young waitresses wore long skirts and long peasant blouses. Their hair was straight and flat, their feet encased in sandals that seemed to have pieces of tires as soles.

"Here's what we have today." A woman handed each of them a small chalkboard.

"No menu?" Nate asked.

"The food changes every day. This saves paper." Her tone had a deep I-don't-care vibe. She walked away without another word.

The chalk on the board was difficult to read.

"Is this…?" Nate asked.

"Everything is made with kale. Soup, salad, bread, entrée." Terri looked at him. "The steak house is about a mile away. They have two-inch-thick sirloins. Charred on the outside, red in the center. Last year we used the peel from one of their potatoes as a canoe. And cheese-cake. *Real* cheese."

"Yeah?" Nate exchanged her chalkboard for his. They had different items on them.

The waitress returned, pad in hand. Her sandals were so heavy she could hardly lift her feet. On her skirt was a long string of tiny bells that jingled with her every step.

"Your mom put you in this getup?" Nate asked.

The girl grimaced. "Grandma. But it was either raid her closet or skip college. She's paying."

Nodding in sympathy, Nate handed her the two chalk-boards. "We'll take one of each."

The girl didn't so much as blink at the huge order. "With or without bacon?"

"With!" Nate and Terri said in unison.

The girl smirked. "In your dreams." She walked away.

When they were alone, Terri turned to Nate and waited. She wasn't going to beg him to talk, but if he wanted to, she would listen.

"So what shade of green are you girls going to wear, and can I apply it on the places you can't reach?"

Terri laughed, glad that he had paid attention to her. "What are you so mad about?"

"I hate my office."

She couldn't help but be pleased by that. "Get Stacy to change the furniture."

He was silent for a moment. "I think the problem is that I can't stand the thought of staying inside all day. The windows face the street and the buildings next door."

She waited for him to go on. When he looked up, his eyes were so bleak that she knew there was more.

"Stacy's father bought the Stanton house. He's giving it to us for a wedding gift."

"That old piece of…?" Terri halted, swallowed. "I'm sure Stacy will make it beautiful."

"No doubt she will. It's just that when it's done, the house will still be smack in the middle of town."

At the sight of his despair, Terri did her best to put aside her own thoughts and hopes. Whatever else he was, Nate was her *friend*. "Look, these are serious problems and you need to talk to Stacy about them. What I can't figure out is why you ever thought that you'd like being in an office all day. When you two were living together in DC, Stacy had to know that you hated your job. She—"

"I never told her."

"What do you mean? You never told her about playing Tarzan and ripping your shirt open to show your bullet wounds?"

"No, I didn't. Stacy and I aren't like that. We don't sit around and reminisce about the past."

Terri didn't like his insinuation that that's what she and Nate did. "Which is why you never heard about Bob Alderson. I think you two need to *talk* to each other. Or did you spend *all* your time in bed together?"

"We didn't—"

"Here it is." As the three waitresses began putting plates and bowls on the table, the first one named them. "Kale salad with cranberries. Kale salad with beans. Kale rolls. Kale and roasted vegetable soup. Kale minestrone." When they ran out of room, the girls pulled a table next to theirs. "Kale potato salad. Kale pasta. Kale and mushrooms. Spicy kale bake. Grilled kale with ricotta. And my favorite, kale ice cream on top of kale apple cake. And four kale smoothies to wash it all down." She stepped back. "Anything else? We could—" Another waitress handed her a ceramic bowl. "Oh yes, baked kale chips. Enjoy!" Smiling, she walked away.

Nate and Terri looked at the two tables full of food, but neither of them said a word. Their disagreement made the air heavy between them.

Nate picked up his fork, lifted a large piece of kale from a salad and said, "I don't eat green food." It was a quote from a *Hobbit* movie and Terri knew it. When they laughed together, the air cleared.

"I can't take any more delving into my life and my mind," Nate said. "I've had it from Jamie and now you. Tell me about Widiwick—without the paint. That makes me think of Della Kissel in her pink…" He waved his hand. "Thing."

"It's a fair. Shopkeepers from Summer Hill set up booths and people come from miles around to buy things."

"Great," Nate said, his mouth full of kale and potatoes. "That's the tourist version. Now tell me the lake story. Start with the name. What does it mean?"

Terri gave a half smile. "Widiwick was started because Billy Thorndyke didn't like his prize."

"Thorndyke?"

Terri's eyes lost their amusement. "You've heard of him?"

"My new office is in the Thorndyke house."

The smile came back to her. She had an idea Nate had heard about her and Billy, but she was glad he wasn't prying. "That's a nice house. Anyway, it was my mother who began the original fair. She wanted to unite the town and the lake so she came up with the idea of the town merchants setting up booths around the lake. And as an incentive to get people to come, every visitor was given a card with each booth's number on it. If they got it initialed at every place, they put the card into a tub, and somebody drew one out. The winner got a prize."

"Such as?"

"It was usually a big box of chocolates. But one year, one of the booth owners, Mrs. Preston from the knitting shop, was down with the flu and her booth was closed. Dad said to skip her on the card."

"Let me guess. Billy didn't do that."

"No. He was eleven years old and—"

"Same age as you?"

"Yes. Same as Stacy and me. That year, Billy rode his bike miles into the country and banged on Mrs. Preston's door until she got out of bed and answered it. She told him to go away but he insisted she sign his card."

"Which made him the only one who had a full card."

"Right. But when Dad gave him the box of chocolates, Billy said, 'Is this all I get?'"

"Ungrateful, huh?"

"Very. But that was the first year that Mr. Stanley Cresnor was there."

"Cresnor Industries. Billions."

"Exactly. And he was in a bad mood because his wife had dragged him away from work for a vacation at a lake. He muttered, 'What'd'ya want, kid?'"

"Ah," Nate said. "Shortened to Widiwick?"

"Yes."

"So what did young Billy ask a billionaire for? A jet?"

"No." For a moment Terri looked into the distance and the way her eyes softened made Nate feel an emotion he hardly recognized: jealousy. If no one had told him that at one time Terri and Billy had been a couple, he would have known it then. "Billy asked to go to a big store in

Richmond and buy all the toys he could put into a cart in four and a half minutes."

Nate leaned back against his chair. "Wow. That is some ambitious kid."

Terri smiled. "Mr. Cresnor was so amused by the idea that he agreed. I mean, how much could one kid get in four and half minutes, right? But he underestimated Billy."

"I'm beginning to like this kid."

"He's one of a kind, that's for sure. The event was to take place the next Saturday, so Billy used the week to organize our entire elementary school. He passed out maps and assigned kids places to be in the store. He got his dad to drive him to Richmond so he could talk to the store manager. The man was so intrigued that he advertised it in the newspaper and put a giant banner across the front of the store. He got a lot of press."

"Did you help?" Nate asked.

"Oh yes. Billy put me in the section with the water toys. On the day, the store was packed with people. They were three-deep around the perimeter, but they let us kids run it all. Billy took a cart, the manager blew a whistle and Billy began running. We kids handed him toys that Billy put in the cart because—"

"That was the deal," Nate said.

"Yes. Billy had to *put* them into a cart. Every few feet a kid shoved an empty basket forward and it was filled in seconds. I ran three carts to the register."

"With all those toys, Billy must have been the most popular kid in town."

Terri smiled softly. "He was, but not for that. It took forty-five minutes to ring everything up. The manager totaled the tabs and handed it to Billy. He climbed up on the checkout counter and read the number. It was a whopper!

When the cheering stopped, Billy reached down, picked up a yo-yo and held it up. 'This is mine,' he said. Then he pulled a piece of paper out of his pocket and handed it to the manager. 'The rest of this goes to them.' There were four names on the list—an orphanage, a hospital, a women's shelter and the local fire department."

"Charity." Nate's voice held awe. "Was that planned?"

"Only by Billy. He hadn't told anyone what he was going to do, not even his parents. Everyone started dancing around, and I remember his mother crying. The press was there and they were so stunned they nearly forgot to take photos of it all. Billy was a hero!"

Nate took a moment to reply. "That's some kid."

"Yeah, he was." She leaned back in her chair. "That's how Widiwick started. Mr. Cresnor now comes to Lake Kissel every year and he grants a wish. Within reason, of course, and only to Summer Hill residents or he'd start a worldwide riot. And it's become a custom that the wishes must be for someone else."

"What a great act of charity. So what kind of things has Cresnor given out?"

"A new van for the church. A two-year college scholarship. A wedding for a couple whose house flooded. My favorite was when a woman asked Mr. Cresnor for the meanest divorce lawyer on the planet for her best friend. Her friend's husband was a real jerk."

"All the wishes couldn't have been unselfish."

"Mr. Cresnor decides. He sits on a big chair and says yes or no. Some years the negotiations go on for hours. He truly enjoys himself! And his wife gets time with him when he's in a good mood. It's a win-win for everyone."

For a while, they were silent, Nate with his head down.

"I got my aerobics for today."

He looked at her.

"Chewing kale? Workout for the jaw? Get it?"

"Yeah. I—" He broke off to take his buzzing phone out of his pocket.

Terri saw the name Stacy, but Nate didn't answer, just put the phone back in his pocket. "Why aren't you answering her calls?"

Nate gave a one-sided grin. "Noticed that, huh? I don't want to have to lie. I still haven't picked up the tent and boxes she sent from Italy. After today, I don't think her parents will let me have them."

"The brunch was that bad?"

"Worse."

She waited for him to go on, but he said nothing. Terri took her cell out of her pocket and sent a text. "There. It's taken care of."

"What is?"

"I told Bob to go get Stacy's things and deliver them to Dad. What other problems do you have?"

Nate grinned. "Now who's granting wishes? Okay, magician, how are you going to fix my office?"

"Can't do that one. That's between you and Stacy. You can't move into the Stanton house for a couple of years so where are you planning to live in the meantime?"

Nate's eyes brightened. "Is that house where we had the pizzas for rent?"

"The daughter of the mayor of Summer Hill staying at the lake? I don't think so. When you entered the Thorndyke house to go to your office, what door did you use?"

"The front one. Why?"

"There's a side door that leads to a full apartment. Billy's grandmother, Babs, lived there. She was a wonderful woman. She used to let Billy and me drink her homemade wine. We thought we were very sophisticated."

"Sometimes it seems like every story in this town leads back to Billy Thorndyke. How is he now?"

Terri looked down at her plate and the piles of green. "I have no idea. When does Stacy get here?"

"Thursday night. You don't have any contact with him?"

"None. Where are you planning to stay after she gets here?"

"I haven't thought about it. What was Thorndyke like as he got older?"

"Smart, athletic, beautiful and big. He ruled our school and he didn't allow any bullying. There was a kid who transferred from the east who picked on the little kids. Billy hung him up on the wall of the gym. He didn't bother anybody anymore. You need to think about where you're going to stay."

"I can see why a guy like that would choose you. He have any girlfriends before you?"

"If you're asking if he and Stacy were an item, they weren't. Billy was unattainable. Personally, I figured he was gay." As she moved a wad of green around on a plate, she smiled in memory.

"I take it that you found out that he wasn't."

She glared at Nate. "How did this go from you to me? Unless you want to be stuck at the mayor's house, you need to find a place to stay in town. I haven't heard that Babs's apartment has been rented. I bet Mr. Hartman would rent it for his daughter just to get rid of *you*."

"I'm not sure Stacy and I will be living together."

Terri drew in her breath.

"I mean, before the wedding. Summer Hill doesn't

seem like a place where people can live in sin." He was smiling at his jest.

"Don't kid yourself. This town is full of sin. You just have to sit outside and see the flashlights to know what's going on."

"Why did Billy leave?"

Terri started to reply, then closed her moth. "The kale ice cream has melted. You want to order some more?"

"Lord no!"

"I agree." Terri looked at all the leftover food. "Let's get this boxed and take it to Elaine. She loves this stuff. She even tries to get Dad to eat it." She looked at the clock on the restaurant wall. "We're going to be late to the meeting."

Nate pushed his chair back. "Then we'd better go." He nodded to the waitress, paid, and they waited for everything to be wrapped. As they left, he said, "Tell me about this Day of the Demons."

Terri waited until they were in the car before she spoke. "After Mr. Cresnor started granting wishes, we got a lot more people wanting to come and see this cute little local custom."

"Sort of like an anthropologist's dream."

"More or less. With more people coming, the vendors started wanting to put up their tents two weeks before the fair. Then six weeks, then three months. It was totally out of hand. So Dad and Uncle Jake decided to cram it all into four days, Monday through Thursday. The fair starts on Friday, goes through to the dance on Saturday night. They disassemble everything on Sunday, starting *after* church."

"You don't really think Jamie will need to be there, do you? I mean, as a doctor."

"Yes."

When Terri didn't say any more, he looked at her. She seemed to be quite serious about it—or about something.

"You'll need to move out by Wednesday," she said softly.

"I thought Thursday morning. I don't need to be at the airport until 5:00 p.m. I could move just after lunch." He sighed. "Maybe I'll stay at Jamie's for a while. I could cook for them. Hallie's getting very big and needs to stay off her feet. The baby's due soon and I could help with that. We Taggerts know about babies."

Terri was looking out the window and thinking of the house without Nate. No more waking up to the smell of coffee. No more spicy chicken dishes. Who was going to groan when she wanted to watch an old movie, but then would sit there with her? What about emergencies? Twice she'd been called out in the middle of the night. Both times Nate had gone with her. He'd calmed a hysterical family while Terri climbed on the roof to chase a feral dog away. The noise had terrified them. The second time, something had overturned a boat and the Enders were sure it was a bear. But it was just a couple of kids who'd sneaked out in the night. She and Nate caught the ten-year-olds and drove them to the sheriff's office. Let their parents take care of them!

How could she and Nate have done so much in just two weeks? How could one person have become as much a part of her life as he had in such a short time? Her dad said that thanks to Nate he'd had two weeks of vacation. Even though she'd never stopped working, Terri felt the same way. Nate was like her, but he was also different. He believed in the old adage of stopping to smell the roses. Terri tended to go from one task to another, with no break in between. But Nate liked to escape. He found hiding places where they could run away from people. In the surrounding forest, they found an old shed, a leftover from when the Kissels owned the place.

They ran inside, feeling that they'd discovered something no one else knew about. When they found six used condoms on the dirt floor, they fell back in laughter.

Nate was great with all the college kids who did the grunt work of the place. They were usually Brody's responsibility, but Nate had such an easy way of solving problems that he'd taken over the job.

Everything was easier and more pleasant with Nate around. And he was endlessly thoughtful. When he saw books in someone's cabin, he asked if he could borrow a murder mystery for Terri. He exchanged recipes with people. He introduced them to each other. More than once he'd dumped a bratty, restless kid onto some grumpy adult, then left them with each other. Thanks to Nate, there were some groups of old and young that were studying turtles or learning about cameras or just lying on the bank and doing absolutely nothing.

"I can't imagine the place without you," Terri said so softly she could hardly be heard.

Nate reached across the console and took her hand. "We'll always be friends. No matter what happens."

"I know." She pulled her hand out of his grip. *Friends!* she thought. *Friends.*

When Nate's phone buzzed, he pulled it out of his pocket and handed it to her. "Would you see who that is?"

"Stacy. You really need to speak to her."

"Not while I'm driving. I'll call her when I get home." He put the phone back in his pocket.

Minutes later, Terri's cell was ringing and caller ID said it was Bob Alderson.

"Terri! Where are you?" His voice was testy.

"In the car with Nate. Why?"

"Put me on speaker and hold up the phone. He needs to hear this."

"Bob wants to talk to you." She held her cell up.

"Nate," Bob said, "can you hear me?"

"Loud and clear. What's up? Want to buy my office furniture?"

"No!" Bob sounded very angry. "I spent hours singing your praises to all four parents. Just when they were beginning to believe that you weren't some girl-stealing jerk, Stacy called. In tears."

Nate glanced at Terri. "Why?"

"She's been trying to get you to answer your phone, that's why. That designer-teacher of hers got called away and Stacy is now on a plane home. She wanted you to pick her up at the airport."

"I... I, uh..." Nate couldn't come up with an excuse for not taking her calls.

Terri turned off the speaker and put the phone to her ear. "He's been dealing with Widiwick business." She was almost snapping. "Remember that? Our biggest event of the year? So when's Stacy get in?"

"Early tomorrow morning. Her parents are spending the night in Richmond and they'll pick her up. Listen, Terri, if Nate's going to be forgiven for this, you better make up some emergency that involves a hospital and kids. And blood. Lots of blood. Everyone is so angry at him that I don't think I can fix it for him."

Terri chose to ignore what he was saying. "Did you get the boxes to my father?"

"Yeah. He didn't know where the two of you were. You two aren't... You know, are you?"

"No, we're not." Her teeth were clamped together. "Okay, thanks for this. We'll get her tent set up first thing in the morning."

"Terri, Stacy is a nice girl. She doesn't deserve—"

"Thanks!" Terri clicked off her phone.

For a while, she and Nate rode in silence. Terri knew she should be thinking about how to make up everything to Stacy, but what blared in her mind was "Last Night." This was the last night that they'd spend together. "You heard?" she asked.

"Every word. Every bone-scraping, hair-raising word. How do I make this right?"

"Why are you asking *me*?"

"Surely some guy has stood you up, not taken your calls, whatever. What did he do to make you forgive him?"

"Never happened. It was always me who did the standing up. Some lake emergency and I never showed up. I had to jump off a dock in my prom dress."

"Yeah? What did you wear instead?"

"Oh no, you don't. This is about *you*. How are *you* going to make Stacy believe that you really do care?"

Twice, Nate opened his mouth to speak, but nothing came out. He gave a sigh of defeat as he drove over the bridge to the lake.

In silence, he parked the car and they went inside the house. They stood by the door, looking through to the outside, neither of them moving.

"You should go pack," Terri said, and Nate nodded. As soon as he was down the hall, she called her father.

"Where have you been?" Brody shouted. "I had to do that damned meeting all by myself. You know I hate those things! You and Nate will have to put up with—"

"Stacy's arriving tomorrow morning."

"Damn! Now Nate will be going on a bunch of those wedding lunches. There'll be no work and we'll have pink doilies everywhere, and—" The misery in his daughter's voice finally hit him. "I'm sorry, baby. I know you're going to miss him."

"I think Nate should move into your apartment."

"Okay. Want me to stay at your place?"

"No!" Terri said loudly, then quieted. "Let Nate use the pullout couch, but you stay there with him." She waited for him to understand.

"You don't want Nate to be staying alone when Stacy gets back, do you?" She answered him with silence. "Oh, honey, this isn't good. He asked Stacy to *marry* him, so he must be crazy about her."

"I know," Terri said softly. "It's just… I mean…"

"You want to postpone the inevitable."

"I guess so. Who knows? Maybe Stacy will return with some Italian guy and…" Her voice faltered. She couldn't keep up the joke.

"Okay. Whatever you want. But listen, honey—"

She heard Nate's footsteps. "I gotta go." She clicked off the phone.

"All done," Nate said, "but you better check. I may have missed a shoe or left my stash of cigars behind."

Terri didn't smile. "You're moving into Dad's apartment."

Nate looked alarmed. "And your dad will come here to stay with you?"

"Actually, you're going to sleep on Dad's pullout sofa. But if you want the apartment to yourself for, uh, you and Stacy, you can have it."

"No!" Nate answered instantly. "This arrangement is fine. Unless your dad snores."

She knew Nate was trying to make a joke, but it didn't cover the fact that he didn't want to be in an empty apartment. Did that mean he didn't want to be alone with Stacy? She didn't dare ask for fear that he'd give an answer she didn't want to hear.

They got the leftovers from the kale feast out of the car and put them in the fridge. "We have to remember to take these to Elaine."

Nate nodded in agreement.

It took them nearly an hour to get all his things together. Nate had missed several items and Terri found them. Since he was staying one more night, his shaving gear was left out. Twice, she'd stood in the bathroom door watching him shave as they went over what needed to be done that day.

As he straightened his toiletries, they glanced at each other in the mirror, but they said nothing.

Once they'd finished, they stood in the living room looking out at the water. "Beer?" Nate asked.

"Sure." They knew that he'd get the beer, she'd get cheese and crackers, and they'd meet in the chairs outside.

They sat side by side, sipping and munching and watching. The fading sunlight was glistening on the water, and far down the lake they could see a flashlight.

"The Phillips," Nate said.

"No, that's Mrs. Jenkins and the blond kid who works in the kitchen."

"When did they get together?"

"Three days ago. Didn't you see her in those tiny denim shorts?"

"Was that the day you wore that green swimsuit that's cut up to your waist?"

Terri took a sip of her drink. "You have to stop that. Can't say it, can't look. Stacy—"

"I know. She doesn't deserve anything bad." He took a breath. "Sometimes it's like I can hardly remember her. I can remember ten years ago when I was with Kit in my first sandstorm. And I vividly remember when that damned camel bit my leg. But my time with Stacy in DC has become a blur."

"Maybe that's because you were in a job you hated." Terri wanted to ask Nate to stay. To tell him to call Stacy and say he'd changed his mind.

But she couldn't do it. She had to live with herself. She knew she was being judged by the town—and knew she was failing. If Nate broke up with perfect little Stacy Hartman for Terri Rayburn, she'd never live it down. Their children would grow up under a stigma.

Oh! she thought. To be able to say, *Let's run away together. Go to Colorado and open a horse ranch.* She'd never been on a horse but maybe she could learn.

But she couldn't do that. Couldn't leave her dad with the lake.

She looked at Nate's profile, saw that his expression was glum. "Can you ride a horse?"

The incongruous question startled him enough to put a sparkle in his eyes. "Quite well. When I was a kid I did some rodeos."

"Bucking broncos, that sort of thing?"

"And a few bulls."

"I'd like to see that."

"Now I'm too old—and I know a lot more about pain."

"So what did you talk to Della Kissel about?" she asked.

When he turned to her, he was smiling. "The same question everyone has. Why did you break up with Billy

Thorndyke? From the way you talk about him, you still seem to think he hung the moon."

She took her time answering. "You have any secrets that you'd die before you told?"

"About a dozen."

"I have one."

"Between you and Billy?"

"More than just he and I know, but…" She trailed off. "Weren't we talking about you? I'm sure that once Stacy is here, you won't remember any of this." She motioned to include the lake, the house and herself.

"Since I heard you yelling at me to get out of your house, it's like time has stood still. I remember being in DC with Stacy, but it's like a movie that I saw long ago." He looked at her. "What would you do if Billy walked through that door right now?"

His question annoyed her. "What would *you* do if Stacy walked through the door?"

"It's not the same thing."

"You think not? It's different because you and Stacy are engaged to get married? Want to see the ring Billy gave me? He cashed a bond from his grandmother to buy it for me." She started to get up but Nate caught her hand and held it tightly. He didn't look at her or speak, and his hand kept her from leaving.

When she began to calm down, he loosened his grip. For a few minutes they sat side by side, fingers lightly entwined, and looked out at the water.

"How about thick, greasy bacon burgers?" she asked.

"As good as water in the desert. And the first one who brings up anything serious has to eat the kale leftovers. All of them."

"That's cruel." She started to get up but paused. "Does

talking about having to deal with tomorrow's temper tantrums and putting up a fancy Italian tent count as 'serious'?"

Nate groaned as he stood up. "Yes! Let's talk about how old that Mason girl is and did you get the thick-cut bacon that I like?"

"Too young, and yes I did. Did you take the sheets out of the dryer?"

"Sure."

"Did you change the bed?"

"How about if I put some shawarma spices in the hamburger meat?"

Terri groaned. "You left those sheets for me to put on the bed, didn't you? Well, I'm not going to do it. It's your job, not mine."

Smiling, Nate stepped aside for her to go into the house before him.

Terri tried to act like it was any other night. Nate found a rugby game on some obscure foreign channel and sat at the end of the couch and watched it. She had an old Josephine Tey murder mystery that she couldn't seem to get into. She thought Nate was absorbed in his game until the announcers started yelling about some great goal, and he didn't blink. It looked like his mind was elsewhere.

She kept her eyes on her book. "What was the food like at the brunch?"

Nate turned off the TV, which made Terri put her book down.

"That woman has the ability to take the flavor out of anything. She had some baked egg thing that was crusty hard all the way through. Bob seemed to like it."

"Bob hasn't lived all over the world and sampled lamb roasted over an open fire."

Nate gave a bit of a smile. "I doubt if he's even tasted Mr. Parnelli's sausages."

He was facing the dark screen of the TV, while Terri had her feet on the couch. She extended her leg and nudged him in the hip with her heel. "Talk! You've been brooding since you got back, so tell me what's bothering you."

"I do *not* brood."

Terri stuck her lower lip out, hung her head and deepened her voice. "I'm so down I ate green food."

Nate chuckled. "I guess that is pretty depressed." He turned so he was facing her, one foot on the floor, the other stretched out on the couch. Not quite touching her, but almost. "I really hate my new office."

"So tell Stacy and change it. Get some different furniture."

"It's not that. It's…"

Terri knew what was wrong but she wasn't going to say it. She'd never seen anyone less suited to sit in an office all day than Nathaniel Taggert.

"Maybe I'm not made for small-town life. Maybe I should return to the Middle East. I'm sure Kit could find something for me to do."

"Running away would sure solve all your problems. No more of the Hartmans. No more office that you can't see out of. You think Stacy will want to leave her parents? Didn't I hear that she's opening a design business in town?"

Nate rolled his eyes. "I'm trying for some sympathy here. Help me out."

"Nope. You have to man up and tell Stacy you hate that office. And what about the old Stanton house?"

He groaned. "What are *you* going to do? I mean, how do you see your future?"

"I'll stay here," Terri said. "I can't imagine not living here. The lake, Dad, even this house. It's where I belong."

"Alone?"

Terri started to answer, but changed her mind. "How about some popcorn?"

"Why do we talk so much about me and never about you?"

"I've told you some of my most intimate secrets."

"Like how you'd like to visit the locker room of the rugby players?"

Terri laughed. "You asked me what I thought of the game and I told you what it meant to me. I like men with meat on them."

"Like Billy Thorndyke," Nate said.

"What is it with you and Billy?" Her voice was rising. "He and I broke up years ago. Since then I've had three boyfriends."

"Three, huh?"

"If you're going to make fun of me, I'm leaving." But she didn't move.

"Let's see. There was the NFL player here at the lake. Who else?"

Terri looked astonished for a moment, then grimaced. "I'm going to kill Della Kissel. I thought I saw her spying on me."

"Why'd you break up with him?"

"He lives in Pittsburgh."

"Steelers?"

She nodded.

"What about the other two?"

"What's caused this interrogation?" she asked.

"Just curious. I'll tell you about all the women in my life."

"I can't imagine why you think I'd want to hear that. Okay! I have a quirk in me that says I want a brain with a body. It took me years to find out that brains and brawn rarely go together. But then, those years were..." She smiled in memory.

For a moment they stared at each other. They could hear a boat motor outside; otherwise it was quiet. But the images in their minds were very loud.

Terri and Nate locked eyes and she could feel herself leaning toward him. Thoughts of honor and integrity, commitment and promises, weren't in her mind.

Nate broke the contact, abruptly. He stood. "I have to get up early tomorrow. I better..." Swallowing, he gestured toward the bedroom.

"Me too," Terri said, and she stood, as well. "Widiwick. Booths."

"Yeah. I, uh..." With a quick nod of good-night, he hurried down the hall to his bedroom and shut the door firmly.

The next morning, as soon as Terri opened her eyes, she knew that Nate was gone. The house had an emptiness that she felt in her bones. She pulled the covers over her head and wished she could go back a few days. Go back to when the smell of coffee woke her, to a time when she'd stumble into the kitchen, yawning, and Nate would be frying bacon.

But she'd known it was all temporary. Only on that first day had she had about an hour when she thought she and Nate could be... Could be more than friends. She'd bragged to her father that it was better to love and lose than...

"Oh hell!" she muttered, and got out of bed. She had to look to the future, not the past. Someday Nate would be married to Stacy Hartman and they'd all laugh in fond memory of these past weeks.

"Yeah, right," she mumbled. She got dressed. It was early, the sun just rising. Today was the opening of the festival and she'd be inundated with work. Good. And where would Nate be? With Stacy? Laughing together as she told amusing stories about her adventures in Italy?

"One time I had a flat tire on the way to Richmond," Terri said under her breath. Changing that on the side of the highway with seventy mile an hour traffic had been a *real* adventure.

As she walked into the kitchen, she saw that Nate had taped a piece of paper on the fridge. It was a drawing of the back of a muscular man wearing a towel and holding a rugby ball. *Hank Bullnose, prop forward, says he'll meet you in the dressing room at noon. Bring sausages.*

Terri knew the cartoon was supposed to make her smile, but instead, it brought tears to her eyes. She ran across the room, threw the door open and went outside to fall into one of the chairs. Her chair. The one next to Nate's. Where the two of them had sat in the evenings and on weekends. Where they'd shared meals and laughter and confidences.

The lake was beginning to come alive. She saw lights coming on, heard a couple of shouts and motors.

It was Widiwick, she thought. It was a festival that had been started by an eleven-year-old boy with a heart as big as the earth. A boy the town came to love to the point where he was their ideal of perfection. WWBD. What would Billy do? they asked one another. It became a motto. Something to achieve.

All through school Terri had been too busy to think about the things other girls did. She wasn't interested in the dances—unless they were to be held at the lake. Then her concern was feeding people and getting them across the docks without falling in after they'd had too much spiked punch.

She'd heard the girls giggling over beautiful Billy Thorndyke. Who was he going to date when he ever did? He couldn't spend his entire life studying and playing sports, could he?

Because Terri had always been exposed to the sexual shenanigans that went on at the lake, she knew more of the world than the townies did. She truly believed Billy was gay. It made sense. He was always with boys, never alone with a girl. Girls threw themselves at him, but Billy ignored them.

When she and Billy were in elementary school together, they'd been buddies. Terri had been a tomboy, strong from all she did at the lake, so she could keep up with Billy on the playground. When the school set up swimming classes at a nearby pool, Billy had been impressed when Terri swam the length easily and quickly.

But by the time they reached the seventh grade, the sexes began to separate. It was like the Garden of Eden and the kids became aware of bodies and feelings they didn't understand. Terri hadn't had time to be part of all that. By that time, she'd grown tall and knew enough that she was a good help to her dad and Uncle Jake. She worked before and after school and on weekends. In the summer she was working every minute.

One day in the last months of their junior year, Billy stopped at Terri's locker and asked what she was doing on Saturday. "Cleaning the oil filters," or some such was her answer.

"I could save you a seat at the game," Billy said.

"That would be nice. There are some bored teenagers at the lake now. They'd probably like to go. Thanks." She turned away to head to class.

Billy caught her arm. "I meant for you. Come to the game and after we can go get something to eat."

"Can't. Sorry. Too much to do." She'd run to her class.

When Terri looked back on it, she was astonished that she'd been so oblivious to Billy's attempts to ask her out on a date. But then, so many of the kids sucked up to her in the hopes of getting something for free at the lake that she'd learned to ignore them. The girls showed up whenever something like a soccer team booked cabins. The boys came to see some female swimmers. And when they did, they acted as though Terri was their best friend.

For all that Terri didn't participate with the others at school, she was certainly feeling what they did. It was just that she kept everything at the lake. There was kissing behind the boathouse. Behind the pizza stand, a guy's hand slipped under her shirt. Nothing was particularly serious, just fun and laughter. And nothing was with any of the Summer Hill kids.

But then, Terri had worked hard to learn not to concern herself with was what was going on in the little town. Since her mother had run off and left her and her dad, meaning all of Terri's life, she'd heard whispers. "Isn't that the girl whose mother...?"

In the ninth grade, there had been that incident in a stairwell when Hector and his friend tried to slam Terri up against a wall. It was after school and the building was nearly empty. The heavy fire door would prevent anyone from hearing her yell. Hector said, "Come on, you know you want it. Everybody says you're just like your mother."

Terri had gone into a blind rage. She'd used her backpack as a weapon and tapped into every muscle she'd made at the lake. She'd had to duck booms and flying oars since she could walk, so she was agile. When she came back to reality, there were two boys on the floor. She threw open the door and ran into the empty hall.

She would have left it there and never spoken of it, but a bunch of cheerleaders, Stacy Hartman one of them, saw the boys crumpled on the floor and asked what happened. Of course the boys had to save their male pride and say they had been attacked without reason. With sad faces of suffering, they let the pretty girls put their arms around them to help them walk.

In the ensuing weeks, the boys exaggerated what had happened in the stairwell to make it seem that Terri had attacked them with weapons.

Terri, her father beside her, had made only one attempt to defend herself by telling the truth. Right away, she saw that it was a lost cause. She was not popular in school and had no defenders, while the boys were the stars of the football team. They were needed; Terri was not.

Brody had been so angry about it all that he'd lost his temper—which hadn't helped. His rage was the final straw. It seemed to be proof that Terri had done just what the boys said she had.

The boys got off with no punishment, while Terri was expelled for three days. Worse was that one of the boys, Hector, blamed the incident for his failure to become a professional football player. Terri had yet another mark against her.

All in all, it had made her disconnect even more from the people of Summer Hill.

But she'd been content. She had the people at the lake, all of whom liked her. And eventually she began planning for college and what she was going to do afterward. Maybe after college she'd go into marine biology. Maybe she'd change from freshwater to salt. Oh! but she'd had plans.

But then, the summer before her senior year, Billy Thorndyke changed her life. The day after school let out, he showed up at the lake and asked Terri to teach him to swim.

"You know how to swim," she told him.

"But not like you do. I might want to join the swim team."

She pointedly looked him up and down. He had on baggy swim trunks and a towel around his neck. He had the body of a football player, not the long, sleek muscles of a swimmer.

He grinned at her insinuation. "Okay, so maybe the coach wants me to improve my running. I thought maybe swimming would help."

She knew he was lying but she had no idea why. She'd have to check the reservations. Maybe some celebrity had booked and he'd learned about it and wanted to be there when he/she arrived. She told Billy to return at two for his first class.

When he came back that afternoon, Terri put him in with her six-year-olds and under. She thought he'd be so insulted that he'd leave, but putting Billy with little kids was like pouring chocolate sauce over ice cream. The children went crazy with delight at the very sight of him. They unanimously decided to see how many of them could sit, lie, hold on to Billy while he swam the length of the pool.

After only ten minutes, Terri gave up trying to restore order for lessons. Instead, she helped the children come up with ways to attach themselves to Billy. After thirty minutes, half the lake was there yelling encouragement to Billy to swim harder. Kids held on to his neck, shoulders, waist, legs.

At the end, he had the whole class attached to him, and there were fifty people around the pool shouting at him to go! go! go!

He made it the entire length, then pulled himself out and took a bow. Only Terri saw beneath his bravado. He was so deeply exhausted, he was about to pass out. To do so in front of all those people would do irreparable damage to his teenage male ego.

Terri decided to be the bad guy. She blew her whistle and told everyone to go away. She then yelled at Billy that he was to go with her so she could give him a lecture about water safety.

Brody was standing in the doorway, his brows drawn together in anger. Terri knew *she* was going to get the lecture for allowing this to happen.

She got Billy up the stairs. At that time, she was living in the apartment at Club Circle and Brody had a cabin. Once inside, she got Billy onto her bed, put a mask on his face and gave him oxygen.

He was shaking his head, but she ignored him. "Just be still and breathe." The stethoscope wasn't in her emergency kit, so she put her hand on his heart to feel how hard it was pounding.

Billy managed to smile under the mask and held her hand to his chest.

She started to pull away, but when he wouldn't release her, everything hit her. She looked into his blue eyes and understood it all. He wasn't gay. He'd just been waiting for her. And he'd known her well enough that he'd not approached her until they were close to graduation. He intuitively knew that if he'd tried to do the boyfriend/girlfriend thing earlier, she would have knocked him across the sandbox.

When he saw that she finally understood, he closed his eyes and his heart slowed down—but he didn't release her hand.

He dozed a bit and Terri stayed beside him.

Brody came in to check on them, saw that they were holding hands and gave a grunt. "Poor guy. I think he was about to give up hope." He left the apartment.

To Terri's astonishment, several people at the lake had seen that Billy Thorndyke was mad for her. Only she hadn't known it.

After that day, she and Billy took their time. He was slow and cautious, never rushing anything. He asked Terri to give him private swimming lessons and she did teach him how to cut the water more smoothly. She taught him to float and do the backstroke.

They began spending more and more time together. Billy started helping her get her work done so they could go out alone.

They made love the first time when they got caught in the rain on the Island. Billy had been gentle and sweet, worried that he was hurting her.

It took a week before the "gentle and sweet" left them and their hormones kicked in. They were young and athletic and adventurous. They made love everywhere and in every possible position.

In normal circumstances, they might have received disapproval, but not in their case. Billy was as popular in town as Terri was at the lake. It was like the prince and princess of two neighboring kingdoms uniting. Terri's family of Brody, Jake and Frank was very happy about the union. The Thorndykes were so glad that their son might marry a hometown girl and stay in Summer Hill that they never quit smiling.

And Terri and Billy were ecstatic. By the end of the summer they were rarely apart. They ran in and out of each other's houses freely. Terri came to know the big old Thorndyke mansion as well as the cabins at the lake.

When school started, Terri's place in the ruthless teenage hierarchy had changed. No one could understand *why* the-boy-every-girl-wanted had chosen her, but he had. Terri was asked to parties and overnighters, and even let in on the school gossip. At the lake, Brody hired three boys to do what Terri did so she could have time with Billy.

Their senior year was sublime. Laughter, lovemaking, arguments, making up. It was all there. LIFE. That's what they'd shared.

And it had all ended in one horrible, devastating, irreversible moment. One day heaven, the next hell.

Billy wanted to go on, but Terri couldn't. The sins of her mother hung over her too strongly. She'd spent her life trying to make people look at her family differently. She could *not* go through the rest of her life with yet another mark against her.

Billy's family left town. He told her they were going to leave—and he begged her to go with them.

"You're asking me to choose between you and my father."

"I am," Billy said. "But in return, I will give you my life. You will have it all."

She couldn't do it. She couldn't go with Billy, knowing

what she did, any more than she could make an effort to take Nate away from Stacy.

She wasn't so innocent that she didn't know how much Nate liked her. Whereas she and Billy had been different people, it was as if she and Nate were two halves of a whole. Never had she ever felt so at ease with a person as she did with Nate.

She'd had to teach Billy things. "No! Pick up that end," she'd snap at him.

One time she was so bad-tempered at his not knowing how to do things, that he'd put his arms around her—then fallen sideways into the lake. It had taken him an hour of kisses to calm her anger down over that.

There was nothing like that with Nate. He'd done so much in his life that there wasn't much she needed to teach him. And his way with people! She'd never seen anything like it. Billy was likable, but Nate went beyond that. He soothed people, made them feel better. He joined them, matched them up. He—

Terri took a breath. They didn't belong to her. Neither man was hers and was never going to be. It should help that each separation was her choice, but it didn't.

The truth was that she knew she could have Nate if she went after him. "Accidentally" landed in bed with him. Wore seductive clothing—or a lack of them. It wouldn't take much to make him forget his promises to Miss Stacy Hartman.

But Terri wasn't going to do it. She wasn't going to be like her mother and leave behind such deep pain that people never recovered.

She wasn't going to be that selfish. She knew that if she seduced Nate, forced him to choose her, Brody would say, "I just want you to be happy." And that was true. But her father'd had more than twenty years of whispers about a wife who'd left him. He didn't deserve more scandal about a daughter who'd slutted her way between a man and the mayor's daughter. Dear Stacy Hartman who'd never hurt anyone. A young woman who was universally loved by all.

If Terri got together with Nate under those circumstances, the town would be rampant with talk of her mother, of Terri injuring a boy who had a promising athletic career, of Terri killing the spirit of Billy Thorndyke, the boy the whole town loved. Add Stacy to that and Terri would have to disappear. Leaving town wouldn't be enough. The town would probably hire mercenaries to go after her.

She closed her eyes for a moment, then slowly got out of the chair. That was enough about the past. Enough wallowing in self-pity. She had a lot of work to do and she needed to put her mind to that.

Chapter 11

"It was the most romantic thing I ever saw in my life," the girl said.

Terri didn't know the girl well, just that she was rarely without a book in her hand and she stayed with her parents in cabin number eighteen. Behind her were two other girls looking up at Terri as though she was supposed to make some comment. She was on a stepladder, staple gun in hand, electric drill in a holster at her hip. "Hand me that yellow box, would you?"

The girl picked up the staples, reached up to Terri and gave them to her.

The big tent Terri was working on had a tear in it the size of an ice crevasse. "You didn't unroll this thing and check it?" she'd asked the three older women putting up the knitting booth.

"Were we supposed to do that? We're very sorry, Terri."

She sighed. They were widows and they'd spent the winter knitting really cute things for their stall. Of course they hadn't looked at the tent for possible rips and tears. "I'll fix it," Terri said, "but only if I get one of those blue scarves."

Smiling angelically, the three women walked away. "I *told* you she'd know what to do about it," one of them whispered.

So they *had* seen the big tear. Terri was trying to decide whether or not to call their bluff when the teenage girls came running. They hadn't stopped talking since Terri began pulling the canvas and stapling the ancient, moldy, falling-apart fabric into place.

"Soooo romantic," the second girl said.

Terri knew they were hinting at something, but she didn't know what. "All right! I'll bite. *What* is so romantic?"

"The house the mayor gave to Nate and Stacy."

Terri stopped stapling. Behind her, the three knitting ladies also halted.

"The mayor and Mrs. Hartman had just picked up that cute Stacy from the airport and—"

"She was in Italy."

"All the way across the ocean."

"Anyway," the first girl said, "Nate was there and—"

"That's the Nate who was here," the second girl added.

"Yes, dear," said one of the knitting ladies, and there was steel in her voice. "We know who Nate is."

"And we also know that he is engaged to Stacy Hartman," said a second knitting lady. There was no steel in her voice, just sadness with a dash of disbelief.

"The house had a big ribbon on the door."

"What house?" a knitting lady asked.

"That old Stanton place," a girl said. "I thought it was falling down. Why would Stacy want that? She's so pretty she could be a model. And she's—"

"Too short to be a model," the first knitting lady snapped. "What was going on at that old house?"

"The mayor gave it to Stacy and Nate as a wedding gift. He gave them a key in a box."

"It had white velvet inside. It was really pretty. And Stacy unlocked the door."

"And inside was a picnic on the floor. With a white tablecloth and candles and a basket of food." The girl sighed loudly.

"And the mayor gave everyone a glass of champagne. I had a sip. It was wonderful!"

"Stacy was so happy she was in tears. She was hugging her parents hard."

"And what did Nate say?" the first knitting lady asked.

"He didn't say anything, but he didn't look too happy. I thought he liked boats better."

"But he carried Stacy over the threshold, then she shut the door so they could be alone." At that image, the girls giggled in a suggestive way.

The third girl gave Terri a sly look. "I thought he liked *you*."

The first knitting lady stepped forward. "Does your mother know you've been drinking alcoholic beverages?"

"She's too busy drinking herself to notice what I do," the girl said with another giggle, then the three of them turned and ran away.

"They're never too young to start being bitches, are they?" the third lady said.

"Terri…" the first knitting lady began.

She turned on the ladder to look down at them. "Nate and I are friends. Got it? I've always known he was engaged. There's never been anything between us of a…a romantic nature. Friends. That's all." She turned back to the tent and began stapling.

Behind her, the three ladies looked at each other in sadness, then went back to unloading boxes.

Good! Terri told herself. She was succeeding at keeping her feelings under cover. Considering how she'd lost it this morning, she was proud of herself. After she'd sat outside and indulged herself in useless memories of the past, she'd given herself a pep talk. Think of the future, not the past! But then, she'd walked into a barren kitchen and realized that Nate was gone. Really and truly *gone*. Everything had hit her with the weight of an outboard falling onto her and she'd burst into tears. Of course that was when her father and Uncle Frank and Elaine had decided to show up with her favorite cream-filled doughnuts. Elaine had immediately taken Terri into the bathroom and splashed cold water on her face.

"I knew it was coming so I shouldn't be upset," Terri said. "Nate and I are friends, that's all. I knew that from the beginning."

Elaine had been silent, but her face told her thoughts. Nate was no longer their darling savior.

When Terri went back into her living room, she had recovered—on the surface, at least. It took only a glance at the two men to see that they were furious, and it was up to her to make things right. "You caught me at the wrong time," Terri said, then went into a defense of Nate. She could tell that they weren't really listening to her. And their support made her feel better. She grabbed three doughnuts and ran down to her boat. What she needed was so much work that she couldn't think.

And she'd done well until the girls decided to tell her the details of Nate and his bride-to-be. She looked back at the tent she was supposed to be repairing and could hardly focus.

"Terri!" a man yelled. "Two people are trying to put up their tents on the same lot. It looks like there might be a fight."

Terri got down from the ladder, handed the staple gun to the man, said, "Finish that," then started running.

"I have my own booth to set up," he called after her. But then he looked back at the three ladies in their pretty hand-knit tops of pale pink, blue and lavender, and gave a sigh. "So what needs to be done?"

By the time Terri got to the cabin, Frank was already there—and he looked as furious as he had been earlier. "Your father gave two people the same booth space."

"I signed up forty-eight hours after registration opened," a tall young man was shouting at a little woman.

She wasn't intimidated. Her head was tilted back until it nearly touched her spine. "So did I. And you know it, because I saw you there."

Terri looked at Frank. "Who was first?"

"Your dad clocked them at the same time, same everything. Identical twins at war."

Terri looked at the stacked boxes. The man's booth was for handblown glass. Tall, artistic vases. Bowls with jewel-like colors in the bottom. Hers were pot holders and birdhouses and other crafts made by disabled children. While charming, they weren't exactly artworks. There couldn't be two booths more different.

"Is there room for them side by side?"

"No. We measured. Besides, they hate each other. She says he's exploiting the masses and he says she's making the planet ugly."

"Coin flip?" Terri said.

"I was going to suggest pistols at dawn and my money's on her."

"We could let them shoot Dad," Terri said.

"Now there's a good idea!" Frank pulled a quarter out of his pocket. "You do it."

She reached for the coin but a big hand took it.

"I'll take care of this," Nate said.

"Don't you have some champagne to drink?" Frank's voice was full of venom.

"Aren't you worried that tone will make you grow cat's whiskers?" Nate shot back.

Terri had to cough to cover a laugh.

Frank gave Nate a glare, then walked away.

"It's not good to anger a man wearing a firearm," Terri said. Oh! but she was glad to see him. She thought that he'd join the Summer Hill crowd and never look back. She turned toward the tall man and the short, plump woman going at each other. Terri was standing as close as possible to Nate without touching him. "I hear you have a new house."

Nate gave a grunt in answer. "Don't you think those pot holders look great with that glass stuff?"

"Fine art with crude crafts?"

"I think they're an excellent match."

"Her proceeds go to charity."

"I bet he could donate 10 percent," Nate said.

Turning, they smiled at each other.

They looked at each other—and for a moment their fingers touched.

"I refuse to move!" the glass man shouted. "I will *not* give away my space no matter how much you beg."

"Beg! Why you egocentric, selfish, elitist! I'll—"

"Terri!" someone shouted. "A tent just fell into the lake and they can't get it out. Could we use your boat?"

"Absolutely not!" she yelled back, then looked at Nate. "You play mediator and I'll rescue a tent."

"Lunch? One? House?"

With a nod, she took off running.

It didn't take Nate long to settle the dispute between the two people. They both wanted the same thing—to sell their objects. Nate made them see that their variety of goods would bring in different clients. The man's glass was so elegant that it would turn off the regular buyer. And her crafts were so crudely made that anyone in twenty-dollar shoes would walk away. Nate challenged the glass guy by saying he couldn't make her things look good. Forty-five minutes later, they were like mother and son working together.

With a sigh of relief, Nate left them. *Where to now?* he thought. Anybody with guns he could separate? Or maybe a fistfight. *Anything* rather than have no excuse to stay away from Stacy and her parents and… And that house.

The reunion with Stacy—the woman he was to *marry*—had been awkward. Since no one was speaking to Nate, all his information about where people were going to be when had come through Bob. Nate was waiting in front of the mayor's house when they returned from the airport.

Stacy, ever happy, ever enthusiastic, had leaped from the car and thrown her arms around Nate. She was smaller than he remembered, shorter, and she seemed almost fragile. But then, he'd had weeks with a woman who would grab the heavy end of a motorboat and lift it.

When she raised her face to his to kiss, he was glad. It seemed like months since he'd touched a woman. Days of yearning, of dreaming, of desiring. He opened his mouth over hers and—

"Nate!" Stacy pushed away from him. "Not here. Not now." She moved to point out that her parents were behind them.

He released her and she stepped away, but not before she winced and rubbed her side. He'd forgotten that he wasn't to be enthusiastic with her for fear of hurting her. With Stacy, words like *gentle* and *tender* were always in his mind.

Mr. Hartman gave Nate a look of reproach and Mrs. Hartman put on her Sunday school teacher face. Yet again, Nate had displeased them.

Silently, he followed them down the street, not knowing or caring where they were going. When he saw the red bow on the door to the old Stanton house, he wanted to turn tail and run. Up close, the house was worse than he'd thought. Peeling paint, rotten window frames. He hated the overall look of it—a sort of White House with its heavy columns—and the position of it smack in the center of town.

When they got there, half a dozen people were already waiting. But then you couldn't do anything at that house that everyone didn't see. There was a big half barrel on a stand: an attempt to look rustic yet actually be sophisticated. Six bottles of champagne were inside on ice.

What was Nate to do? Was he to declare that he hated the place right there in front of everyone? He glanced down at Stacy as she held his hand. Her face was a poster for happiness. She was so ecstatically happy that tears gleamed in her pretty blue eyes.

Nate said nothing as he helped Stacy cut the big ribbon with the huge scissors, then stood back as she unlocked the door. When she paused, he knew he was to carry her over the threshold. What else could he do?

When they were inside, Stacy did give him a little snuggle. As the growing crowd showed its delight—people seemed able to smell free champagne—she shut the door so they were alone.

There was a picnic set up on the floor with white cloths, more champagne and a basket full of what Nate was sure was Mrs. Hartman's bland food.

He set Stacy down and even opened his mouth to speak, but she didn't seem to notice.

"I have loved this house my whole life! It's something Dad and I shared. He got a key from the caretaker and on Sunday afternoons we used to sneak in here. I know every inch of it. Come on! I'll show you."

She grabbed his hand, pulled him to the stairs and he followed her up. With more excitement than he'd ever seen in her, she showed him room after derelict room. Paneling and wallpaper hung down in strips. Two ceilings were falling. She wouldn't let him enter one bathroom because the floor was rotten.

"I can walk on it but you'd go through."

The way she said it made him feel like the Hulk, green and cumbersome.

Downstairs were the big rooms. A hideous kitchen, a family room with dark paneling. Stacy loved the little alcove to the side.

"We can snuggle there on rainy days and read."

The built-in seat was so narrow that half of him would hang over the side. But he said nothing.

The dining room had bow-front windows that looked out into… The backyard was filled with broken concrete blocks, rotting piles of lumber and a couple of old appliances. He turned to her in shock.

"I know," she said. "It's awful, isn't it? But don't worry. I'll clean it up. I'll make it into a truly beautiful garden."

Then what? he wanted to ask. Their view would be of a bunch of flowers? He thought of the view he'd grown used to: the lake, the tall trees on the edge, the people in the distance.

With this house, there was no privacy anywhere. Every window looked into someone else's house. Maybe their kids would talk to the neighbors from one window to another.

"What's that look for?" she asked.

"I was thinking about our kids."

"That's so sweet," Stacy said. "Do you think they'll be dark like you or as pale as I am?"

Nate had never imagined having blond children. "Like you," he said, and managed to smile a bit. When she patted his arm, he realized how hard he'd been working out lately. In the gym with Jamie or lifting machines made of iron because Terri had tricked him into cleaning an old machine shop. For the first time in hours, he genuinely smiled.

Stacy had her back to him and didn't see. "Maybe our children will be runners and not bodybuilders."

Nate's smile disappeared. He'd told her more than once that he was a powerlifter, not a bodybuilder. Well, maybe he wasn't strictly a powerlifter, but... "I have to go," he said.

She whirled around to face him. "Go? I just got here. I haven't seen you in weeks. I thought we might..." Smiling, she lowered her lashes. "We could christen the house."

"I'd love to but I promised Brody that I'd..." He couldn't think of an excuse.

"Brody? Oh. At the lake. You don't need to leave. Bob said he'd put up my tent."

Nate took a step backward. "Bob? Are you kidding? He's a would-be politician. All he can do is eat rubber chicken. I have to lift the poles." He couldn't help it but he held up his arm and flexed his bicep. It was something he'd been doing a lot in the last few weeks because every time he flexed, Terri gave a very satisfying expression of appreciation.

But Stacy's frown didn't change. She was utterly unaffected by his display of muscle.

He took another step back. "I really do need to go. They're expecting me. And I have to oversee your booth. The boxes you sent fill a dump truck."

"I guess," Stacy said, then regained her usual happiness. "You're right. I have much more in the basement of Mom and Dad's house. Why don't you go to the lake to work on the tent and send Bob to me?"

Nate had an idea that suggestion was supposed to make him feel guilty—or maybe jealous—but it didn't. "Great idea! I'll do it." He got to the door before he turned back. In a few steps he crossed the distance between them and pulled her into his arms. He had to bend down to reach her and she had to stand on her toes, but their lips met.

This time, it was Stacy who got passionate and Nate who pulled away. "Keep up with that and I'll never get out of here."

"That's the whole idea," Stacy said with absolutely no humor.

"You're so cute." He touched the tip of her nose with his finger, then was out the door before she could say another word.

He drove much too fast to get to the lake, and when he saw the chaos he was relieved. He needed that to take his mind off his own problems.

There were pickup trucks everywhere and it looked like a hundred people were unloading them—and they were all arguing about how to do it. Some booths were tents, some were being built out of pine, some were prefabricated of plywood. Sellers did a lot to attract customers to them.

A straw hat blew across the gravel and landed at Nate's feet. He picked it up and smiled at the middle-aged woman chasing it. She looked as though she didn't know whether to cry or kill someone.

"I hate my husband," she said. "Really and truly *hate* him. I should have listened to my mother and dumped him twenty-four years ago."

Nate slid an arm around her shoulders and handed her the hat. "What do you say we go beat him up?"

"Only if I get to help."

Thirty minutes later, he'd settled six arguments and had found Terri and her uncle Frank, then got the glass guy and the pot holder woman together.

Best of all, he'd made a date to have lunch with Terri. No! he corrected himself. No date with Terri. They were in business together and needed to discuss it.

And, he promised himself, as soon as Widiwick was over, he was going to spend a whole lot of time with his bride-to-be and rediscover what had made him fall in love with her in the first place. Yes, he thought. That's all he needed. Time with Stacy and it would all come back to him.

By twelve thirty, Nate was hungry, thirsty and ready to throw people in the lake. The petty complaints they came up with were appalling. "My space is too far from the toilets," a man said. Nate bit his tongue to keep from saying "Use a tree."

Two women were arguing over the colors of their side-by-side booths. Nate started to step in but Reverend Nolan caught his arm. "Save your breath. Those two are sisters." Nate nearly ran away.

When it was almost time to escape to some peace and quiet, he saw Mrs. Lennon alone in the midst of what looked to be a hundred pots, ranging from new to old tin cans, all ready to be filled with flowers. Her tent was up, a light tan trimmed in dark green, and she had a big sign: Garden Day.

All in all, a nonangry person looked like a haven. "You okay? Need any help?" he asked.

"You couldn't possibly move that big urn to the front, could you?"

"Sure." Nate slid his forearms under the iron pot, lifted with his legs and carried it to where she pointed and set it down.

"My goodness, but you are a strong young man. You must have to work to keep the girls away."

Nate picked up another big pot and moved it to the front. "I just wish all of them thought that," he mumbled. When he stood up, Mrs. Lennon was staring at him, her eyes asking what he'd meant. "Sorry, I shouldn't have said that. I better go."

"How about a tall glass of homemade lemonade?"

"Who do I have to murder?"

She motioned him to the back of the tent where she'd set up a little table and two chairs. A big container of lemonade and a box of cookies were on top. "Help yourself." He took a seat and she sat across from him.

"Whoever thought up this festival should be shot," he said. "I mean the very first person who invented it, not the Widiwick part."

"Hmmm," she said. "You must be referring to Terri's mother, Leslie. Lovely woman."

Nate smiled. "Any objection to telling me about her?"

"None at all. Leslie was my friend and she's the one who made this place—all of it, the whole lake—what it is. Jake and Brody were just a couple of ex-GIs who wanted to build some houses. It was Leslie who had the vision of what it could be. She designed the club, made a circle road. She made a *community*."

"I was told that—"

Mrs. Lennon's face instantly turned to anger. "I *know* what you were told. But it's not true. Why would a woman who lived for her family run off with some man? She was mad about Brody and hardly ever set her daughter down. She designed this place for families. She—"

Mrs. Lennon took a breath and calmed herself. "It doesn't matter now. I don't know what happened to Leslie Rayburn but I don't think she ran off with a man."

"Didn't she leave a note?"

"I heard that she did and people said it was her handwriting, but Leslie called me that morning. She said she'd spilled a hot cup of tea over her right hand and it was in bandages. *How* did she write a note?"

"Did you tell the sheriff about this?"

"Of course, but we had old man Chazen then and he wouldn't listen to anyone but Della Kissel. He said no one could understand what a woman like Leslie thought. Maybe she'd planned it in advance." Mrs. Lennon turned her head away for a moment. "I'm sorry for getting so angry."

"Did you tell Frank?" Nate asked softly.

Mrs. Lennon looked back at him. "I did. He wrote everything down and I think he threw it in a box. Brody won't listen to anything." She tightened her lips. "You're going to break Terri's heart, aren't you? We'll add you to the list of people who have done it."

Nate was startled by the quick change of subject. "Do you mean whatever happened with Billy Thorndyke?"

"Yes. No. I mean what this whole town has done to her."

Nate saw that her face had an expression of guilt. "You know something, don't you? Leslie—"

"This isn't about Leslie."

"Mom! Are you here?" The voice came from the other side of the tent.

Instantly, Mrs. Lennon stood up and began to speak quickly and softly. "There are ugly secrets in this town and they should be exposed. Let the light shine on them. It's not fair that girls like Stacy Hartman get so much and the Terri Rayburns of the world get so little. They should—"

"There you are." Kris looked from her mother to Nate and frowned. "I need help out here and I think other people do too." She pointedly glared at Nate.

He put his empty glass down and stood up. "That was very interesting, Mrs. Lennon. I had no idea so much was involved in running a flower shop. And yes, I think you're right. I should send Terri some flowers of thanks. You choose and send me the bill." He gave a smile at Kris and left them.

It took some work, but Nate managed to escape long enough to get to his car. He backed out around a dozen other vehicles and made his way to Terri's house. As soon as he parked, he felt the first peace he'd experienced in what seemed to be a long time.

He practically threw open the door. "I'm—" He stopped himself from saying "I'm home."

The house was empty. There was food on the kitchen counter and a note from Terri.

Everyone has been giving me things to eat—just before they tell me Dad screwed something up. Sorry,

but I can't be there for lunch. Too many wars going
on to take time off. Tell Stacy hi from me. Maybe
we can double-date some time. You love Widiwick
yet? —Terri

Nate read the breezy little note a couple of times, smiling. There was a Post-it on the fridge. *Sandwiches inside.*
She'd left him two big subs with some of Mr. Parnelli's
spicy beef. He took one and a beer and went outside to
the chairs to sit and watch the chaos.

He sent a text to Hallie asking if he could spend a
few days with her and Jamie. After today, he didn't think
Brody would want him back as a houseguest.

Only if you cook for us, she wrote back.

"At least someone wants me," he said as he bit into his
sandwich.

He was so relaxed that he was half-asleep when the
door into the house was thrown open.

"What the hell are you doing here?" Frank Cannon
yelled.

Nate turned in the chair and looked at the angry man.
"Having lunch. Can I get you anything?"

"No. This is *not* your house and you have no right to
treat it like it is."

Nate got up, lunch things in hand and started back to
the house, Frank close behind him.

"You know what Terri did this morning?" Frank asked.

Nate was throwing away his trash and straightening
the kitchen he knew so well. He didn't answer because it
was a rhetorical question.

"She defended your ass, that's what. In case you haven't
noticed, we're all PO'd at you."

"I noticed," Nate said. Brody had walked past him three

times with no greeting. Elaine had waved but it wasn't friendly.

"Terri told us to stop it. She said we were angry at you for being an honorable man. She said we were hating you for what we *liked* about you."

Nate paused, his hand on the counter. He could imagine Terri saying those things. She took friendship to its highest level. "Terri and I never did anything inappropriate."

Frank looked like he might explode. "Inappropriate?" He said the word as though it were filthy. "You kids today make me sick. You think that if you say it in a PC way then it's okay. Do you *really* think what you did to Terri was 'appropriate'? Just because you didn't pay her the courtesy of showing her the lust I saw on your face, you think it's all right? You should have left when you saw that she liked you so much. You knew you were engaged! But your ego liked having a pretty girl look at you like she did. What I want to know is what you're playing at." He stared at Nate, waiting for an answer.

"I don't know," Nate said, and the honesty he felt came out in his words. "I'll leave."

"Yeah. I think you should. And stay away."

"I have to help..." He motioned toward the lake.

"Of course you do. You worked hard to put yourself in the lives of the Rayburn family. You made them *need* you. But they were just something to entertain you, weren't they? Something to occupy yourself while you waited for the mayor's daughter to return."

Nate could think of nothing to say. Turning, he left the house.

Chapter 12

It was Wednesday and Terri was ready for the whole festival to be over. It seemed to be worse this year. Four years ago they'd put a limit on the number of booths and that had caused a war. Brody had lost his temper after about three hours and said everyone could apply and he'd let them know who got in. The hint was that there would be a random draw. But he and Frank and three retirees had sat down with beers and chosen people they liked.

Elaine had stopped that favoritism and made the process more fair. So now they had a cross section of sellers, all of whom wanted the best spots.

Terri ran from one place to another, repairing things and trying to solve arguments. But she wasn't very good at diplomacy. She found herself muttering, "Where is Nate?"

She'd seen him often, but every time she got near him, he said he had to go somewhere else. Behind him trailed the usual chorus.

"Nate fixed it"

"Nate solved it."

But she knew that today something was different.

"Are you all right?" she asked when she caught him running from one disaster to another.

"Fine. I need to…" He waved his hand in a vague way.

"I know. You have to go solve some problems." Yesterday she'd had to miss lunch with him. "Want to try for lunch today?"

"No!" he nearly shouted. "I mean, I have too much to do. I'll see you… Whenever."

As Terri watched him leave, she was frowning. What was wrong with him?! She was the one who was being left behind. Last night she'd stayed in her dad's office until after ten. Anything rather than go back to her empty house. The night before she'd found one of Nate's socks stuck in the dryer and she'd almost started crying. Again.

She'd angrily wiped at her eyes and told herself to get a grip.

Nate was with the woman he loved and probably spending fabulous nights of joyous sex with her. He had everything he wanted in life, so why did he look like he was miserable?

Three times she'd tried to talk to him, but he always ran away. *Some friendship*, she thought. They'd gone from sharing bottles of beer, sharing their *lives*, to not even speaking.

By about two, she was beginning to see some progress. The past participants had their booths up and were arranging their displays. Best was that they were generously helping the newbies.

Smiling, flexing her sore shoulders, Terri walked along the road. Nearly all the cabins had something set up in the front. Sometimes the owners used their porches to display things they'd made during the year. Candles were a popular item. The photo school—the one Nate had started—was advertising for students and displaying their shots.

She was near the bridge when she stopped to look at Stacy's tent. It was magnificent: pristine white, a tall, slender, pointed section in the center. Like the petals of a flower, the wings spread out and were held up by tall poles. It was a piece of art!

Inside were beautiful rugs and furniture, nearly all of it upholstered in white silk. Exquisite little pillows in brightly colored silk were scattered about.

Whereas many of the booths looked like the homemade items they were, Stacy's was professional. Glamorous. Anyone walking past would stop and gawk.

As Terri gazed in awe, she heard a short scream and saw what appeared to be a foot flying up in the air. She ran.

Stacy was hanging from a steel brace for the tent roof, her feet dangling, and the ladder was on the floor. Terri picked up the ladder, helped Stacy get her feet on it and held it.

"Thank you so much!" Stacy said. "I thought the thing was secure but it wasn't."

Now that she was inside the tent, Terri saw about twenty boxes that hadn't been unpacked. "Do you need some help?"

"Would you? Could you? Please? I have so much to do and everyone is so busy."

Terri pulled her knife out of her belt and began slicing tape on the boxes. "So where's Nate?" She hadn't meant to ask that, but it had come out.

"I have no idea." Stacy pulled what looked like an

Aladdin's lamp out of a box. "Do you know what's wrong with him?"

"Not a clue," Terri said honestly as she unwrapped a white ceramic lamp. The decor seemed to have Moroccan overtones.

"May I vent? I know you and I have never been close, but right now I have no one to talk to and Nate is driving me insane."

"Vent away." Terri reached for the scarves Stacy was unpacking.

"When Nate and I lived together in DC, he was the most wonderful man I ever met. You should see him in a tuxedo! He's big but if his clothes fit, he can look quite elegant."

Terri was just glad when Nate took a shower. How many times had she told him, "You stink"?

"We went to dinner parties and galas. It was all like a dream. We had the most beautiful apartment. Everything was white. Carpet, curtains, upholstery, even the dishes. *We* were the color in the place."

Terri remembered their worry of dropping pizza on white furniture. "Did you cook?"

"Oh yes. My mother taught me and I'm rather good at it. I believe in healthy and fresh. Nate and I went to a farmer's market every Saturday morning and chose all our vegetables. I steamed everything. I made some rather nice sauces—nothing too spicy, but delicious."

Terri was holding the ladder as Stacy stapled up some big, handwoven cloths. Nate's many jars of spices were still in her kitchen. "I tend to live on pizzas and barbecue. And beer. That doesn't sound like you and Nate."

"Not at all. He's quite good at choosing wine. We had

red and white at every meal. Nate knows which glasses to use for every course."

"Does he? I guess you know that he worked here while you were away. I never saw him drink anything but beer."

"And I never saw him with anything but wine."

The two women looked at each other.

"Which one do you think is the real Nate?" Terri asked.

"Mine," Stacy answered quickly. "He was so smooth with all those politicians we met that I'm sure he's learned to adapt to wherever he is. So, at the lake he dresses and eats like them. Oh, sorry. I didn't mean any offense."

"None taken. Weren't you originally supposed to meet Kit's son?"

"Yes." Stacy got down from the ladder and held out the staple gun to Terri. "I think you're better at this than I am. Would you mind?"

"Not at all." Terri climbed up and Stacy handed her the fabric. "Tell me about him."

"Rowan is a beautiful man. Tall and slender and graceful. I would imagine that he's an excellent dancer."

"Didn't you meet him and Nate at the same time?"

"Yes. And…" Stacy paused, a long blue cloth in her hands. It was intricately embroidered in silver thread. "This is terrible to say but everyone has a physical type they like, and Rowan was… Well, he was…"

"Your type?"

Stacy gave a little laugh. "I shouldn't say that since I'm going to marry Nate, but yes. Nate is really… Well, you know. Larger."

"Yeah, I know." Terri thought of Nate just back from the gym, muscles bulging, sweat dripping off him.

"I'm not complaining because Nate is a wonderful

lover. Very thoughtful and…" Stacy smiled. "Long-lasting, if you know what I mean."

All Terri could do was nod.

"But the size of him is a bit off-putting. I've suggested he try yoga and I do believe I'm making progress. Anyway, Rowan…" Stacy grimaced. "Beautiful or not, he was a jerk! I don't know what his father had told him about me, but Rowan acted like I was a girl who couldn't get a date. He seemed to think *I* was pursuing *him*. He made some remarks that were so cutting that I wanted to dump my wine over his head."

"But Nate stepped in and calmed you both down?"

"Yes, he did. Did you know that Nate was a diplomat?"

"I did," Terri said. "So you and Nate moved in together right away?"

"Not instantly. Actually, it was never official. I just sort of stayed. But then my parents were going crazy about Bob and me getting back together. I needed to tell them that there was someone else."

"How did your parents like Nate?"

Stacy groaned as she began pulling picture frames out of a box. "They were awful! My father said Nate looked like a guy who pulled up the anchor on a ship. Dad said Nate could never be the—" She broke off with a sideways look at Terri. "I talk too much."

"Nate could never be the mayor of Summer Hill?"

"Right." With a sigh, Stacy plopped down on the wicker sofa. "It's been awful between my parents and Nate. They don't like each other at all. Mother keeps locking up her Lladró figures for fear Nate will break them, and Dad…" She shrugged.

Terri didn't dare sit on the white fabric so she threw a green scarf over the seat.

"I don't know what to do. I love Nate. He's so interesting and we like exactly the same things and…" Stacy looked at Terri. "At least I thought so. I'm not sure he likes his office or the Stanton house."

"Did you ask him?"

"Of course, but he just says he has so much work to do that he can't talk about it now. He seems to love the lake. In DC he never once said that he wanted to be near water. And I modeled his office after the apartment we were in. I thought he *liked* it. But now I'm not sure he even likes his job. Last night I tried to talk to him about his future clients and when his uncles could help him open the office. But he wouldn't talk about it. He just said he had to go."

"Go where?"

"He's staying with Dr. Jamie and his wife. I told Nate we could camp out in the Stanton house, so we could be alone. But he said his cousin needed him and…" Stacy threw up her hands. "I don't know what's going on with him. I was only gone for a few weeks, but it's as though everything has changed. It's like he doesn't even *want* to be with me."

"I think you two need to sit down and talk," Terri said. "You should be honest about what you want out of life and honest about yourselves."

Stacy turned toward Terri. "I've never been dishonest with Nate. Do you know something that I don't?"

"Just that he's been quite grubby around here and he seems to enjoy the physical labor. He hasn't been like the man you described."

"Yeah, well, men like to watch football. They all have that part of themselves."

"Rugby."

"What?"

"Nate likes rugby."

Stacy was quiet for a moment. "He hasn't been, you know, having…?"

"An affair? No," Terri said. "Not even a hint of sex. I never saw him going after any of the females here, even the ones who let him know they were willing."

Stacy gave a sigh of relief. "We just need time. Tomorrow I'm making a picnic for Nate and me. It's to be at six, after everything is set up. I thought we'd go to Moonlight Beach. Would you join us?"

"I'm not sure—"

"Please?" Stacy asked. "Nate seems so at home here. Maybe you can get him to relax, to open up, to *talk*. If he'd just tell me what's wrong, maybe I could fix it. Maybe—"

"Okay." Terri stood up. "I need to go. Other people…"

"Sure. I can do the rest of this." Stacy smiled. "I'm sorry you and I missed out on a lifetime of friendship. You've been great today."

"Uh… Yeah, me too." Terri said as she practically ran back to the road.

Terri was in the kitchen going through the cabinets trying to find a blue pan that she'd seen Nate use. It was oval and had a rough coating inside. He'd said it was perfect for fish and that's what she had. Mr. Allen had given her a big striped bass in thanks for figuring out how his tent was to be put up. He'd held the poles while she screwed them together. This was his first Widiwick and he was very excited.

When the doorbell rang, Terri grimaced. It was nearly 9:00 p.m., she was hungry and she did not want to have to solve even one more problem.

She wiped her hands on a towel, took the frown off her

face and went to the door. When she saw Nate through the glass, she smiled so wide her skin nearly cracked. She flung open the door. "Why didn't you use your key?" It wasn't easy to keep from throwing her arms around his neck. It seemed like years since she'd seen him.

He stepped inside and he started to say something, but then he glanced at the kitchen and saw the long white package on the counter. "Is that a fish?"

"Mr. Allen gave it to me. I was going to cook it but I can't find that big blue pan."

Nate went into the kitchen, opened an overhead cabinet and pulled the pan from the top shelf. "I was going to hang it on the wall, but it's so heavy that I'd have to use a grappling hook."

Terri laughed, glad to again feel the easy, light camaraderie between them. She leaned on the counter and watched him season the fish. How often she'd watched him cook!

Nate put oil in the heavy pan, then set it on the stove and turned on the burner.

"Did the Turner Twins help you today?" Terri asked.

"Those two pretty boys don't know which end of a hammer to use." As he got a potato out of the pantry and began to peel it, he smiled at her. "Why did they call Jamie this morning?"

"Mr. Arnold thought he was having a heart attack, but it was just anxiety. Mrs. Mellerson was there in one of her low-cut tops. Besides him, Jamie had to deal with two smashed thumbs, four splinters, a twisted ankle and a sprained wrist."

Nate put potato slices in the hot pan. "I know that later he had to deal with an allergic reaction to a bee sting. He sent the boy to the hospital."

Terri was watching him. For all his small talk about the day, she could see that he had something more serious he wanted to say, but it looked like he needed time. "How's Hallie?" she asked.

"Big. Tired. She hates Jamie. He thought for sure that it was twins as they run in our family. Jamie is a twin, but she's carrying only one huge baby."

As Nate turned over the browning potatoes, Terri gathered her courage. "How are you and Stacy?"

"Fine."

If this were a few days before, she would have called him on the tight tone of his voice, but she didn't. "Did you tell her that you hate your office and the Stanton house?"

"No. We haven't had time to talk about that. I'll tell her after Widiwick. On Sunday, maybe." He took the potato out of the pan, put it on a plate, then reached for the fish. "I need to talk to you about something. Maybe you've noticed that your dad and Frank are angry at me."

Terri grinned. "You mean the way Uncle Frank sneers at you? My dad wants to tie rockets to your ankles and launch you. Yeah, I've noticed."

As he put the fish in the pan, he didn't laugh and she could tell that something was bothering him. She braced herself. He was going to tell her of his great love for Stacy. Would he use terms like "light of my life"? Please not "soul mate." She was so sick of that term.

"I owe you an apology." He sounded as though he was announcing the end of the world.

"For not putting the sheets on the bed?" There was no smile from him. "Okay," she said. "An apology for what?"

"I knew what was going on." He glanced at her as though this was something she'd understand.

"What was going on?"

"With you and me that first day. I saw it."

"Saw what?" When Nate looked up from the fish, she could see his pulse pounding in his throat. Wow! Whatever he was trying to say was certainly difficult for him.

"I saw the way you looked at me."

"You mean when I yelled at you to get out? Sorry about that, but I thought you were an Ender in the wrong house. How you got the key was a mystery." She was smiling.

"No, not that." He took a breath. "You let me stay because you liked...liked the look of me."

"I guess so," Terri said. "You're certainly not ugly."

"I'm afraid I played on that knowledge. See, I was angry with Stacy for leaving. I'd come all the way here from Colorado for her. I was planning to move to *her* hometown, but she appreciated my sacrifice so little that she ran off to Italy. How could she leave the country when *I* was *here*?"

Terri lost her smile. She hadn't thought about it but it was rather inconsiderate—dare she say selfish?—of Stacy to do that. "I'm sure she didn't mean to hurt you. She just took an opportunity when it was offered."

Nate waved his hand. "I realize that now. She was right and I was wrong, but that doesn't matter."

"Oh? So what exactly is the problem?"

"You."

"Me? How am I a problem between you and Stacy?"

"You're not." Nate paused. "I'm not explaining this well. That first day we met, I knew you...you were interested in me in...in that male-female way. Not friendship, but as something else. That was okay on your part, but not on mine. I knew I was engaged and that nothing could happen between us. But I stayed anyway. And I think that staying may have encouraged you to think there could be something else."

"Possibly." Terri still didn't understand what he was trying to say.

"I didn't tell you about Stacy until the last minute. Until I *had* to. I was enjoying that a woman was paying attention to me when the one I loved wasn't." He looked back at the fish.

At last, Terri was beginning to understand. She'd thought that her father, or maybe Uncle Frank, had arranged the mix-up and had gifted her with this beautiful man. But after he told her about Stacy, she felt that she'd been stupid and naive. At the memory, Terri could feel the blood rising in her face. "It's okay," she managed to say.

"No, it isn't, because I've known all the time."

She looked at him. "What have you known?"

"About what's between us. What we never speak of. The...the attraction."

If a person could blush all over her body, Terri was doing so.

"Because I knew about it, I was wrong," Nate said. "I shouldn't have walked around shirtless so often. I know how much you like...rugby bodies."

"Ah." Terri was at last fully understanding what he was saying. He had done things on purpose. Nothing had been an accident as she'd thought. "You pulled off your sweaty shirt and asked me to rub you down."

"Yes, and at that house when it was raining, I knew you could see me when I undressed." He stood up straighter, as though preparing himself for punishment.

"And when you dived underwater to get the garbage up, you were shirtless. Later you said that when a pretty girl..."

Nate nodded. "I said that when a pretty girl watches, I tend to strip off. That was true even in the danger of that water. And by the way, there's something big down there and it's not farm machinery."

"We'll look into it," Terri mumbled. All he was mentioning was the physical. What was important to her were their moments together. Their easy laughter and talk. Sharing what was inside their minds. But he seemed to care only about what their bodies wanted. Was that all she had meant to him? Who had the hots for whom?

Terri clamped her teeth together. "I guess it was all a challenge, like a peacock showing off his tail feathers to a pretty hen. And I'm the hen."

Her tone made Nate look at her in alarm, but she smiled sweetly.

He slipped the fish out of the pan onto the plate beside the potato. "That isn't it at all. The point is that I take the blame entirely onto myself. I should have been more honest with you from the beginning. And I should have moved out immediately. I shouldn't have led you on." He looked at her. "Terri? Are you all right?"

"Considering that you're making me sound like Della Kissel, I'm just great. Should I put on an old-fashioned negligee and come on to the young bucks around the lake?"

"I didn't mean it like that."

"So how did you mean it? Explain it to me."

He held out the plate of food he'd just cooked for her, but she didn't take it. They were still standing in the kitchen. "It's more serious than that. More than once I thought about breaking up with Stacy. I thought..." Nate took a breath. "I've done my best to treat Stacy honorably, which meant that I couldn't give in to my baser urges. If I had, that would have meant that I wasn't being honorable with *you*. I made you think… I mean, not that I haven't thought about…"

"Thought about what?"

"Us. You and me. Together."

"I think I understand. You're saying that you've been working hard to decide which of us two women to choose?"

Nate's eyes went back and forth, as though he was trying to figure out if her question was real or a trick. "I guess so."

"You're saying that I was a woman living all alone, then big gorgeous you showed up, and I dreamed of having you? But no! You're engaged, therefore you should have moved out so poor me, a woman who obviously can't get a man of her own, wouldn't be heartbroken when you went back to the woman you truly love. Is that right?" She didn't give him time to answer. "What a dilemma for you." Terri's voice rose. *"'Should I choose sweet little Stacy or strong, sassy Terri? Both women want me so very, very much. But I just can't make up my mind.'"*

Nate looked trapped, frantic. "That isn't what I meant," he whispered.

"Explain to me what's so wonderful about you that you've managed to make *two* women fall in love with you. From what Stacy told me, you're whatever we women want you to be. You're wine for her and beer for me. Tell me, Nathaniel Taggert, who are you really?"

Nate's eyes looked bleak. "I'm beginning to think that I don't know."

"I can tell you that *I* don't know." She glared at him.

Nate took a step back. "I think I should go."

"You think your ego can get through the door? I sure

hope you don't meet a woman on your way out. You might have to choose from *three* women, all of whom are, of course, just dying to have you. A decision like that would probably tear your tiny dinosaur brain into so many pieces even sonar couldn't find them."

"I better leave."

"You think?"

Without another word, he left the house.

For a while, Terri stood there, staring at the space where Nate had been. Part of her thought she should be upset. Shouldn't she be gnashing her teeth? Wringing her hands? Feeling like she should throw herself into the deepest part of the lake and never come up?

She had just been nasty—really, *really* nasty—to a man she liked so much that she'd… Well, she'd almost been willing to leave family, friends and all she knew in the world just to be with him. But tonight she had irreparably broken the bond between them. Cut it with a chain saw made of words.

But another part of her felt only freedom. Stacy Hartman had won and Terri had lost. It was over. Again, Terri had lost a man she liked very much. First Billy and now Nate.

Only she'd never actually had either of them. She and Billy had been too young to be serious about the future. And she'd always known that Nate could never be hers.

He'd asked her what she saw as her future. The truth was that she'd never thought about it. Maybe she'd always assumed that her future would just happen. She'd meet a guy, fall in love, get married, have kids. Normal.

But with the way Terri conducted her life, that was *never* going to happen. Except for Billy, then Nate, if a man got near her, she backed away. She was not going to give people reason to believe she was like her mother!

So where had that taken her? Nearly every girl she'd gone to high school with was married. Half of them had kids. But Terri was still tiptoeing around like one of the Players to secretly meet some football player in his cabin.

And now that Nate Taggert had made it clear he wanted pretty little Stacy and not workhorse Terri, she was again on her own. If she'd learned nothing else in the last weeks, it was that she wanted a boyfriend, wanted a *life* outside of taking care of the people at the lake. When someone rang at 3:00 a.m. saying a bear was in the garbage, Terri wanted someone who'd help her with the job.

So now what? Did she return to her old life? Hey! Maybe she'd get an invitation to Nate and Stacy's wedding. That would be fun. She shook her head.

Stacy had invited her to a picnic tomorrow. Because Nate would be there, Terri hadn't really considered going. Her fear had been that she'd say or do something that might let Stacy know that Terri and Nate had been— were— What? Had been roommates? Were friends?

Or used to be, she thought.

She remembered what Nate had said. He'd known she was "attracted" to him so he'd stripped off whenever possible.

In that aspect, Terri was innocent. Yes, she'd worn shorts and high-cut swimsuits, but she always did. She'd done nothing different that was meant to turn Nate on.

She looked at the plate of fish and sliced potato. It was the last meal Nate would cook for her. She grabbed the plate, a glass and a bottle of wine, and sat down at the dining table. As she ate, she planned—and thought that a little revenge wouldn't be out of order.

She picked up her phone and called Elaine. "Do you have any really tiny bikinis?"

"None of those Brazilian string things, but some are just a few triangles. Who wants one?"

"Me."

"Oh," Elaine said. "Any reason why?"

"Stacy Hartman invited me to a picnic tomorrow."

"Ooooh." There was a smile in Elaine's voice. "How about a transparent cover-up and some sexy sandals to go with it?"

"That sounds great. I'll—"

Elaine cut her off. "I'll just bet the Turner Twins would love to go with you as your date." She sounded quite excited.

"They're next on my list to call."

"This is wonderful, honey. I'll pack up everything and you can get it tomorrow. I'll put in some sunscreen that the boys can rub on you. That should make Nate..." Elaine didn't finish the sentence.

"Insane with jealousy?" Terri asked.

"My thoughts exactly," Elaine said. "I'm going to the shop right now and get this ready. Please don't ever forget that your dad and I love you, sweetheart."

"Thanks, and it's mutual," Terri said, and hung up.

The next person she called was Mr. Parnelli. She asked if she could hire him to make a fabulous picnic for her.

He said, "For you, Terri, it's free and I'll make you a meal to remember."

She thanked him profusely, then called the Turner Twins. She didn't bother with a preliminary explanation. "Is it possible that you could pretend I like you and go on a picnic with me tomorrow?"

"Which one of us?" asked the one speaking.

"Both of you."

There was a pause, then a bit of a laugh. "You wouldn't be trying to make Nate Taggert jealous, would you? We saw him with cute little Stacy."

"Maybe," Terri said.

"We're in! Just tell us when and where."

She did, then hung up, smiling.

By the time she'd cleaned up the kitchen and showered, it was time for bed. The house was quiet and the moonlight came through the glass doors into her bedroom. She remembered how she and Nate had grabbed food and run away in her boat to the Island. For a moment the memory of that sweet time flooded her so thoroughly that her knees nearly gave way.

But then she remembered how angry she'd been when he spoke of "poor Bob." *Poor* because he'd lost darling little Stacy. "He knew," she whispered. It hadn't been innocent on his part, but he *knew* how she was feeling that day. Through every word, every look, he knew what she was thinking and feeling.

As she climbed into bed, she hoped that the bikini Elaine gave her would be microscopic.

Chapter 13

Stacy frowned as she packed the big picnic basket. All in all, she was beginning to wish she'd stayed in Italy. Dealing with fabrics and decisions about furniture and flirty Italians who seemed to have a hundred hands now seemed glorious. And so very simple!

She'd spent a lot of time planning her booth at Widi-wick. She was really hoping to get some commissions in Richmond or Charlottesville. She'd spent so much on fabrics that she'd had to ask her dad for money to buy the beautiful tent. Before she asked, she'd planned what she'd say to him to persuade him that the tent was an investment.

But her father hadn't balked. In fact, he'd asked what else she needed.

"An Italian sports car?" she'd joked.

"Whatever you need, pumpkin," he'd said.

Her mother was on the extension. "Did you meet anyone?"

"Lots of people," Stacy said. "I got two contacts for silks, and one for hard-carved—"

"No, I mean a man," her mother said.

Stacy had to count to ten before she could reply. "No, but then I *am* engaged," she said. "How is everything there?"

"Good," her father said, "but we really miss you. We think you should come home soon."

It had taken Stacy a while to reassure them that she was fine, but when she got off the phone she was worried that something specific was bothering them. Then she'd had to run to class and forgotten about it. Whatever was happening in Summer Hill seemed far away.

Everything started falling apart when her teacher had to leave early. Stacy had been disappointed, but she was missing Nate and her family and her little hometown, so she was all right. She called Nate to tell him she was returning early. It went to voice mail. She packed, then called again. Voice mail. She made plane reservations, called. No answer. She began calling Nate every half hour. In the car to the airport. At the airport. Nothing.

She didn't want to call her parents because that would mean she'd have to tell them Nate wasn't picking up his phone. She'd already been told about the disastrous brunch at their house.

Her parents' dislike of Nate was becoming a serious problem. When she couldn't contact him, she'd had to swallow her pride and ask them to pick her up at the airport.

As she'd feared, they went into a mini tirade about Nate not being reachable.

Stacy defended him. "He works for the government. Maybe he had something important to do for them."

"I thought he quit that job," her mother said.

Stacy had no answer for that. She just gave them the

flight information and told them it was time for her to board. The truth was that she was very annoyed with Nate. Couldn't he at least pick up his phone?!

But by the time she got back to dear little Summer Hill, she was willing to forgive him for everything. Surely he had a good excuse.

He'd been waiting for her and she was so glad to see him! Her father had prepared a lovely little ceremony with champagne and hors d'oeuvres to present her and Nate with the fabulous Stanton house.

But Nate had just stood there staring. Not frowning, not smiling. Just nothing. But then he'd abruptly grabbed her and kissed her in an intimate way in front of the townspeople who'd gathered. Stacy had been quite embarrassed.

Once they were alone inside the house, Nate had been so cool that it was as though they were strangers. She'd practically thrown herself at him in invitation for a tryst on the floor, but he'd refused. When he'd nearly run from the house, leaving her standing there alone, her pride had been hurt.

Since then, there had been nothing. Absolutely and totally *nothing*. They hadn't spent even ten minutes alone. Stacy had tried to talk to Nate, to snuggle with him. She'd suggested they rent a hotel room.

Nate had said he wanted to talk, cuddle, spend the night with her—all of it, but right now he had to… Whatever.

Since she returned, he'd been so distant, so distracted, that she'd called Bob and asked if he knew what was going on.

"Nate's staying with Brody Rayburn and I think there may be a problem about the office you got him. And the house," he added in a low voice.

"What kind of problem?"

"That's for him to say, not me. Want to hear about this girl I met?"

"Sure," Stacy said. She knew when Bob didn't want to talk about something.

Today had been the last day of preparation for Widiwick. Tomorrow the booths would be open and people would be coming to look and to buy. Stacy had high hopes about showing what she could do in terms of design. She'd prepared a big binder full of rooms she'd done. That they had all been in her parents' house at their expense didn't count. She just wanted to show people what she could do.

In DC she and Nate had talked a lot about their futures. That he was willing to move to Summer Hill had been tremendous. They'd talked about getting clients for his business. Between his uncles and her father, he'd have many people to do work for.

Nate had taken an interest in her business, even getting her a job decorating an apartment for his cousin.

Everything had been perfect. All that she'd ever hoped for. But now it was like something had happened while they'd been separated. She desperately wanted him to talk about whatever was bothering him. If, as Bob said, he didn't like his beautiful new office in the Thorndyke house, he should tell her. She'd *make* him tell her!

As for the Stanton house, he couldn't possibly not like that grand old place, could he? What was not to like? Spacious rooms. A large garden area. Located near everything. He could walk to work. No, that house was gorgeous—or would be after she restored it to its original magnificence and filled it with beautiful furniture. She was thinking of white silk for everything. Damask, raw silk, jacquard, duchess. She'd use a lot of texture and just a little color. Yes, that would be nice.

She looked back at the picnic basket. After she'd at last finished with the tent this afternoon, she'd driven out to a nearby restaurant and bought everything for this picnic. She especially liked the green eggs. They'd steamed them in kale-infused water. She knew Nate would love them! In DC they'd always eaten healthy and fresh. Besides, she wanted to get his weight down. He really did look good nude—if she remembered that far back—but enough was enough! If he packed on another pound of muscle, she'd have to shop for him at one of those dreadful big-and-tall shops.

Again, she thought of trying to get him to join her in yoga classes.

She looked through the basket. Everything was ready and she looked forward to this evening. Considering Nate's mood, she was glad she'd invited Terri.

While she was in Italy, Nate had asked about Terri, and she'd told him why Terri had been suspended from high school. What she didn't tell him was that she had been one of the cheerleaders who had come down the stairs to see Hector and Jay crumpled on the floor. Jay had a black eye and Hector's lip was bleeding, and they could hardly stand up.

Some of the girls helped the boys while the others ran and called for help. The boys were in such bad shape that they'd left the school in an ambulance.

Over the years, the memory had faded until she hardly recalled it, but Nate seemed to think Terri got a raw deal. And maybe she had. Maybe Billy and his family leaving town hadn't been *all* Terri's fault, just some of it.

Whatever the truth, Stacy was glad that Nate was trying to iron out the problems between the lake and the town. Her father had tried to do that but he'd had no success. He said that Brody Rayburn ran the lake like his own fiefdom and no one could penetrate his rule.

If Nate could, Stacy thought, well maybe he *was* suitable to become mayor of Summer Hill as she and her father had talked about.

At the thought, her frown was replaced by a smile. She grabbed the basket of food, then remembered to get the notes she'd taken when Billy called. She was curious as to how Terri was going to react to hearing about *that*. Like the rest of the town, Stacy was very curious about why Terri had dumped a lovely man like Billy Thorndyke.

Oh yes, she was very much looking forward to this little get-together.

Chapter 14

Nate was outside, waiting for Stacy beside his car. He had on baggy shorts, heavy leather sandals and a blue T-shirt that looked like it had been washed on a rock. She made a mental note that she needed to go shopping for him.

He gave her a kiss on the cheek and took the big basket, a tablecloth and a couple of aluminum chairs. "Don't like to sit on the sand?"

"Certainly not my favorite thing to do." She smiled, but as he'd done since she returned, he looked distracted. *Deliver me from moody men!* she thought.

He opened the car door for her, then got into the driver's seat and pulled away from her parents' house. "When your father had his law office, did he do any work for the man who used to own the lake?"

"Dad was Mr. Kissel's attorney. He set up all the contracts."

Nate glanced at her with sparkling eyes. "What do I

have to do to get him to tell me about what happened back then? At least I think that's when this lake-town feud started."

"I can tell you whatever you want to know."

Nate gave her a sweet smile, picked up her hand and kissed it. "You can? Tell me every word of it."

Stacy pulled her hand away. "Oh no, you don't. You don't get what you want until I get what *I* want."

"And what is that?" he asked softly, sex in every syllable.

"Not that! You missed that boat at our house! What I want today is for you to be *my* Nate, not the sullen, silent bear you've been since I got back."

"A bear, huh?" He was teasing.

She didn't smile as she looked at his arms bulging in the T-shirt. "You look like you've been doing very heavy weights."

"You don't like it?" He flexed a bicep.

She still didn't smile. "I think a person's body should do all forms of exercise: weights, aerobics, stretches. They should—" When he started to frown, she quit. "I know the whole story from the beginning. Want to hear what Della Kissel did?"

The humor came back to Nate's face. "And I have to behave to hear it?"

"Well, you don't have to be exactly angelic," Stacy said as they crossed the bridge to the lake. She started to tell him to go left, but he turned beside a house and went down an alleyway she'd never seen before. He certainly did seem to know his way around the lake. "Once upon a time…" she began, "Sheriff Chazen and Princess Della Kissel were engaged to be married. However, no one thought they were in love."

"Then why in the world would he want to marry her?"

"Because Princess Della's much-older brother, King Kissel, owned the lake and all the land around it. It was a very rich kingdom."

Nate smiled at her fairy-tale spin on the story.

"But the poor king's beloved wife had passed away and he was ill. Sheriff Chazen wanted to marry Princess Della because she would inherit everything."

"Nice," Nate said. "So what was this, uh…princess like when she was young?"

"She wasn't really a fairy-tale princess because she wasn't at all nice, and even the king knew she wasn't. The problem was that King Kissel didn't want to leave his kingdom to her and the sheriff, but he didn't know what to do."

"I know this part. He met Brody and Jake in a restaurant."

"The king knew Sir Jake to be a hardworking, reliable young knight, and Sir Brody was recommended to him. Together, they planned to build a new kingdom that would house many of the deserving citizens. But there was a problem."

"Let me guess. Della met Brody," Nate said. "Even now she never takes her eyes off him."

"Oh yes, the princess saw the young, handsome, virile Sir Brody and decided she *had* to have him. She had no doubt that she would get him, for she was used to a life of being given whatever she wanted. On the first day she saw Sir Brody, she went to Sheriff Chazen's office, returned his ring and said she was going to marry someone else."

"Della must have been livid when Brody met Leslie."

"Ah yes, the beauteous commoner, a stranger in town, the maiden Leslie. They saw one another across a room and—zap!—true love claimed them. Without thought of the consequences, they married and she was instantly in the family way."

"But in this case, there was no happily ever after," Nate said.

"I guess not." Stacy looked out the window. "The fairy tale ended abruptly on one dark and stormy night."

Nate parked behind a house, then turned to look at her. "Did Leslie's, uh...leaving cause the hatred between the town and the lake?"

Stacy's voice lost its storytelling tone. "Dad said that's what set it off. Sheriff Chazen was angry about all of it. He told people that Brody was trying to con the dying Mr. Kissel out of millions. When Leslie ran away, he said that was proof that Brody Rayburn was no good. Unfortunately, a lot of people believed him."

She looked at Nate. "Dad said the sheriff kind of went crazy with his hatred of all things to do with the lake. If a town kid got caught speeding, he'd be sent home with a warning. But if a lake kid was caught, he'd be put in a cell in the back of the office and have to wait for his parents to show up."

"Why didn't the people stop him?"

"I don't know. I think maybe it was the times. People didn't stand up to authority. And if they did protest, Sheriff Chazen tended to get revenge—like not showing up when he was needed. But Dad said that he did more good than bad. Until..."

"Until what?"

"The Fourth of July weekend when I was twelve, the whole town was getting ready for a parade and a fair. We were going to have rides. A couple and their sixteen-year-old daughter had rented a house at the lake for that month, but something made them have to go back home on the fourth. Their daughter begged to be allowed to stay here and they said okay. It was only for two days."

"What happened?"

"They didn't know anyone in town so no one knew the girl hadn't gone with them. She went to the grocery and the sheriff stopped her and asked to see her license. She was a new driver and she'd left it at home."

"He didn't put her in a cell, did he?"

"Yes. The bad part was that he forgot about her. He and all three deputies were out in the crowds so the office was empty. He left that girl in the cell for forty-eight hours with no food or water."

Nate looked at her in horror.

"It was awful. Her parents came back and couldn't find her so they called the sheriff. The girl was passed out on the floor of the cell and had to be revived. She spent days in the hospital. Eventually, she was okay physically, but mentally, she was seriously traumatized."

"Was the sheriff prosecuted?"

"No." Stacy let out her breath. "He knew what was coming. He went to a cabin in the woods and drank bottles of whiskey. When they found him, he'd been dead for days."

"Some ending for a fairy tale!"

"But don't they all end like that? The evil queen sends the hunter after the beautiful young girl, that kind of thing."

"But in those stories the evil queen ends up being dissolved or something. Nothing bad has happened to Della. She still follows Brody around, still spies on people, still spreads rumors and makes people miserable." He was getting angry. "She still—"

Stacy put her hand on his arm. "Are you all right?"

"Sure." He opened the car door and got out. "What fabulous food did you bring for us?"

"I went to a new restaurant just out of town. I think you're going to love it."

"If you do, I'm sure I will." He opened the trunk as Stacy got out.

"It's called Kale House. Just wait until you see the green eggs. They're delicious and so very good for you!"

Stacy had spread the cloth on the sand, put the chairs beside it, then pulled out all the pretty containers and set them on the cloth. Nate had done nothing but look out at the water. His gaze was so intense that he looked like someone in the crow's nest of a ship searching for whales. "Thar she blows," she muttered.

"Did you say something?"

"Nothing important. Why don't you tell me what you've been doing for the last few days? Any funny stories?"

Nate had skipped the chair and was sitting on the edge of the cloth. "Nothing worth repeating. Just a lot of people trying to get the most and the best. What about you? I'm sorry I didn't get to your booth often enough."

"That's all right. Terri helped me."

"Did she?" Nate turned his intense glare from the water to her. "You two talk about anything interesting?"

"Not really. Just you." Stacy was glad to see him lose his faraway look. "Don't look so scared. It was just girl talk. Here, try one of these eggs."

He took it and stared at it. "Green food."

Stacy was getting tired of his odd comments. "Yes. Food is sometimes green. If you don't like it I can—"

Nate popped the egg in his mouth.

Stacy was about to remark on his grimace when she looked behind him. "At last, she's here. Wow."

"Who is?" When Nate looked up, he was so startled he began to choke. He grabbed a bottle of water.

"Terri looks fabulous. I've never seen her like that." Stacy glanced down at her outfit of white shorts that almost reached her knees and a navy halter top that only showed a few inches of midriff. "I feel completely overdressed. Is that bikini even legal?"

At that, Nate stopped guzzling water and turned back around—and the sight made the egg and water fill his throat so that he started coughing and sputtering.

Stacy absently patted his back as Terri and two gorgeous men walked toward them. "Terri, you look great. Where did you get that suit and that cover-up?"

"Elaine's. Today I'm a walking advertisement for her shop. You should stop by some time. Do we set up here?"

"Sure. Anywhere. And I will definitely shop there."

Terri motioned to the young men who flanked her to put the cloth and the basket down. "Your food looks like it's from Kale House."

"It is. Have you eaten there?"

"I went with a friend and we ordered everything on the menu. You can't have too much green food."

"That's what Nate calls it too." She glanced at him, but he had his back to them as he tried to calm down from his coughing attack. "I haven't met your friends."

"They're Turners," Terri said in dismissal.

"Brent," one said.

"And I'm Brett."

"It's nice to meet you. I guess you've met my fiancé, Nate."

Nate had finally turned around to face them, but he said nothing.

"We've seen him around, but we haven't had a lot of conversation."

Stacy noted that Nate kept staring at Terri. While it did annoy her, she really couldn't blame him. Terri was five-nine or -ten and most of her seemed to be long, slim legs. There wasn't an ounce of fat on her. Actually there was hardly an ounce of anything on her. Her red bikini was so small it almost didn't exist. She had on a white cover-up but it was a soft, completely transparent cotton voile. Nothing was concealed.

All three of the men were gaping at her while the twins unpacked the picnic basket.

"Mr. Parnelli made a meal for me," Terri was saying. "He makes his own sausage and all the pasta is home-made. Help yourself."

"Dad bought some of his food," Stacy said. "Too spicy for me, but Nate might like some."

Nate didn't say anything, but he was staring at Terri in a way that Stacy really didn't care for. "Terri," she said, "you'll never believe who called me last night. Someone you greatly admire."

"Chris Hemsworth?"

"No, but close. Billy Thorndyke."

Terri was leaning back on the cloth, all of what looked to be four feet of her legs before her, but she abruptly sat up straight. "Billy? How is he? Where is he? What's he doing now?"

Stacy smiled warmly. "He called me with a job offer. His uncle now owns the Thorndyke house and the old stable. He's going to make the house into apartments and divide the stables into two houses. He wants me to decorate them and your father to handle the rental."

"That's really great." Terri gave a quick glance at Nate, who still hadn't said a word. "But didn't you put an office on the ground floor?"

"I did, but there's still the upstairs and isn't there an apartment downstairs? I only went to a few parties there. What's the upstairs like?"

Brett handed Terri a sandwich, ciabatta bread slathered in mustard, with sliced beef, pickled peppers and home-grown tomatoes. She bit into it. "This is so good. Best I've ever had. Soooo spicy." She glanced at the pretty little containers on Stacy's cloth. "Is that a kale salad? The one with cranberries?"

"Yes, it is. Want some?"

"No, thanks. This is enough. Oh, thanks." Brett had leaned forward and used a napkin to wipe a bit of mustard from the corner of her mouth. "Food like this makes me such a pig. Could one of you get me a cold beer?"

Brent opened one and handed it to her. "Now, where was I? Oh yes, dear Billy and that wonderful house. The attic is huge. Billy and I used to spend a lot of time up there. We'd..." Terri gave a little giggle. "Never mind what we were doing. But yeah, I could see that you could divide it up easily."

"Billy mentioned his grandmother's place downstairs. What's it like?"

Terri smiled. "It's very nice. When I was there, it was packed with years of family things. How did Billy sound?"

"Good. He asked about you. Asked if I'd give you his contact info." She looked at Terri in question.

"Sure. I'd love to have it." She watched as Stacy pulled an envelope out of her handbag and handed it to her.

"Billy said he had to go to class. He's just finishing school and—"

"School in what?"

"Law, I guess. Didn't Billy say he wanted to be a lawyer?"

Terri looked out at the water, her voice quiet. "Billy wanted to save the world. Damn! I miss him. Is he married? Children?"

"Neither," Stacy said. "I *did* ask about that."

Terri was silent for a moment, then she said, "But *his* office is there." She didn't look at Nate but jerked her head toward him. "Be careful not to rent to any single females. They'll be attracted to him. Overwhelmed with attraction. Lots of *attraction*!" Abruptly, she stood up and dropped the cover she wore to the sand. Her long body was sleek, tightly muscled—and barely covered. She was like a model for a statue of a Greek goddess.

"How about a swim?" she said over her shoulder to the twins. She didn't give them time to answer before she started running toward the water. The twins followed her.

Stacy watched them until they reached the lake and began to swim, then she turned to Nate. "What the hell did you do to her?"

Nate had reached across the cloth to pick up one of Mr. Parnelli's sandwiches. "Me? I didn't say a word."

"You've done something to make Terri angry and I want to know what it was."

"Nothing," he said. "I did *nothing* to her." He dropped the sandwich back onto the cloth, but Stacy didn't stop staring at him. "I made a remark about Terri being attracted to somebody and she didn't like it. That's all it was."

Stacy looked around the beach. There were some couples and a few families, several of whom she knew, and the lifeguard in his high tower. The last thing she wanted to do was get into an argument in public.

They sat in silence as they watched the people splashing in the lake. Most of them were tossing a ball and giving rides to children. But Terri was cutting the water with long, strong strokes. The twins were trying to keep up with her but couldn't do it. "She's really fast," Stacy said.

"She's holding back."

There was such admiration in his voice that she looked at him sharply, but his eyes never left the trio in the water.

After about thirty minutes they returned—and everyone on the beach, young and old, paused to watch Terri stride across the sand.

"I think I should take one of your summer jobs here," Stacy said when Terri put the cover-up back on. "It would get me in shape better than forty minutes a day in a gym."

"Sure," Terri said. "We'll get you to help the guy who cleaned out the old motor shed. He always needs help with everything he does."

When the twins turned away to hide what looked to be laughs at some inside joke, Stacy frowned. What she'd hoped would be a pleasant outing was turning into a disaster. Something was going on, and they were all part of it but she wasn't.

"I need to…" Terri waved her hand. "I should check on some Widiwick business so I'd better leave." She looked at the twins. "You two can stay if you want."

"We're with you." Brett started to fling things into the basket. But he pulled something heavy, wrapped in black cloth, out of the bottom, handed it to Terri, and she took it.

"I nearly forgot. This belonged…" Terri hesitated. "To my mother. I thought you might like to use it in your booth. It kind of fits your theme."

Stacy took it and peeled back the cloth. Inside was a bowl on a short pedestal with a finely sculpted dragon wrapped around it. "It's beautiful."

"It's also valuable," Nate said. "It's seventeenth-century silver. You can't leave this out in your booth."

"I agree," Stacy said. "Too many people and I couldn't guard it properly. But it is quite lovely. Where did your mother get it?"

Terri held it up to the sun. It needed polishing but the cloth had kept it from turning black so the light flashed off it. "I have no idea."

Nate stood up and took the ornament out of her hands. "You're drawing attention to it." He quickly wrapped it back in the cloth. "Where was this kept?"

"In the hall closet in the top. How valuable is it?"

"Very. I've seen ones like it in palaces. You should have it appraised, insured and keep it in Brody's safe."

Stacy, sitting on the cloth, was looking up at the two of them. Both were tall and strong. And they were standing very, very close. Turning her head, she saw the twins watching her. It was as if they expected something from her, but she didn't know what.

Terri took a step backward, away from Nate, then held out her hand. He gave the bowl to her. "We're going," she said. She looked at Stacy. "I'll see you tomorrow and good luck on your booth. I hope you get twenty commissions." Terri was walking backward, both twins beside her. "If you need anything, you have my number. Thanks for the info on Billy. I'll call him tonight."

"I think it's time you did, don't you?" Stacy said.

"Yes!" Terri grinned. "I do think now is exactly the right time." She gave a wave, then headed toward the road.

She was almost there when the lifeguard began blowing his whistle loudly and urgently.

Terri didn't hesitate. She tossed the silver bowl at a twin and started running, her long legs eating up the distance. She slowed at the picnic cloth and tossed the cover-up down.

Nate was waiting for her. "Man overboard. Probably drunk." He nodded toward a boat, turning about in the water, its motor going.

When Terri started running again, Nate was beside her.

Behind them, the twins stayed with Stacy. "Why is Nate doing this? Shouldn't the lifeguard be going out to help?" she asked them.

"He's just a kid and he knows to leave this to them," Brent said.

"To them?" Stacy asked. "I don't understand. Why is Nate doing this? He's not a lifeguard. He's a diplomat. He *talks* to people. He—" Her voice was rising.

Brett slipped his arm around her shoulders. "Nate will be fine and he knows what he's doing. He's had a lot of practice."

His twin looked at him sharply.

"I mean, Nate learns fast and he's good at swimming."

"He's spent the last twelve years in a desert," Stacy said. "He can ride camels. He can—" She broke off as Nate and Terri hit the deep water. They were swimming together, side by side.

The lifeguard's tower was empty since he was by the lake getting everyone out. She ran to it and climbed up the side so she could see. Nate and Terri were swimming—exactly alike, she thought. They looked like the swimmers in the Olympics, their faces under the water most of the time, their arms extended, their feet making only small movements.

Heavens! but they were beautiful! Like human dolphins. Slicing through the water like they'd been born in it, their movements synchronized, perfectly in time with each other.

The twins had climbed up the other side of the tower. "I had no idea Nate was so graceful in the water." When Stacy looked at them they gave weak smiles. She got the idea she wasn't supposed to see something. But what?

When Nate and Terri reached the boat, Stacy drew in her breath. Everyone on the beach was watching in silence and they could hear the motor running. It was like a multibladed guillotine in the water. If any of them hit the whirring rudder they would be cut into pieces.

Brett was hanging onto the tower with his arm through a rung. He was still holding the silver bowl.

Stacy watched as Nate put his hands on the side of the boat and pulled himself up. Looked like all those muscles of his were being put to use. But Terri swam to the far side of the boat, out of sight of the people on the beach. "What's she doing?"

"He knows Terri can find the guy, but she can't lift him into the boat. That's what Nate does."

"What he *does*? How many times have they rescued people?"

"Four," Brett said, then backtracked. "I think, but I could be wrong."

Nate and Terri rescued four people together, Stacy thought. But he'd not mentioned that in any of their phone calls or emails.

She looked back at the boat. Nate had turned off the motor and he was leaning over the side, pointing to Terri.

He went to the other side of the boat and Terri swam around.

"Shouldn't someone call 911?" Stacy asked.

"The lifeguard did. The EMTs will be waiting at the dock for them. They know they can't get to the scene as fast as Nate and Terri can."

"And they know this from practice, do they?" She looked back to the water because the people had begun to count. It didn't take much to know that they were counting the seconds Terri had been underwater. "Thirty-six, 37, 38." Stacy began counting with them. "Forty-eight, 49, 50." *Please*, she prayed.

Nate put his foot on the side of the boat. He was going down to get Terri.

But then she came up, and her hands were under the arms of a young man whose head was to one side. She held him up to Nate, who pulled the guy into the boat and began resuscitation on him.

With what looked to be a very practiced gesture, Nate dropped his arm down toward the water. Terri grabbed his wrist with both her hands and Nate lifted her straight up.

They didn't seem to speak but just set to work on the young man.

From the shore, no one could tell what was going on inside the boat. Was the man alive or not? The onlookers seemed to collectively hold their breath. Not even the kids were restless as they stood there in stony immobility and waited.

Finally, Terri stood up straight, faced them, then held her arms up, her thumbs pointed to the sky. He was alive!

Nate started the boat motor and took off so fast that Terri would have fallen if he hadn't caught her. He grabbed her by the waist and pulled her to the seat beside him. They disappeared around the bend.

For a while Stacy just stood there, clinging to the life-guard stand. The people on the beach were laughing and some of the kids were dancing. What she heard most was "Nate and Terri." Only it was said as one word: nateandterri.

"You want us to give you a ride back to town?" Brett asked. His tone was as to someone who'd just seen the death of a loved one. Sad and full of caring.

If there was one thing Stacy didn't want, it was to be the object of pity. She gave the smile that as a cheerleader she'd learned to put on after the team lost. "No," she said brightly, "I need to clean up and…" She couldn't think of an excuse. "My booth."

"But how will you get back?" Brent asked.

"Nate warned me that something like this might happen so he left me his car keys. He told me he and Terri worked together, but I had no idea they were so good. It was like watching a ballet, wasn't it?" She smiled broadly.

The twins looked dubious, but then nodded. "You're sure you don't need us?"

"Of course not." *I had no idea I was so good at lying*, she thought. *I'm an absolute master at it.*

It took a few moments to get rid of them, then Stacy stood by her basket full of uneaten food and looked about the bystanders. Who could she get to tell her the *truth* of what was going on?

To one side, digging up shells, was Colby Felderman. He was nine years old, went to her church, was in her mother's Sunday school class and was a great talker. She knew his parents lived in a house at the lake.

"Hi, Colby," she said.

"Hi, Miss Hartman. Did you see it?"

"I sure did. I have some food here that needs to go to Nate but I don't know where he lives. Do you know?"

"With Terri. Up there." He pointed toward a house on a bit of land that stuck out into the lake.

"That's a pretty place. Have you seen Nate up there?"

"Sure. He and Terri sit in the chairs and drink beer."

"Every night?"

"No. Sometimes they have parties and everybody goes."

"That sounds like fun. Does Nate help around here, at the lake?"

"He does everything."

"With Terri?"

"Oh yeah. My mom says they're in love but too dumb to know it. But I don't think Nate is dumb. He fixed the motor on my dad's boat. And one night he and Terri took my brother to jail, but Dad got him out."

"That doesn't sound dumb to me either," Stacy said softly.

"I gotta go. See ya in church."

"Yes, I'll see you in church."

Chapter 15

"Where's Nate?" the man asked Terri. It was Saturday and Widiwick was in full swing, with hundreds of visitors.

"I have no idea."

"But I need him to carry one of my sculptures to a truck. It weighs about four hundred pounds."

Terri was stapling the side of a tent that had fallen down. "I don't know where he is. Go ask Stacy Hartman."

"What does she have to do with anything?"

"Stacy and Nate are engaged to be married."

"Married?" The man looked shocked.

"You've never heard of it? Marriage has been around for a while."

"I thought you two were—"

She stepped around the man and started toward her next job.

"Terri, I'm serious," he called after her. "How am I going to move this thing? It's a polished tree stump with a piece of glass on the top."

"How did you get it there in the first place?" When he started to speak, she put up her hand. "Don't tell me. Nate did it. I don't know how we ran this place before he showed up. Go find Stacy and ask her. I haven't seen him." She picked up her pace and went to her utility truck and got in.

For today, no cars or trucks were allowed on the road that encircled the lake. People had to park on the outside and walk. That caused a lot of grumbling but it saved them from running over each other.

Terri needed a break from the noise and the questions and the general chaos of the fair. They didn't have a count, but it looked to be the biggest one yet. A vendor said she'd stamped over two hundred tickets as the people tried to get them ready to be put in for the Wish drawing. Summer Hill Residents Only seemed to have been lost along the way.

Mr. Cresnor had been sitting on his throne chair off and on since yesterday morning. Terri hadn't okayed it but the kids on the staff had started gluing seashells to the big wooden chair. As soon as the children saw it, they added things. One of the girls who worked in the kitchen was in charge of the glue gun. Matchbox cars, diaper pins, hair clips, feathers, and lots and lots of fake jewels were being glued on. Mr. Cresnor sat in his chair and approved or disapproved what could be added. His wife said he was in heaven.

Smiling, Terri waved to people as she entered Elaine's shop. There were six college girls working today and from the sound of it, they were mostly running the register.

One of them pointed toward the storeroom door. It looked like Elaine was hiding out. Terri went inside, closed the door behind her and leaned on it, her eyes closed.

"Come on," Elaine called. "Sit down. Have you had anything to eat?"

"Not since 6:00 a.m." Terri stepped around some open boxes, past shelves that were nearly empty, to get to the little table by the back door. It was set with soft drinks and sandwiches wrapped in plastic. Gratefully, she sat down. "Are you going to run out of stuff to sell?"

"Close. I've had eight requests for suits and cover-ups like you wore. I want you to be my model more often."

"Sure. I'll get a tattoo on my forehead that says I got it at Elaine's."

"No one will see it. Now if you put it on your behind, everyone would see it."

Laughing, Terri took the drink Elaine held out to her. "Really, how are you doing?"

"Financially, excellent. I actually have sold out of nearly everything. Next week I'll have to go to New York to buy more."

"Take Dad with you. Have lots of sex and cheer him up."

Elaine didn't smile. "You, Brody and Frank all need cheering up."

"A three-way? No thanks."

Elaine still didn't smile. "How are you? And don't you dare say, 'Fine.' What's going on in that busy mind of yours?"

"Nothing. I've had too much to do to think about anything." Elaine was glaring at her. Terri gave a deep sigh, picked up a sandwich and unwrapped it. "I haven't seen Nate since the picnic on Thursday."

"You mean, not since you two saved that man's life?"

Terri shrugged. "I guess so. We got him to the ambulance, then Nate left." She finished the sandwich and reached for another one. "To be fair, the picnic was awful. I was angry and I said too much. Poor Stacy. I don't think she had a clue what was going on."

"Have you talked to her since then?"

"I'm too cowardly for that. I figure that by now she's been told and I fear her wrath. 'You lived with *my* fiancé?' That sort of thing." She dropped a crust of bread onto the table. "I *am* like my mother," she whispered.

Elaine stood up and clasped Terri to her.

Terri clung to her tightly and for a moment there were tears in her eyes. She pulled away. "I'm all right."

Elaine sat down across from her. "Terri." Her voice was terse. "I haven't been here that long but you have to get over this obsession about what-my-mother-did. Her sins are not yours. You aren't responsible for them." She picked up Terri's hands and held them. "Honey, you work all the time. You are twenty-six years old and you've hardly had any life outside of work. The *only* reason you became attached to Nate was because he showed up inside your house. If he'd been staying somewhere else you wouldn't have looked at him."

"No. I would have *looked*."

"Looked, lusted, then done nothing." Elaine sat back in her chair. "You need to have some fun."

Terri was getting suspicious. "You've got something in mind, don't you?"

"The dance is tonight."

"So?"

"What are you going to wear?"

"Black pants and jacket. Uncle Frank and I will be on drunk duty."

"You and Frank and Brody. Three old men."

Terri started to reply, but then squinted her eyes. "What are you planning?"

Elaine got up and went to some dresses hanging inside plastic bags. She removed one from the back. Inside was a very plain gown, off-white, with a high, rolled collar and long sleeves. It was very modest.

"It takes a perfect figure to pull this off and you can do it."

She'd expected Elaine to pull out some ghastly concoction that sparkled and bared her legs. But this was as covered up as a nun's habit. It would cling, true, but there'd be no skin showing.

"Try it on."

"I need to…" At Elaine's look, Terri broke off. "Okay." She pulled her T-shirt over her head and stepped out of her shorts and sandals, leaving only her two pieces of underwear. She held up her arms as Elaine slipped the dress over her head, then tied it in the back.

Terri looked at herself in the mirror. The dress fit perfectly. The sleeves were bat wing, and the fabric was a slinky silk charmeuse. All in all, the dress covered her from neck to toes. Not even her arms were showing.

"It's nice," she said. "A far cry from the bikini. It's— Holy hell, Elaine!" Terri had twisted around to see the back—except that there wasn't one. There was a little shoestring tie across her shoulders, then nothing else all the way down to…to… "Is my crack showing?"

"Of course not." Elaine turned her to face the mirror. "I knew it would be perfect."

Terri reached her arms back to feel how much skin was exposed. All of it. The band of her bra was showing. "What underwear am I supposed to wear with this thing—not that I will wear it but I was just wondering."

"None whatever. Full commando."

"I can't—"

"Terri, when you get to my age and everything is going

south, you need strong foundation garments. But you, my dear, are so young and firm you could run hurdles and not bounce. You are to wear nothing whatever under this gown. No panties to show a line, no bra to show seams. Naked. Like a wood nymph."

"No," Terri said, "absolutely not." She reached for the tie but Elaine put her hand over it.

"When you're forty-five I want you to tell me about the parties you missed and the dresses you didn't wear be- cause…because… What was your reason again? You're afraid of what people will say?"

Terri was looking at herself in the mirror. The dress was really pretty. It slid down her body as though it had been poured over her. The only flaws were the seams in her undies. If she wore nothing under the dress, those lines wouldn't be there.

Elaine had been dressing people for twenty years, and she knew that look. She handed Terri a big round mirror and turned her around.

The dress really did expose her entire back. What with all the lifting of motors and chains, etc., there was a lot of muscle there. Muscle that gave shape to her back.

Sometimes, Terri thought, she did get fed up with try- ing to live down what her mother had done. Worse was that it didn't seem to be working.

She moved the hand mirror to the side and looked at the front of the dress. "Full commando, huh?"

"Absolutely."

She and Elaine smiled at each other in the mirror.

As Nate drove to the dance, Stacy's words were ringing in his ears. She'd been told that he and Terri had "lived" together and he'd tried to explain. But it hadn't gone well, especially not when he added the truth about not liking the office she'd created for him.

"I was trying to help *your* career—the one *you* said you wanted. I wasn't trying to make you give up your free spirit to work in an office. It's what I did to make a home for the man you told me you were. I never saw you in any clothes that weren't made by some Italian designer. Forgive me, but I thought that was who you were. But no. It seems you're denim and boat shoes and you want a woman who drools over you."

"Terri doesn't—"

"If you defend her to me, your fiancée, the woman you asked to *marry* you, so help me, I'll make you sorry. Damn you! But you've cast me in the role of some uptight, priggish female who's trying to force you to…to play bridge and someday be the mayor of a little Southern town. I don't know if you're the man I fell in love with or you're some guy who spends his days in a motorboat. And you know what, I don't think you know either. Nathaniel, you don't need to decide which woman you want, you need to decide who you actually are."

With that, she left the room and Nate nearly fell into a chair. It seemed that everyone he knew was angry at him.

Nate wasn't there. That was Terri's first thought as she searched the crowded dance floor. She had a red cashmere shawl that Elaine had lent her over her dress. An end was flung over her shoulder and pinned. But it was warm inside and unless she wanted to start sweating, she was going to have to remove it—and reveal her bare back.

Her second thought was that she was an idiot. Why was she standing against a wall and looking for some other woman's man? Or was he? She'd seen Stacy at her booth during the two days of the fair. She'd been talking enthusiastically to the many people who stopped to look at her designs.

One time Stacy had given a quick wave and a smile at Terri. She knew Stacy had been told about her and Nate "living" together. She'd expected Stacy to be livid. You know, like in every book and movie and girl fight since the beginning of time. Women didn't fight to the death over recipes. They went to battle over some man.

But Stacy's smile had been genuine. *Or was it?* Terri wondered. Should she watch alleyways for possible assassins?

She looked up to see the Turner Twins standing in front of her. They had on identical tuxedos, perfectly fitted and classically plain. It cost thousands to look that simple— and it made them look even more gorgeous than they usually did. "Got your names sewn into your cuffs?"

"We'll take them off and you can look."

Terri couldn't stop her laugh. "Don't you two have dates?"

"The world is our date," Brett said.

"If we need a chaperone, will you volunteer?" Brent asked.

At first she didn't know what they meant, but they were looking her up and down with little smirks. The floor-length dress with its long sleeves, and the big wool throw covered her.

"Who dressed you? Your grandmother?"

"Actually, it was Elaine." Terri unwrapped the throw and handed it to Brett. When they saw the dress clinging to her body, their eyes widened.

"Hi, Terri," called a teenage boy from behind them. He was with a pack of other boys.

"That dress is on backward," one called.

"Will you dance with me?"

"With *all* of us?" another boy snickered.

The twins' faces showed that they didn't understand what was going on. Terri smiled at them. "Put that in the coat check, will you?"

She lifted her chin, stepped between them and walked onto the dance floor, exposing the backless dress.

Behind her was a very satisfying silence from the twins. When she reached the dancers, she looked over her shoulder. They were staring in openmouthed astonishment.

Terri didn't dance much, although she was repeatedly asked. She was sure that if she moved too much she might pop out of the gown. Slow dances made her partner wonder where to put his hands—or he put them all over her bare skin.

It wasn't until after eleven that Nate showed up. He was in a tuxedo, as perfectly fitted to him as a tailor could make it. His broad shoulders, small waist and heavy thighs were accentuated. Terri had never seen anyone as beautiful as he was.

She was fighting the hands of a seventeen-year-old boy as he tried to slide into areas that were covered by silk.

Nate picked the kid up by the waist and set him aside, then stood there looking at Terri for a moment before extending his hand to her. When she took it, the lights changed. A soft spotlight shone on the two of them and the rest of the room darkened. The music changed to soft and easy.

She didn't have to be told that he'd arranged this.

The smile he gave her seemed to say that he knew what she was thinking. He pulled her to him, her back to his front.

They'd never danced together but they'd worked and lived together. Their bodies were well suited. Even in four-inch heels, Terri wasn't as tall as he was, and their athletic bodies matched.

This is the other Nate, she thought. The one Stacy had told her about but she'd never seen.

She followed him as he spun her around, dipped her down, his arms supporting her. It was a ballet of a dance: elegant, graceful, refined.

Just when she thought it was over, the music changed to down and dirty rock and roll.

Nate pulled off his jacket, tossed it onto one of the twins, then loosened his tie.

The crowd looked at Terri. What was *she* going to remove? She raised her hands and turned around slowly. It was easy to see that she was saying that she had on *only* the dress.

There was a murmur around them: laughter, giggles, teenage smirks.

For all that Nate was big and covered in muscle, he could certainly move! His hips began to gyrate and Terri followed him. Grinding, hunching, moving together but not touching.

They went down, hips almost to the floor, never ceasing to move in the ancient way of a man and a woman, then they came back up.

The music changed again. Harder, faster. The audience around them was clapping.

Terri heard them, but she only saw Nate. Just him. It was like only he existed and no one else. Her body was doing the thing she dreamed of doing with him, had fantasized about. She was actually feeling his hands on her skin!

When the music stopped, Nate picked her up in his

arms and she put her head against his chest. She could hear applause but only he mattered. His heart, the warmth of him. The skin of his neck was against her forehead, his hand on her bare back.

For a moment she thought he was going to carry her outside, but he didn't. He set her down on the ground and when her feet faltered, he pulled her back against him. His hands entwined with hers. The soft, sweet warmth of them! Their hand-holding was as intimate as kisses.

Slowly, she became aware of being watched. The people from the lake were smiling in that way they do when they think they're seeing True Love.

But the townspeople were frowning. A dance was one thing, but holding hands with the mayor's daughter's fi-ancé was quite another.

Terri put a smile on her face and stepped away from Nate. "Thank you," she said loudly, then like Cinderella, she turned to flee the ball. Prince Nate belonged to a prin-cess, not the boat girl.

But Nate wouldn't let her run away. His grip on her hand was almost painful. She frowned at him to let her go, but he didn't. Instead, he pulled her back to him in a slow dance, holding her hand over his heart, his cheek on her head.

"Stacy gave me my ring back," he whispered.

Terri's heart leaped at his words, and she worked to calm it. "Bad scene?"

"Brutal. It hurts to hear the truth about yourself."

There were other dancers around them and now that they weren't doing a show, she could think more clearly—or as clearly as she could with Nate's body pressed against hers. "And now you expect you and me to get together?"

"That was my hope, yes." He twisted her full circle and

drew her back, smiling in a way that said he was at last getting what he wanted.

Terri took a breath and kept her voice low so only he could hear her. "I've lived my whole life with whispers about my mother being a loose woman."

"That has nothing to do with you."

"Think not? I know you've heard about the two boys I knocked down in high school. They were trying to rape me. They said I was like my mother and that I wanted it."

Abruptly, Nate stopped moving and pulled away to look at her. His eyes were very, *very* angry.

Terri glanced at the couples around them. They were staring. She put herself against Nate. "Please. Not here. Not now."

It took him a moment but he started to move stiffly to the music. She could feel the anger in his body.

"If you and I...if we were together I'd be known for stealing the man the mayor's daughter was to marry."

"I do have free will." Nate's teeth were clenched in anger over her reveal of the high school incident.

Terri ignored his words. "Our children would have double my problems. Mother *and* grandmother were harlots. I'd be afraid to let my daughter out of the house. A son would fight all the time. They—"

"That wouldn't happen." Nate tried to pull away from her, but she held on and kept up a semblance of dancing. Her voice was low and near his ear. "And *you*! You'd be so hated for hurting the mayor's daughter that you'd never get any clients. What are you going to do? Follow me around all day and pull tourists out of the water? Are you willing to go from international diplomacy to being Terri's 'boy'? The guy who helps her? They'd say you were my wife. Can you handle that?"

Nate stopped moving and stared at her in horror. "This is ridiculous. You can't let other people rule your life."

"We shouldn't, but we all do." She was aware of people staring at them. She took his hand and led him outside into the cool night air. When they were alone, she turned back to him.

"You've thought about this, haven't you?" he asked.

"I've thought of nothing else since the picnic. I thought maybe…" She trailed off.

"Thought what? That I'd come to my senses and seen how blind I've been?"

"That did cross my mind." With a smile, he took a step toward her and she knew he meant to kiss her. It's what she'd dreamed about since the day she met him. But she stepped back. "You have to go away."

"No," Nate said.

"Not forever. Just until the town recovers."

"You want me to tell you what I think of this town?"

"No." She put her hand on his chest. "In your peace-making career did you ever advise people to take a break from each other? To give everyone time to settle down?"

"I don't like it when you're so smart."

"Me neither," she said. "I hate it! I wish I could stick my chin in the air and tell them to go screw themselves. Then you and I could… We could—"

Nate pulled her into his arms and stroked her hair. "It's all right. Don't cry. We'll do whatever you want. Whatever you *need*." His hand slipped down to her bare back. "You thought about our kids, did you? We Taggerts tend toward big families." Both his hands were on her skin, his fingertips sliding under the silk at the sides. "I love this dress. Really. It's the best dress I've ever seen in my whole life. Do you actually have nothing on under it?"

She pushed hard against his chest to stand a foot away from him. "I'm serious about this. You can't stay here. You need to leave Summer Hill now. Tomorrow everyone will be talking about how we danced together so wantonly on the same night that we broke Stacy's heart."

"Actually, she looked more relieved than upset. Her father was downright jubilant."

"You're making jokes but the town won't be. They'll say—"

"I don't want to hear another word about this town! Come away with me. My family will buy you a lake somewhere. You and Brody and—"

Terri turned away and started walking.

Nate caught her arm. "I apologize. I'll come back in the fall and we—"

"That's too soon. Make it a year."

"Absolutely not! That's too long."

"Unless you can rewrite my life, that's half the time it should be."

A couple came outside, looked at Nate, then began whispering to each other as they moved on.

"They're friends of Mayor Hartman." She turned away.

"Terri, you can't live in this fear. You can't—"

She spun around to face him. "What do you know about it?" She was angry. "What right do you have to judge *me*? My father and I have spent twenty-four years trying to show this town that we're respectable people and you want me to throw it away in one day? Why? Because you can't wait a few months to get what you want? And besides, maybe you'll change your mind. Maybe I'll be the next Stacy."

Nate's face lost its anger and his hurt showed as he stepped back from her. "You're right. A hundred per cent right. I'll, uh… I'll see you in a year. Maybe. Who knows what the future holds?" He put his hands in his pockets, turned his back on her and walked away into the darkness.

Chapter 16

"I am not going to cry," Terri chanted to herself. "I'll see him again. It isn't over. I'll—" The door to her house was standing open. She often forgot to lock it, but she didn't usually forget to close the door.

There was a flash of lightning, the beginning of a summer storm.

Terri went inside the dark house and reached for the light switch, but another flash revealed Nate in front of the windows. He was just standing there in his white shirt and black trousers, saying nothing, but he was watching her—and she knew what he was thinking.

But wasn't that their problem? They ate alike, worked alike, thought the same things.

Tonight, she thought. *We have tonight.*

She let her keys slide to the floor, then she stood and waited for him to come to her. It took only a few steps and he had his arms around her.

He'd kissed her before but it was nothing like when his

lips touched hers this time. He was a man who was hungry for her, who desired her down to his very soul.

Hours, days, weeks of longing were in his kiss. His lips opened over hers, his tongue sought hers. His hands encircled her body, pulling her close to him.

Terri had dreamed about this moment, fantasized about it. But the actuality was better. Their bodies were perfectly suited for each other. Strong and tight; muscular and solid.

When he stepped away from her, she started to go with him, but he held his arm out straight, his hand lightly on her collarbone.

She stood still, puzzled by what he was doing. Did he mean for this to end at a kiss? Would he kiss, then run away?

Terri frowned at him. "We can—"

Nate drew back his hand—and when he did, Terri's dress fell forward. She caught it. He had unfastened the tie in the back.

With a wicked little smile, Nate looked at her.

Terri moved her hands, gave her shoulders a twist, and the silk dress fell to the floor.

She had the great satisfaction of seeing the smile leave Nate's face. His eyes went to her feet, then slowly moved upward over her naked body. All of it was exposed to his view. By the time he reached her eyes, there was sweat on his brow.

Oh! The deep feeling of triumph to see lust in the eyes of the man you love.

Holding her arms out to the side, she gave a slow turn so he could see all of her, front and back. She was proud of the body she'd achieved from a lifetime of work.

When she turned to Nate, his eyes were wild. He pulled her against him, his clothes against her bare skin.

"I don't want to hurt you," he said.

She knew what he meant: pretty, delicate little Stacy. She gave a snort of contempt. "Try it."

It was as though her words released something in him. When he picked her up, her legs went around his waist, his hand running the length of one of them from waist to ankle, all while his lips never left hers.

She didn't know when he unfastened his trousers, but by the time he got to the wall, he was ready for her. He entered her with all the force of his desire. She arched her back against the wall and pushed against him, taking him deeper and deeper inside her.

As his strokes began, Terri lifted her arms and put her hands against the wall, pushing hard. Nate could take it. He could hold her full weight, easily stand up against her strength. He cupped her backside and pulled her even closer.

When he came, Terri was clawing at his back, trying to rip the shirt off him.

"Sorry," he whispered into her ear. "Next time is yours."

He carried her down the hall to what had been his bedroom.

She expected him to lay her down gently, but he didn't. He dropped her so she bounced on the mattress.

"I spent night after night imagining this." He was looking at her beautiful nude body on the bed.

"And here I thought you never noticed me."

"In those shorts?" He was slowly unbuttoning his shirt, taking his time. "Did you cut them off?"

"Maybe." She turned onto her side, drew one leg up and put her hand on the curve of his backside. "Was it too much for you to handle?"

When Nate took his shirt off, Terri drew in her breath. She was going to get to touch what she'd seen so often!

"You shortened your shorts and I lifted so heavy I nearly detached my pecs."

She got up on her knees and ran her hand over his chest, over the curves of the hard muscles. "It was worth it."

With a quick gesture, he let his trousers fall to the floor—and Terri saw him hard and upstanding, ready for her. She ran her fingertip down the side of him.

"Not too much for you?" he asked huskily. "All the men in my family are—"

"Do shut up," she said pleasantly, and he did.

They made love all night. With Terri on top until her legs gave out, then Nate rolled her beneath him.

At first he was cautious about putting his full weight on her, but she just laughed. "I'm not a Townie." They knew who she meant but she didn't say the name. Reality, consequences, and worse, separation, would happen tomorrow.

But now, for this one night in heaven, they had each other.

Only once did Nate try to persuade her out of the year-long separation. Terri said, "We can't build a life on the tears of an innocent person."

After that, they didn't talk much. But then, they'd done that and nothing else for weeks. Talked to cover their longing. Talked of work and other people and past experiences that hid what they'd really wanted to say. They'd shared experiences instead of emotions. Confessions of past feelings instead of declarations of true love.

There had been gentle hints of future wants and needs. Bits of hope that somehow they'd be together.

All these were replaced with touching, tasting, tongues,

fingers, hands. Exploring bodies they'd seen but had been forbidden to touch.

They showered together. Ate spicy sandwiches, then licked mustard off each other's skin.

Laughed. Every touch, every gesture made them laugh. Happiness that had been delayed, suppressed, came out in a joy that started inside them and erupted. If laughter could be said to come from the pores of their skin, it did.

As the sun rose, the light from inside them began to fade. They lay still, her head on his shoulder, bodies wrapped together.

There were no words that could be spoken. It had all been said. They must part. Not for themselves, but for those they loved—and would love. The sacrifice they were making was for people who did not deserve pain or in some cases, *more* pain. It was for the protection of the children they would have.

"You—" Terri began, but Nate put his fingertip over her lips.

He stroked her hair in a gentle way. So gentle, so sweet, that she fell asleep. And when she awoke, he was gone.

Chapter 17

Nate was in DC, sitting on the hated white couch in the apartment he and Stacy had stayed in. He was bent over, head in hands, and trying not to think that his life was over. A year! He was to stay away from Terri for an entire *year*.

When footsteps came down the hall, he didn't look up.

"Might I ask what you're doing in my apartment?" Rowan asked.

With a sigh, Nate leaned back and looked at his cousin. "Why are you here?"

"I live here, and right now I'm on holiday."

It wasn't easy for Nate to pull his mind away from his own problems, but Rowan looked awful. He had a big bandage on his forehead, a greenish eye and a bruise on his jaw. "You get shot again?"

"No. Blacked out and fell down the stairs, or the other way around. I don't remember clearly." He sat down on the opposite couch. "What about you? Last time I saw you, you were in a hospital. You looked better then than you do now."

"Felt better then."

"Ah," Rowan said. "Your girl dump you?"

"Girls. Plural."

Rowan raised his eyebrows. "That's the most interesting thing I've heard in days. Tell me about it."

For a moment they sat in silence, two very handsome men, physical opposites. Rowan was as slender and lithe as Nate was big and solid. But both of them had eyes sunken with misery.

"I guess you could say I have memory problems too. I was in love with one woman, spent a couple of weeks with another one and could hardly remember the first one. First one won't speak to me and the second one told me to come back in a year. I think your dad set me up with the second girl."

Rowan gave a tiny bit of a smile.

Nate grinned. "The second girl, the one I like, has an old boyfriend coming back to town. Everyone likes him but the whole town wants to hang me from the court-house." When Rowan looked skeptical, Nate said, "First girl's father is the local mayor."

Rowan laughed. "I think maybe you win—or lose. So what are you going to do?"

"Can you arrest the old boyfriend? Hold him in prison for a year?"

"Is this year to allow the town to get over what you did to the mayor's daughter?"

"Yeah," Nate said. "And so Terri doesn't have *another* mark against her in that damned town."

"Is she the one you and I went to dinner with? Yes, and

I know her. Stacy Hartman." Rowan stood up. "Are you planning to stay here in DC or go back home?"

"Haven't decided."

"Who is the second girl?"

"Terri Rayburn from the lake."

"I think I met her one time when I was with Dad. Tall girl? Can swim well?"

"Legs like a thoroughbred." Nate stuck his hands in his pockets and stared at the floor.

"You hungry? We can order in from a place down the road. They have a chopped kale salad that's good. Or do you want a Taggert feast of meat on top of meat?"

When Nate looked up, there was a sparkle in his eyes. "Kale, huh?"

Rowan knew it was a joke at his expense, but it didn't bother him. "If you're no longer welcome in Summer Hill, what are you going to do to earn a living for the next year? Don't you have an office there?"

Nate sat up on the couch. "A big one. Stacy modeled it on this apartment." He looked at the white furniture with distaste. "She thinks this place is beautiful."

"Yeah?" Rowan smiled. "I agree. Simple. Clean."

"You remember the Stanton house?"

Rowan put his hand to his forehead. "Stanton house? Big place smack in town? Falling down but could be restored?"

"That's it."

Rowan opened a drawer, pulled out a stack of menus and looked through them. "That's a great old house. I always liked it."

Nate shook his head. "You *like* that house?"

"Very much." Rowan handed Nate a menu. "Italian. Lots of meat. If you can't read it, I can translate. Call and order while I take a shower." He left the room.

Nate looked at the menu but didn't see it. Likes kale, loves the Stanton house, his apartment is all white. Maybe Kit had been right in matching his son with Stacy. And maybe he'd been right in putting Nate in Terri's house.

But Nate had messed it up. He'd been so jealous that Kit had given his son a beautiful young woman that Nate had... He took a breath. He'd done whatever he had to do to win her—including becoming someone he wasn't. He didn't want to think this was true, but maybe he'd tried to be a Montgomery—specifically, he'd tried to make himself into Rowan.

"I gave Stacy beer when she wanted champagne," he whispered.

Rowan appeared in the doorway, a towel wrapped around his waist. "Did you order?"

To Nate's eyes, Rowan was too thin. In good shape, but with little muscle on him. But maybe that's what Stacy liked. From the way she was always trying to get Nate to reduce his size, he thought so. "Not yet," he said, and pulled out his phone.

By the time their meal arrived, Rowan and Nate were so glum they were hardly speaking. They sat at the glass-topped table, heads bent. That Rowan didn't get plates and proper silverware out showed that he was in a serious funk. He moved a plastic fork around in his lemon pasta that was still in the foam container.

"Can you get me a picture of William Thorndyke?" Nate asked. "But then, maybe I should check at a church because by now the kid is probably up for sainthood. Terri will float away on a cloud with him."

"Rayburn! I just remembered. Didn't her mother run off with some man?"

"Yeah," Nate said gruffly. "Her mother did."

"I was a kid but I remember when it happened. We were in Dubai at the time. Dad got angry and wanted to go home and find out what *really* happened. He was on the phone yelling at somebody."

"I wasn't there then or I'm sure it would have been me."

Rowan ignored Nate's statement. "It was the sheriff. Dad was yelling that Lisa—"

"Leslie."

"Leslie could have been murdered and her body thrown in the lake, but the sheriff wasn't investigating."

"I can believe that. I was cleaning up garbage around the old dock and I saw something down there. It looked like…" Nate's eyes widened like in a horror movie.

"Like what?"

"Like…" Nate's voice fell to a whisper. "It looked like the roof of a car."

Rowan looked at his cousin, trying to read his mind. "Maybe Dad was right. Could have been an accident."

"She left behind a note," Nate said.

"Any reason not to believe she wrote it?"

"Yeah. Everyone who knew her says she was mad about her husband and kid." Nate took a breath. "Frank said that Leslie Rayburn didn't exist before she came to Summer Hill. You have access to FBI files? I'd like to do some research."

"I do." Rowan was smiling. "Anything to get my mind off what's in my brain!"

Nate took out his phone and started typing a text. "Frank gave me his cell number."

Send me your files on Leslie. Everything you have.

He added his FedEx account number and the address of the apartment. At the end, he inserted: My FBI cousin is with me. He'll search all. He put his phone on the table.

"The files should be here in a day or two. If Frank is even speaking to me, that is. I'm going downstairs to the gym."

"I'll go with you." They both needed the physical exertion.

At 4:00 a.m. the next morning, Rowan flung open Nate's bedroom door. "They just called me from downstairs and said there's a man in the lobby with a bunch of boxes and he wants to come up."

Nate had had a hard time going to sleep and he was groggy.

"It's your sheriff."

Nate's eyes opened. "Frank?" He threw back the cover, pulled on jeans and a T-shirt, and slid his feet into sandals. "I'll go down."

"So I don't have to hear him say what he thinks of you?"

"That and so I can get my hands on the files before he changes his mind." He quickly left the apartment. If he hadn't been on the eighteenth floor he would have run down the stairs. As it was, the elevator seemed to take forever.

Frank Cannon, looking worn-out and angry, was standing in the big marble lobby, his hand tightly gripping the bar of a tall luggage cart. Half a dozen beat-up old file boxes were piled on it. He gave Nate a look that said he hoped he and his descendants went up in smoke.

Nate didn't say anything, just gestured toward the elevator, then stepped aside. Silently, Frank pushed the cart inside.

Inside the elevator, cheerful music was playing. It seemed out of place considering the dark looks of the two men standing on opposite sides of the cart.

The elevator stopped on the sixth floor and a white-haired lady got in, her little dog in her arms. The door closed.

"How's Stacy?" Nate asked.

"Tearing into the Thorndyke house remodel with a fury. She gave away all that white furniture and the bucking bronco pictures, and she's sending you the bill. I think she's keeping the barbed wire as a special memory of you."

Nate nodded. The woman got off at the tenth floor.

"Brody and Elaine?" Nate asked.

Frank's jaw was barely moving. "He's staying in his office. Somebody asked him to help back a boat into the water and Brody told him what he could do with the boat. In detail. Elaine put everything in her store on sale. Looks like she may leave town."

Frank pushed the red button, the elevator halted and he looked at Nate. "Why aren't you asking about *her*?"

Nate stared straight ahead. "Because I know about her. She's doing her job but she's quiet. She won't participate in anything. At night she sits in one of..." He hesitated. "In one of our chairs and watches the water."

Frank stared at Nate's profile for a moment then he pushed the red button again and the elevator started. Nate was right. "So who's the FBI cousin?"

"Kit's son."

Frank gave such a loud sigh of being pleased that Nate rolled his eyes.

Rowan was waiting for them at the open apartment door. He was fully dressed in a crisply ironed shirt, trousers with a crease down the front and Italian loafers.

Frank looked from him to Nate in his T-shirt that said "Shhh... I'm dreaming of beer," jeans and ugly black sandals, then back again. "You the son Kit wanted Stacy Hartman to meet?"

"I am," Rowan said.

"Smart man, your father."

Behind him, Nate glared, and Rowan suppressed a laugh.

Frank finally let go of the cart. "You two kids get busy reading. I drove all night to get here so I'm going to bed." He looked at Rowan in expectation.

"Both beds have been slept in. I can change the sheets, or—"

"Show me to *your* bed," Frank growled, then followed Rowan down the hall. He paused at the doorway. "He made up his bed," he said loudly, meant for Nate to hear. "A real gentleman." Frank went into the bedroom and firmly shut the door behind him.

When Rowan got back to the living room, he looked at Nate and laughed.

"I'm glad you think it's funny. I told you the whole town hates me." Nate was taking the boxes off the cart and stacking them on the dining table.

"I'm astonished that he even let you touch the files."

"Don't rub it in." Nate pulled the lid off the box marked Leslie. There were file folders inside, all of them worn from what looked to be years of use. Inside were newspaper clippings, pages with old-fashioned typing and some handwritten papers that had been torn from spiral notebooks. There were lots of photographs.

When Rowan picked up a folder, he caught three photos before they fell out. He looked at the stack of boxes, then at Nate. When he spoke, it was with the voice of an FBI agent, not a cousin. "Put that cart in the hall, then help me move the long couch. We need to clear a wall so we can put all this up where we can see it."

Chapter 18

Hunger woke Frank, but he didn't get out of the bed immediately. He didn't know what kind of sheets were on the bed but they sure beat the close-out-sale kind on his bed. There were nice curtains on the windows and he could see a line of sunlight between them.

Yesterday when the text from Nate came through, Frank had wanted to throw his phone down and stomp on it. That boy had turned the whole town upside down! The mayor was angry, Brody was furious, Elaine had been crying and little Stacy Hartman looked so mad he was afraid she'd take a bulldozer to the Thorndyke house.

The mayor called to ask if Nathaniel Taggert could be forever denied entry into the town. Frank said, "Wish I could but ol' Thomas Jefferson said I couldn't do that."

By the time the text from Nate appeared, Frank was ready to turn in his badge. "Like hell I'll send those files to that bastard," he mumbled.

But an hour later, he changed his mind. This was his

chance to have someone look into his files on Leslie. He well knew that no one else would look at them. Not anyone in Summer Hill, not any other law enforcement people he knew, no lawyer, no one. Their opinion was that she ran off with a lover and disappeared. The end. That no record of her could be found before she arrived was proof of what a lowlife she was.

Frank had known Leslie. She was a kind, sweet young woman. She was what he needed since Jake thought his little brother was a waste. In one of his many belittling gestures, he'd hung a pair of handcuffs on the wall over his desk. "Having them here will save the sheriff some time since he arrests you about three times a week."

It was Leslie who never lost faith in him. He never told anyone but he used to spend afternoons with her and the baby. Between her housework, baby care and helping with lake business, she was overwhelmed. He got good at diaper changing. And Leslie used to listen to him bellyache about his brother, about how he didn't know what to do with his life.

After the storm and Leslie went missing, Frank told Sheriff Chazen that he didn't believe that damned note she supposedly left behind. He didn't believe she had a lover. "I was at her house one or two afternoons a week," Frank said. "She wouldn't—"

"Are you telling me *you* were one of her lovers?" the sheriff said.

"No! I never touched her. I helped with the baby."

Chazen sneered. "Unless you want me to tell people you're involved in this, I suggest you get the hell out of here."

Frank didn't walk out the door, he *ran*. It was the most cowardly moment of his life and he'd regretted it every day since.

Wanting to overcome his cowardice of that moment, needing to take away the shame he felt, had been the driving force of his life. He'd thought that if he became the sheriff, he would have the resources to investigate Leslie's disappearance.

He put himself up as a candidate for election, gave gung ho pep talk speeches, and he won.

Within a month he'd found out that a small-town sheriff had little power—at least not the kind he needed. He couldn't get a federal investigation going, couldn't get the Big Boys with all their money and tech equipment to get involved.

Frank had done the second-best thing. He'd started gathering local info. He interviewed people who'd known Leslie, people who could have seen something that night. He went through old newspapers and collected data.

As the years went on, he started spreading out to include people Leslie's disappearance had affected. Namely, Terri.

One year she'd had trouble with a couple of boys at school. As sheriff, Frank had stepped in. It wasn't really his job but Terri was like a daughter to him. Unfortunately, she was as stubborn as her father was. She refused to tell Frank everything that had happened with those boys. He had an idea but without Terri's word on it, he could do nothing. "You'd lock them up?" she'd asked. "Put them in jail?"

"I'd enjoy doing it," Frank answered.

Terri clammed up and said nothing. He knew she was protecting the boys. An early indictment could affect their entire lives.

Terri never complained about the harassing she received in school and in town that he knew was aimed at her. When she broke up with Billy Thorndyke at the end of high school, she'd refused to tell anyone what had happened. Maybe if Elaine had been there then, Terri would have confided, but she wasn't.

When Jake died unexpectedly right after Terri graduated from college, Frank had gone into full battle mode. He told Brody he could not—NOT!—let Terri give up her life to help out at the lake.

"Let her have some *fun*!" Frank had shouted. "Give her some freedom. Let her travel. Let her meet some guy who didn't grow up in this town." Frank never mentioned that Terri needed to get away from Leslie's reputation hanging over her head, but they both knew what he meant.

But to keep Terri from returning, Brody would have had to order her to stay away. And he couldn't do that. Terri was all he had left and he missed her fiercely.

Through all the years, Frank kept investigating Leslie's disappearance. It wasn't as though Summer Hill was a hotbed of crime and he had too much other work to do. When he got nowhere, he tried to solve the mystery of the Thorndyke family's abrupt move out of town. He even called the family in Oregon, but all Mr. Thorndyke would say was that he'd received a job offer from his brother and had taken it.

Frank had even swallowed his pride and once a month he'd listened to Della Kissel's hateful gossip. He'd drink tea in her cluttered little house and sit through endless hours of her heavy-handed flirting. "I've always liked sheriffs," she'd purr.

Frank would act as though he was having trouble holding himself back. While it was true that her snooping had helped him solve several petty crimes, he felt that he'd paid a heavy price to get the information.

Everything Frank learned, did, heard, he recorded and put in the "Leslie file." He kept the boxes at home in a fireproof container and had never let anyone see them, didn't even let anyone know he had them.

Until Nate Taggert arrived in town. And right now, Frank hadn't decided whether or not that was a good idea. Nate had left behind anger and resentment, and Terri was a ghost of her usual self.

Reluctantly, Frank got out of the bed, took a shower, then pulled on clean clothes from his duffel bag. It was about noon and he was ravenous.

When Frank stepped out into the hall, so much anger ran through him that he thought he might explode. There the two of them were, calmly sitting at the fancy glass table and eating pizza. Taggert had a beer and Kit's kid had a glass of wine.

Frank felt rage come up from his toes to reach his hair. "You lazy bastards!" he yelled. "I came all this way to give you those files and look at you. Sitting there getting drunk. Did you two rich kids even open the boxes?"

As he spoke, he was stomping down the hallway. Neither of the young men moved or changed expression. They didn't look the least guilty or ashamed of their laziness.

"I ought to—" Frank began, but then Rowan nodded toward the far wall.

Frank glanced to his right, then back at the two of them. "I nearly had a wreck getting here and—" He stopped, blinked a few times, then turned back.

The two couches had been shoved up against the wall of windows, and the upholstered chairs had been placed on top of them. The two solid walls were covered with papers pinned on them. Side tables had more papers piled high. Above the couches, photos were taped on the glass. Hand-

lettered signs had been put up. Terri and the football boys.
Leslie's last days. Garden Day. The storm. Chain saw. Dock.

Slowly, Frank went to the first wall. A copy of Leslie's
driver's license had *forgery* written on the bottom, and a
note saying Leslie Brooks didn't exist before she arrived
in Summer Hill, Virginia. He knew a lot of it, but there
were new details. What did the local florist shop have to
do with anything? There were several headings that he
knew nothing about. One was "Cabin twenty-six."

There was a computer screenshot of an underwater
chain saw. In the background was a reflection of the Kissel clubhouse. Frank put his hand on it and turned to look
at Nate and Rowan. "I'm not sure but I bet this is the one
my brother accused me of borrowing and losing. He kept
the box as a reminder of something that I didn't do."

Nate swallowed his mouthful of pizza. "I found the
empty box when I cleaned out the motor shed. I think that
saw might have been used on the posts of the old dock.
When I was down there, they didn't look broken but *cut*."

Frank had been working on this for over twenty years
and he'd *never* been able to get anyone interested in what
he thought. For a moment, he was so overcome with emotion that he felt tears welling up. He got himself under
control. "Get up and tell me everything. Don't leave out
a word. Taggert! Get me a beer."

It took over an hour for Nate and Rowan to explain what
they'd discovered. Nate had called a man at the lake and
he'd taken a few underwater photos, including the one
showing the chain saw. He'd said it was too deep and too
murky around the old dock to see clearly, but yes, it was
possible that Nate had seen the roof of a car. To be sure,
they'd need divers with scuba gear.

Frank listened as he finished the last of the pizza and said, "But it's nothing, is it? Just unrelated facts."

Rowan and Nate looked at each other.

Nate answered. "We believe that everything that happened to Terri was caused by whatever was done to Leslie."

Frank was so pleased by Nate's phrasing that he almost smiled. "It all works together."

Nate took a chair off the couch—Rowan had covered the white upholstery with sheets—and sat down. "I can't go back until Terri's name is cleared, so whatever it takes, I'm ready to do it. Maybe I can't solve the mystery about her mother but I'd sure like to get my hands on that Thorndyke loser. My guess is that he did something rotten, then made Terri swear not to tell."

"Yeah?" Frank smiled. Three beers, half a large sausage pizza and having two kids interested in his life's work was making him happy. He picked up his cell phone and tapped in a number. "Hey, Billy!" he said into the phone. "I gotta guy here that wants to talk to you." He held out the cell phone.

Nate took it and put it on speaker. "You're the yo-yo kid?"

There was a chuckle on the other end of the line. "I guess so. I hadn't thought of it that way."

"So how come you left behind a mess for Terri to take the blame for?"

"Terri?"

"Yeah, Terri! Ever hear of her?" Nate didn't wait for an answer. "That whole town blames *her* for your family leaving. They think *she* did something to make the Great and Wondrous Billy Thorndyke run away with his tail between his legs. She *still* can't go into that damned town without someone making a crack about it." Nate stopped ranting but there was no sound. "Are you listening to me?"

"I didn't know," came a whisper. "No one told me. Oh, poor, poor Terri."

Nate's body stiffened and he handed the phone back to Frank. "I think he's crying."

"Billy?" Frank said as he took the phone off speaker. "Are you okay?" He listened. "I understand. Yeah, sure. Sorry about that. We'll be there soon." He looked at Nate in question and he nodded. "Okay, see you then." He clicked off the phone. "Billy is leaving as soon as he can and he'll meet us in Summer Hill."

Nate sat back down. "Great," he said in sarcasm. "The love of my girl's life is coming back to town. Me and my big mouth."

"What did he say?" Rowan asked.

"Billy's parents have kept in contact with a few people in Summer Hill, so he figures they knew that Terri was being blamed. They just didn't tell their son. He said he wanted to call her, call some of his old friends, but his parents kept saying that he should make a clean break," Frank said.

"How old is this boy that he still lets his parents make his decisions?" Nate's voice was disgusted.

"He should be like you and defy his elders like you did Kit?" Frank shot back. "Look how that's worked out."

Rowan waited for a reply but the two big men just glared at each other. "If you two bulls want to fight, let me know so I can leave. Otherwise, I need to visit some people to make arrangements to search the bottom of a lake. Anyone want to go with me?"

Frank and Nate didn't move.

Rowan rolled his eyes. "We're out of beer and I will *not* buy any while I'm out. If you want some, you have to come with me. *Both* of you."

Chapter 19

Rowan arranged everything. Nate wasn't sure, but he thought maybe Rowan stretched the truth so he could use his FBI resources. "They'll meet us at the dock in Summer Hill at 8:00 a.m. the day after tomorrow."

"Divers?" Frank asked.

"And a truck with a crane. Whatever is down there, we're going to take it out."

"What about Brody?" Nate looked at Frank.

"And what about permission to excavate?" Rowan asked. "I can't get a court order based on no evidence."

Frank said, "Brody is in charge of the trust that owns the place. He'll probably go into a rage but I'll take care of him."

The two younger men nodded.

The next morning they removed everything from the walls and tables, put it back in the boxes and packed the car. They rode together in Rowan's car, leaving Frank's truck and Nate's car behind in DC. Frank protested until

Rowan reassured him that he'd get someone to drive it to Summer Hill.

"If *you* say so," Frank said, making Nate roll his eyes.

Rowan was the first driver, Frank beside him, Nate in the back.

"I have no reason to think there's a connection," Nate began, "but Thorndyke and Kris Lennon left town at the same time."

"Kris's mother, Abby, was Leslie's friend," Frank said.

"Yeah, at Widiwick, she told me—"

"Who won the prize this year?" Rowan asked.

"Cresnor gave it to some kid who plays the piano. He gets her a Juilliard audition and if she gets in, he pays for a year. If she makes good grades, he forks over for four years. Now tell me what Abby said."

After Nate finished, Frank told of an interview he'd had with the woman who'd hired Leslie when she first showed up in Summer Hill. The facts of it had been in his files, but he was able to share more details. "Meryl said Leslie was all class. She didn't have references and wouldn't tell much about herself, but the dress she had on cost a lot. Meryl said she was shocked when Leslie said she was going to marry Brody Rayburn. Good-looking man but *not* Leslie's class."

Nate frowned. "I guess she was one of them who thought Leslie did run away with some man."

"Naw. Meryl said half the men in town—including Lew Hartman—came on to Leslie and made fools of themselves, but Leslie was a real lady. She only saw Brody."

They didn't want to get to Summer Hill too early so they spent the night in Richmond. Over dinner they grew serious. They were finally realizing what they were doing.

"We might find nothing," Rowan said.

"*Something* is down there at the bottom of the lake," Nate said. "But it's probably just some old farm equipment Kissel got rid of."

After dinner, they went to their separate rooms. They were a quiet group. "Hope they have sheets like yours," Frank said to Rowan, then pushed the elevator button.

"Tomorrow," Nate said. "Tomorrow may change everything."

Terri was watching Billy try to tie the rope holding the boat to the cleat. He'd forgotten what she'd taught him when they were kids. Of course he'd been away from boats and even water for a long time, and that should have made her more forgiving.

But it didn't. She just compared him to Nate. Nate could tie knots, could back up trailers, could… Could do whatever needed to be done.

"You haven't changed," Billy said as he stood up. "You're still annoyed that I'm not half merman."

Terri wasn't sure but she thought she heard at least two girls sigh at the sight of the big blond man. He looked over her shoulder and smiled in the direction of the sound. Blue eyes, white teeth, streaky blond hair. Put a horned helmet on him and he could star in a Viking movie.

Terri had never realized how much she preferred dark men: hair, whiskers, eyes, honey-colored skin. And oh yeah, chest hair that grew from the middle and fanned out.

"You okay?" Billy asked.

"Sure." She frowned at being brought back to reality. A year. A whole year before she'd see Nate again. Or maybe he'd forget about her and not return at all. What man would put up with her life? Or with separation for a year? Was she expecting him to do without *sex* for an entire year? No women at all? Maybe—

"Hey!" Billy said. "Is that frown for me? Sorry I couldn't remember the knot."

"You should get Nate to do it," said Mr. Weber, a Rounder whose boat Billy had been trying to fasten to the dock.

"Ah, yes," Billy said, "the magical Nathaniel. The man who can do anything."

Terri shot him a look to cut it out, then turned back to Mr. Weber. "Nate left and he won't be back until… I don't know when or if—"

"He's by the old dock."

Both Billy and Terri stared at him.

"Come on, Terri." Mr. Weber's voice was teasing. "Are you going to tell me that something is happening at this lake that you don't know about? There's a whole lot of commotion over by the old dock and—"

"There was an accident?" she asked. "Is Dr. Jamie there? He looks like Nate."

"I may be old, but I'm not senile. It's Nate and the sheriff with some big equipment. And there are men and women wearing FBI jackets. I'm going over there to see what's going on. I'm—" He didn't finish because Terri had already run to her boat, Billy right behind her.

As Terri rounded the corner, she saw the people gathered where the old dock used to be. There were about half a dozen men and women in blue jackets with FBI in huge letters on the back. A truck with a crane on it towered over them.

Standing together in a quiet, solemn group were her father, Uncle Frank, Nate, and she was pretty sure that was Rowan Montgomery. She hadn't seen him in years. They were listening to what a man in diving gear was saying. Terri would have yelled at them for not telling her what was going on, but the looks on their faces were so serious that she said nothing.

She stopped her boat several feet away and told Billy to anchor it. The solemnity of the people seemed to make the air feel heavy and Terri had a sense of foreboding. Her father was looking at something and as she got closer, she could see that it was an iPad.

It was Nate who saw her first. There was a darkness in his eyes that she'd not seen before. He hurried forward and, forgetting their agreement, put his arm around her and started to lead her back to her boat.

"The divers found a car on the bottom of the lake and photographed it. Your dad says it's your mom's car." Nate looked up to see Billy standing in front of them. "You're Thorndyke?"

"I am."

"Take her home. We don't know what's inside and—"

Terri twisted out of Nate's grip. "I'm going to be with my dad. Whatever is in there, he'll need me." She looked at Billy. "Take my boat and go get Elaine."

"You're sure?" Nate asked.

"Completely."

Nate nodded to Billy and he left, then Nate took Terri's hand.

"You and I shouldn't be seen together," she said. "We—" The look he gave her made her take a breath. She knew that whatever was going on took precedence over a broken engagement and town gossip. She wanted to ask him questions of how and why and what had made him do this, but now was not the time.

When her father looked up and saw her, he had tears

in his eyes. Terri went to him, hugged him, then stepped back and linked her arm tightly with his.

They watched, clinging to each other. Frank came to stand beside them as the divers went down, holding on to the chain hooks needed to attach to the car.

It was slow going and Terri looked up when she heard the motor of the boat. Billy was coming toward them, driving at full speed. As bad as he was at mechanics, he did indeed love to go fast.

Elaine was holding on to the sides, her carefully coiffed hair blown flat back. She leaped into the water before Billy fully stopped and ran to Brody and fell into his arms.

When Terri stepped back, Nate was there. He led her to the side, pulled her into his arms and held her. She clutched him tightly.

"Sorry," he said, "but I couldn't stay away."

She had her head pressed hard against his chest. "Stacy hates us."

"It's deserved," Nate said. "Are you back with…with…?"

"Billy? Naw. He can't even remember what a half hitch knot is." Her tone made him sound useless.

Nate's arms tightened so much that Terri thought her ribs might crack, but she only smiled. They'd heal.

For a long moment they held on to each other in silence. Behind them was the noise of the truck and people talking. A crowd was beginning to gather and boat motors were idling.

"On that day when you cleaned up around here, you saw something, didn't you?" she said.

"Yeah," Nate said. "I was so busy showing off to you that it didn't register until later. The posts from the dock had been cut, not broken, and I saw something on the bottom. It was a while before I realized that I might have seen part of a car."

"Uncle Frank always said my mother didn't leave us." She pulled away to look at him. "But maybe she ran her car off the dock and left with…him."

"Maybe," Nate said. "And maybe he cut the posts. It's just that she disappeared so completely. Rowan checked all files and she vanished."

"She could have—" Terri broke off when they heard a shout. The car was coming up.

Nate took her shoulders. "You don't have to see what's in there. If you want to leave, you can."

She didn't answer and started back toward the group, but then she took Nate's hand. It suddenly occurred to her that maybe she didn't want to know the truth. All her life her uncle Frank had put doubts in her mind. He'd been fierce that Leslie had *not* run away. As for Brody, he'd refused to talk about his wife's disappearance. Never a word spoken about it. Terri had made up a hundred scenarios of what had happened to her mother. As a kid, aliens and fairies played a part in the stories. She'd clutched onto anything rather than believe what people whispered about her mother.

The car came out of the water slowly, back end first. An old Toyota, rusted, covered in years of underwater debris, emerged.

Elaine with Brody, Nate with Terri, and Billy beside Frank, stood together as they watched Rowan look inside. He shook his head no. There was no one inside.

Terri could feel hope leaving her. Her mother had *not* been lost in the storm and accidentally driven off the pier. It looked like she'd hidden the car, discarded it so no one would find it. Did her lover steal the lake's chain saw and cut the posts?

Rowan and the FBI agents and even the bystanders were looking at the group with sympathy. The poor Rayburns, their faces seemed to say. The wife ran away with another man and left them.

"Oh hell!" Nate said, and dropped Terri's hand. There was a crowbar on the side of the big truck. He grabbed it, ran to the car and broke open the trunk.

The lid flew up—and everyone close enough to see inside froze in place, unable to move.

Frank shoved his way through them, then he too stopped. Immobile.

Brody was still standing with Elaine, and he didn't seem to want to see what they were looking at.

It was Terri who stepped forward. Nate put his arm out for her and had it securely around her before he stepped back to let her see.

Inside the trunk was a skeleton. There was a rusted metal belt around its middle, shoe buckles by its feet—and handcuffs around its wrists.

When Terri's knees weakened, Nate picked her up, carried her away from the car and set her on a rock nearby. Standing, he held her against him.

"That wasn't natural. She was…"

"I know," Nate said softly. Neither of them wanted to say the word *murdered*.

Terri was clutching him about the waist. "Someone did that to her."

"Yes. And we'll find…" He trailed off because that didn't matter now. He and Rowan would move heaven and earth to find out who had done this to Leslie Rayburn, but that wasn't going to bring back Terri's mother.

Gazing over her head, Nate watched as Brody, holding hands with Elaine, went to the car. "I gave her that belt on our honeymoon," he said softly. Rowan caught him when he almost collapsed, then he and Elaine led him to Terri's boat. Elaine drove it as they went back to Club Circle.

Frank was still standing there. He hadn't moved since he'd first seen what was in the trunk. Rowan looked at Nate and gave a sharp jerk of his head for him to come and get Frank.

To the left, Billy Thorndyke was standing back, waiting to be needed. Nate nodded to him, then he bent to Terri. "I'm going to help Rowan and Frank now, okay?"

She nodded.

"Thorndyke will see that you get home and I want you to stay there. Rowan called Jamie and he'll be here soon and he'll talk with you. He knows all there is to know about trauma and grief." He kissed her forehead. "I'll be with you as soon as I can and we're going to dispense with this stupidity about what the town thinks. Understand me?"

All Terri could do was nod.

Billy was standing close and waiting.

"Take her home," Nate said, then added, "and if you touch her I'll break every bone in your body."

"Good," Billy said. "I'm glad she found you."

Nate watched them walk away, then went back to the rusty old car. The others had moved away, but Frank was still standing and staring at the gruesome skeleton.

Nate stepped beside him.

"The bones in her wrists are broken," Frank said softly. "She tried so hard to get out that she broke her bones. Those are the handcuffs Jake got for me. He etched my initials on them." His voice was rising. "They were on the wall but they disappeared in the storm. Jake said I took them. And he said I took the chain saw. All I did was get mad. Why didn't I put them together with Leslie's disappearance?" Frank looked at Nate, his face red with growing rage. "If I'd been smarter, faster, maybe I could have saved her. There was air in that trunk. I bet there was enough air in there that I could have—"

Nate grabbed Frank, pinning his arms down. It was an unbreakable grip. Frank fought him. He twisted and turned, kicked, but Nate held him. Frank was strong but Nate was stronger and he didn't let go.

Tears came, but Frank kept fighting.

Behind them, Jamie had arrived and was filling a syringe, but Nate shook his head. Frank needed this release.

Slowly, Frank began to weaken, his energy gone. His face was buried in Nate's shoulder and tears had soaked the cloth. When Frank was near to collapsing, Nate nodded to Jamie.

"I'm going to give you something to relax you," Jamie said and gave Frank the shot. It took both of them to hold the older man when he started to fall. An ambulance pulled up, and the EMTs put Frank onto a stretcher.

He held up his hand for them to stop, and Nate stood by his side. "Sorry for it all." Frank's voice was slurred. "But you found her." With trembling hands, Frank removed his sheriff's badge from his chest and held it out to Nate.

"I can't take that."

"You think those guys in their fancy jackets are going to let you hang around without any authority?"

"Rowan will—" Nate glanced over his shoulder at his cousin. Already, Rowan had changed into the agent he was. No, he wouldn't let a civilian hang around. Nate took the badge and, groggily, Frank smiled in satisfaction.

At last, Frank let his body give in to the sedative and his eyes closed. "Now maybe the town bastards will leave our Terri alone."

Nate nodded at the "our."

"I'll make sure they do. Rowan and I will make you proud."

Nodding, Frank gave a weak smile. "Poor Leslie. We all loved her so much. Who would do this to her?" They loaded Frank into the ambulance.

"Yes. Who would do this to her?" Nate whispered as he walked back to Rowan and the other agents and the car. Who would murder the mother of a small child and—

Nate cut off his thought because standing to one side of the growing crowd was little Della Kissel—and from the way her eyes were glittering, she was spreading her venom. He didn't have to hear her to guess what she was saying. Probably something on the lines of "Leslie had an argument with her lover. She deserved what she got."

Nate could feel the badge on his chest as though it were a brand. At the moment it felt like it was glowing—and it weighed about a thousand pounds. While wearing the badge, he couldn't do what he wanted to do, which was threaten the dreadful little woman so strongly that she shut up. Scare her to silence.

Ah, he thought, if he was sheriff maybe he could lock her up.

And be like Sheriff Chazen?

He took a breath. Diplomat, he told himself. I am a diplomat and Della Kissel is an enemy warlord. He went forward.

Chapter 20

It was early evening before Nate could get away to go to Terri's house. During the long day he'd frequently glanced toward the house to see if she was watching. But he never saw her or Thorndyke. Busy as he was, he wondered what the two of them were doing there. Alone.

Nate had introduced himself to Frank's three deputies, all of them young and eager to follow his lead. Nate wanted to tell them he knew nothing about investigating a murder, but he looked into their eyes and didn't say that. It was clear they didn't either.

By six, everything had been cleared away from the old dock. Rowan had called his father and asked for help in getting an immediate forensics report. "I'm calling in every favor I can," he told his dad. "But I need help."

Kit said he'd do all he could.

Nate drove to Terri's house, then sat in the car for a few minutes while he gave himself courage. The medical examiner had arrived and from his quick examination of the skeleton, he'd been able to tell of the horror Leslie Rayburn had gone through in her attempt to get out. As far as they could tell, she'd been handcuffed, her ankles tied together, probably gagged, then thrown into the trunk. Maybe she'd been held in there and her car parked on the dock while someone cut the pier's big posts.

Whatever happened, it had been long enough that Leslie'd had time to fight so hard that she'd broken both wrists and an ankle. All done while she had a deep gash on her head.

"With a dent like that in her skull, she must have been bleeding a lot," the ME said.

Now in the car, Nate removed the badge from his shirt. Sheriff Chazen hadn't even looked for Leslie. Hadn't believed all the people who said she hadn't run away.

Nate put the badge in his pocket, got out of the car and went to the house. The door was unlocked. Billy Thorndyke was sitting in the living room, reading. The house was quieter than Nate had ever heard it. Even the outdoor sounds were silenced. No boat motors, no one yelling. Not even the birds were singing.

Nate didn't have to be told that Terri was asleep. Jamie had sent a text saying that he'd spent over an hour talking to Terri and had given her some strong sedatives.

Billy put his book down and got up. "I made some spaghetti. Want some?"

Nate was too tired, too beaten up by the hideous day to do anything but nod, then he went down the hall to Terri's room. She was asleep on top of the covers, still wearing her shorts, T-shirt and even her sandals. She was curled up, her knees nearly to her chin. She looked like a tall baby.

As he watched, she gave a little hiccup and he knew

she'd been crying. He couldn't imagine what she'd been through at finding out her mother had been murdered.

Nate removed her sandals, then her shorts, pulled the covers back and put her under them. She seemed to give a sigh of relief. He gave her a soft kiss on the lips, smoothed her hair back and left the room.

Billy had put a huge bowl of spaghetti on the dining table and a plate of several pieces of warm garlic bread dripping butter. A tall glass of beer was by the plate.

"I guess I'll leave," Billy said as he backed up.

"Sit," Nate said as he began to eat. "How was she today?"

Billy sat at the table. "Quiet. Hardly said a word—except about you. 'Nate will fix it.' That's what she kept saying."

Nate looked at Billy. He was young, tall and he had quite a bit of muscle on him. Some of it was genetics, but Nate knew the amount of time he had to have spent in a gym. Deltoids like his didn't come from mowing the lawn. Nate well knew the energy that heavy workouts used. He pushed the plate of bread toward him.

"Thanks," Billy said, took a piece, then got up to get both of them another beer. "I hear you're the new sheriff."

"It's temporary."

"Frank wants to retire so maybe—" He stopped at the look Nate gave him. "Right. You want to hear about Terri. I guess you know that Dr. Jamie came by and they talked for a long time. He seems to know a lot about trauma."

Billy paused, waiting for Nate to say something, but he didn't. "Terri seemed to be less restless after he left. Can you tell me what you've found out?"

"I want to know what you did to Terri just before your whole family ran out of town in the middle of the night.

As far as I can piece together, you did something really bad, then made her swear to tell no one."

Billy's fair complexion showed the blood that rose in his face. "Good deductions. I think maybe you should keep that badge."

Nate's look didn't soften. He pushed his empty plate away, got up, picked up the beer bottle and motioned for them to go to the living room. He took the couch and Billy sat on the chair across from him. Nate waited in silence for the younger man to begin.

"You know Kris Lennon who owns the Garden Day florist?" Billy said.

"I've met her."

"When she was still Crystal Wilkins and in high school, I… I got her pregnant." He looked at Nate but he said nothing. "I wish I could say that Terri and I had a fight and were broken up and that I was angry. Or that I…" Billy took a breath. "But there was nothing like that. I was happy and in love and seventeen years old. I was driving home from football practice, it was raining and Crystal was walking in the road. She was drenched, and she was crying because her dad had thrown one of his fits and said she couldn't go to some dance. I stopped the truck, she got inside and I pulled over to the side of the road to listen to her. When I hugged her, it was purely to comfort her, but…" He shrugged. "Six weeks later I had to tell Terri that Crystal was pregnant with my child. It was the worst moment of my life."

"And Terri's." Nate's voice was hard, unforgiving.

"I made it worse by getting her to swear that she'd never tell anyone what really happened."

"She's kept that promise. She never even told Brody.

You got that vow from her, then your whole family left town."

"They wanted to protect me and our name. And they wanted the baby. But Mrs. Wilkins was encouraging her daughter to get an abortion. She never said so, but I think she was afraid of her husband. Rodney Wilkins was—"

"Yeah, I know. Banged up in an accident. Not mentally stable and he drank a lot."

"More than that. He tended toward violence, but Kris and her mother hid it. Mrs. Wilkins was afraid that when her husband found out that I had…had impregnated his daughter he might…"

"Come after you with a gun?"

"Yes. My parents made a deal with Crystal and her mother. They would adopt my…my child and in return, they'd—"

"Give Kris money."

"Yes." Billy was sitting in the chair, slumped down, his hands in his pockets.

"Your family couldn't stay in town because they couldn't raise the child and keep your reputation as the Saint of Summer Hill."

"More or less," Billy said. "The truth was that back then I was so upset about losing Terri that I couldn't think about anything else. When my parents said we had to leave town, I begged Terri to go with us. Pleaded."

"So I heard," Nate said in disgust. "You made a real spectacle of yourself with all your theatrics. What people saw was their beloved yo-yo boy begging the daughter of the town's infamous adulterer. And she was saying no. To them, you were the innocent one and she was the monster."

"I wasn't aware of any of that. I thought only of myself, not of the two girls whose lives I was ruining."

"Where's your child?"

Billy looked away for a moment. "My daughter was stillborn at seven months, two weeks and three days."

"But your parents gave Kris the money anyway?"

"Yes. At my insistence."

"And she and her mother returned to Summer Hill and bought a florist's shop."

"Eventually, yes. First, she went to college. I think she wanted to prove to everyone that she was more than just the town drunk's daughter. And also, there was gossip about why they'd left so abruptly after Rodney's death."

"His death sure came at a convenient time, didn't it?"

"No one *ever* asked about that. It was a taboo subject. After his death, they were free. Kris and her mother flew to Oregon. My parents met their plane and took them to the apartment they'd rented. They were given the best of care."

"And Kris got to see a different way of life."

"She did. She and my mother bonded a bit. She'd always wanted a daughter."

"Meanwhile, Terri was back here in Summer Hill being whispered about."

"I am ashamed that I didn't know that. My parents and Mrs. Wilkins were saying that Kris and I should get married and raise the baby together. I was sick about it all." Billy stopped talking and looked out at the water. "I didn't know *any* of it," he whispered. "Not then and certainly not afterward."

Nate had had enough experience with people to know when someone was honestly remorseful. To tell this guy what he should have done would serve no real purpose. Sometimes, forgiveness was the best solution.

Nate knew that Billy had been raised in Summer Hill,

so he must know people. "I got Della Kissel to help on the case."

It took Billy a moment to understand Nate's words—and his tone. Nate wasn't going to keep on about what had happened. He was going to move forward, not stagnate in the past. "That's not possible. My guess is that Della is telling people that the way Leslie was found is proof that she was running away with someone."

"That's just what she was saying," Nate said, "but I made her an honorary deputy and sent her to find out who was in cabin twenty-six when Leslie disappeared."

"Let me guess. Della said Leslie was having an affair with whoever was in that cabin."

"Exactly. Whatever was going on, I'd like to talk to the man."

"You think he might have…done that to Leslie?"

"It's the only lead we have."

"One thing I know about Della Kissel is that she would do anything for Brody," Billy said. "When Terri and I were kids, she used to spy on us. One time we found her hiding in a closet in the boathouse. Another time, she was under a table. She said she was looking for her compact. Terri and I learned to search everywhere."

"And you started going to the Island."

"She told you about that?" Billy was smiling in memory.

Nate didn't reply.

"What's this about you and Stacy Hartman?"

"A broken engagement," Nate said quickly. "Tell me what you know about what happened in high school with those football boys."

"Hector and Ryan? Hector is—"

Nate lifted his hand. "I know about him. But I've not heard anything about the kid Ryan."

"That's because they moved away the next year. I have no idea what happened to him." Billy was looking at Nate. "You have something in mind, don't you?"

"I don't like that Terri is blamed for things she didn't do and I'm trying to figure out a way to stop it." He glared at Billy. "If the lies and innuendos are to stop, you're going to have to tell the whole town the truth about what you did."

"I will. Without hesitation. Kris is another matter. She came back here to show the town she was respectable. She won't like telling why she and her mom fled."

"I really don't care about her reputation," Nate said. "Terri's had enough blame put on her."

Billy smiled. At first it was just a bit, then he broke into a real grin. "'Nate will fix it.' It looks like Terri was right. Whatever you need from me, I'll do it."

"Thanks," Nate said.

Chapter 21

When Terri woke, she knew something was wrong, but she didn't know what. Nate was in bed with her—or was she dreaming that?

She turned slightly to see his whiskery cheek. Light was barely coming in between the drawn curtains. She could feel the warmth of his body all down the length of hers, and she moved her leg so it was near the center of him.

He moved in his sleep, his arm tightening on her as though he thought she might run away.

At that thought, her memory came back to her. She remembered the skeleton in the car trunk. Remembered the handcuffs.

Her mother had been murdered! She didn't run away with another man. She'd been handcuffed and put into the trunk of her own car, then driven to the dock and…

Nate's other arm encircled her and he drew her close.

"You…?" she whispered. "She…? How did…?" Terri didn't know where to begin.

Nate stroked her hair out of her eyes. "What do you want to know?"

She was glad he wasn't going to patronize her with a sugarcoated version of the truth. "All of it. What happened and what you're planning."

"Sure?"

"Yes." Her back was to his front and she thought that when she was in his arms she could handle anything. Quietly, with great patience, he told her what they'd been able to piece together. Someone had handcuffed and tied Leslie Rayburn, put her in the trunk of her own car and driven it through a storm onto the old dock.

"Then he cut the posts to the dock away," Terri said. "I guess he wanted to make sure it wasn't used anymore and risk discovery."

"That's our guess too, and it worked since no one saw the car in all these years."

"Until you." Terri kissed the back of his hand. "You found it." Turning over to face him, she kissed him on the mouth. Oh, how good it felt to be able to touch him! On their last night together, a year's separation had seemed so practical. She would stay at the lake and Nate would be... She didn't know where he would go, but she did know they had to wait to give the town time to calm down. But now she wanted to feel him close to her. As close as possible.

Nate pulled back to look at her. "You're sure you want to do this?"

"Yes." She moved her leg between his. "Did you take off my clothes?"

"Some of them. Thorndyke—"

She gave a little chuckle as he kissed her neck. "I think Billy is afraid of you."

"He should be. He—"

"Wait!" Terri pushed on his shoulders. "What about the note? Who wrote it?"

"Someone who knew Leslie's handwriting and could imitate it."

His hands were running down her body. She still had on some clothes and Nate was deftly removing them.

Terri wanted to ask more questions, but at the moment she could think of nothing but his hands and his lips on her skin.

Besides, something Dr. Jamie had said yesterday was coming to her. "There is always a good side," he'd said. "You just have to find it." He'd made her realize that the cloud that had hung over her since she could remember—that her mother had abandoned her and her father—was no longer there. Her mother had wanted them. She didn't discard them and run away with someone else. She wasn't—as Terri feared—now living somewhere else with another family. She wasn't helping another daughter buy a new dress. She wasn't taking her other children to swimming lessons. Wasn't laughing with them and never thinking about the two people she'd left behind.

"Nate," Terri whispered. "We can—"

"Yeah," he answered as he rolled on top of her. "We can do anything. Do it *all*."

As he entered her, she felt the freest she'd felt in her lifetime. With Nate's slow, long, deep strokes, she felt something else rise in her: hope. It was not an emotion she was familiar with. Her life had always seemed to be preordained. She had to always be good to atone for her mother's sins. She'd had to…

She bent her leg and pushed on Nate so he rolled onto his back, taking her with him.

When he looked up at her face and saw the beginning

of a smile, he understood. For all the tragedy of the situation, it meant he and Terri could be together. With the infidelity of the past removed from Terri's life, all that was wrong was a broken engagement. Not a reenactment of the past, just a normal thing.

They knew that the future belonged to them. They were conjoined beings who no longer had to face the world separately.

They made love for an hour, until exhaustion and hunger made them stop. Nate would have to go back to the crime scene, but he needed a shower. Terri joined him. "You know I can't resist water," she said.

By the time they got out, it was midmorning and Nate finally checked his phone. He had thirty-two messages—none of which he read. "I have to go," he muttered.

"Oh?" Terri dropped the towel to the floor. "Sure?"

Nate stepped back to look at her nude body, rosy pink from the hot water. He remembered her long, long legs around him, her ankles on his shoulder. "I'm the sheriff now so I have to—"

"You're what?"

"Jamie gave Frank a tranq and put him in the hospital, so Frank temporarily gave me his badge. I need to—"

Terri threw open a closet door, pulled out a blue robe, put it on and headed for the kitchen. "I'll make you a sandwich and you can eat it in the car. What's Rowan doing to find out who…who did it?"

Nate hastily pulled on his jeans and T-shirt. He picked up his shoes and socks and followed her to the kitchen. "Why the change of heart?"

"I thought you were just a bystander, getting in the way of the FBI, but as sheriff they'll have to let you in on this. You're clever. You can figure out things."

Nate took a handful of corn chips. "When you thought I was a civilian, you wanted to spend the day in bed with me. But now you want me gone?"

"That's right."

"Jamie will probably release Frank today and I'll give his badge back."

Terri stopped putting mayonnaise on bread and stared at him. "I retract the clever part. If you think Frank Cannon will *ever* take that badge back, you are dreaming. And as for getting out of the hospital, I'll bet you twenty grand—which I don't have—that he's on his way to his fishing cabin—and no one, not even Dad, knows where that is. Since I won't lose, I'll add five to the bet that he left his phone behind so no one can reach him."

Nate was staring at her.

She piled the bread high with cold cuts, tomatoes, pickles and lettuce. "You have the badge with you?"

Silently, Nate pulled it out of his pocket and pinned it to his shirt.

"Looks good, and you'd better get used to it."

"Terri," Nate said with great patience, "I am not into law enforcement."

"What about your years with Kit?"

"That was a fluke and Kit was there overseeing it all. I'm good with numbers. My degree is in business."

"Isn't that what you ran away from to go with Kit? But your degree will help you organize that mess Uncle Frank has in his office. He hires secretaries but they quit because he won't tell them anything and because he's an all-round pain to work for." She held out the sandwich with the bottom half wrapped in a paper towel, and a can of lemon-lime soda. "No beer on the job." She was smiling happily.

Nate hesitated.

"You meet your deputies yet? Nice boys, aren't they? Uncle Frank could never stand anyone challenging him so he tends to hire boys with no spirit. Don't yell at them or they'll cry." She shoved the sandwich and drink into his hands, then got behind him and pushed him toward the door. "Go help Rowan and hire a secretary who does some work. Uncle Frank tended to hire them by how good they look in a bikini."

Nate stopped by his car, opened the door and started to get in. Terri was smiling at him in a way that said she was quite pleased by it all. "Actually, I did hire a secretary," he said.

"If it's some beach bunny, I'll fire her."

"No, she's a friend of yours." He got into the car and smiled back at her. "I hired Della Kissel." When Terri's face changed to shock, Nate closed the door and backed out of the driveway.

The first thing Nate did when he was out of sight of the house was call Jamie and ask how Frank was doing.

"I have no idea. The hospital said he woke up about 2:00 a.m., put his clothes on and left. Brody said Frank probably went to his fishing cabin. I left you two messages asking if you knew where he went. Where have you been all morning?"

Nate gave a deep sigh. "Talking to someone who appears to be smarter than I am."

"That would be Terri. My dad said that if we men keep marrying women who are smarter than we are, how come the next generation of males isn't any brighter?"

Nate wanted to laugh but the way he was feeling, it seemed to be a valid question. Sheriff? He did *not* want to be a sheriff! "If you hear from Frank, tell him to get his butt back to Summer Hill."

"I will, but the rumor around town is that his cabin is in Wyoming. Rowan said he's driving and he left his phone behind."

"I owe Terri twenty-five grand." Nate's voice was heavy.

"Should I ask what that means?"

"No. Definitely not. Talk to you later." He clicked off.

Nate hadn't actually hired Della. He'd just entrusted her with one simple task. She was to work with Brody's secretary, Anna, to try to find out who rented cabin twenty-six in the year Leslie Rayburn disappeared. He didn't have any belief that the two women would be able to do it since the records kept at the lake didn't go back that far. But maybe they could find out enough that Rowan could use the US government files to fill in the rest.

Anna wasn't in the office, but Brody's door was half-open. Nate pushed it wide. Inside, the room was in chaos. File drawers had been opened and emptied, with all the contents on the floor. Hundreds of papers were taped to the walls. Sitting on a rug in the middle of the mess, her usually tidy hair tangled, her clothes rumpled, was Della.

Nate's first reaction was to yell. But his years with the foreign service had taught him to stamp the anger down and think before letting go.

As he calmed himself and looked about, he saw order in the chaos. Each of the many piles of folders had a piece of paper on top and a character description. Troublemakers. Suspiciously Nice. Sneaks. Adulterers. Flirts. Teenage Misfits. Hiding secrets. Former Big Shots. Spies. Good People.

There were about twenty piles, each with multiple files under them. He noted that the Good People stack contained only three folders.

Della looked up at Nate standing in the doorway. "Brody may be as beautiful as a Greek god, but he can't organize anything."

Nate sat down on a wooden chair, one of the few empty surfaces in the room. "I think most people put files in order by numbers. Dates or account numbers, something like that."

"What use is that?"

Nate could see that she was genuinely asking a question. He wanted to answer it but damned if he could think of an answer. "Did you find the man?"

"Oh sure. I found him two hours after you asked me to. Six phone calls, a computer search with a bit of a hack, three more calls, and I got him. He—" She looked around her, searching for something, then gave a little smile and pulled a piece of pink paper out of the inside of her bra and handed it to him. She batted her lashes at Nate. "I do so love a man with a badge."

Nate took the paper and looked at the name and phone number on it. "If you're this good at research, maybe Frank should deputize you," he joked. "Did you call this number?" When she didn't answer, he looked at her.

Della's eyes were wide, as though she'd just seen something alarming.

"What is it?"

"Really?" she whispered. "Me? A deputy?"

Frank is going to go back to hating me, Nate thought. *If he ever returns, that is.* No! He couldn't think that way. *When* Frank returned.

He listened as Della told him that Leslie Rayburn was at cabin twenty-six because she'd been visiting the widower's twenty-year-old daughter. She'd been dumped by her boyfriend and was sure her life was over. "Leslie was like a mother to her," the man had said. "So kind and caring."

When Nate left the office he was torn between hearing more good about Leslie and having his only lead crushed.

Chapter 22

Nate was sitting behind Frank's big oak desk when Rowan walked in. He looked around at the wood-paneled walls, the worn wooden floor. There were ledgers on the four desks, but no sign of a computer. "This place looks like a set for a 1950s movie."

"I think there's an abacus around here somewhere," Nate said, frowning.

Rowan sat down on a wooden chair. "How's Terri?"

Nate's frown deepened. "Great. She's decided I'm going to be the town sheriff and arrest bad guys—after I find a murderer, that is."

Rowan nodded as though he agreed with that. "What's down the hall?"

"Three jail cells. I think they were used on the Andy Griffith set."

"The town gossip is that Della is going to be your head deputy."

"I'm *not* the sheriff. If Frank doesn't come back, the town will elect someone else."

Rowan was looking at Nate in speculation. "You look good behind that desk. Maybe you should consider—"

"Shut up," Nate said. "You hear anything from forensics yet?"

"Not a word and I couldn't tell you if I did."

"What does that mean?"

"It means that you're not officially the sheriff until the mayor swears you in."

Nate groaned. "In that case, I never will be. He wouldn't let me be the town road sweeper."

"Nevertheless, you need to get his say-so before I can tell you anything."

Nate knew his cousin was lying—or twisting the truth around. "Your dad tell you this?"

"Yeah," Rowan said with a sigh. "It's blackmail. No expedited forensics report until you make up with your former fiancée's father. And I'm to go with you to hold your hand or let her hit you. Not sure which."

"I'd rather face men with guns," Nate muttered as he stood up.

Rowan walked to the door. "So what are you going to do to decorate this office? And will you get new uniforms? Hey! I know. Isn't your ex a designer? Get her to come up with some new uniforms."

"Right," Nate said as they walked toward the town hall. "She hates me so much she'd do pink with purple trim. But it doesn't matter because I am *not* going to be a sheriff. Not here or anywhere else."

"I thought you said Terri liked your being the sheriff."

"Yeah, well, after I make it clear that that's not what I want to do, she'll see reason."

"I bet you'll have as much success as Dad does when he stands up to Mom."

This statement started them making declarations about

how they would rule their own households. And both men truly believed what they were saying.

It was Rowan who told the mayor's secretary that they needed to see the man.

"He's in a meeting," she said. "And you don't have an appointment." Her eyes were on Nate and her distaste was evident.

Rowan held out his credentials. "We do need to see him. If you haven't heard, there's been a murder."

"With that woman who ran away with some man? She—"

Nate stepped forward, but Rowan put himself in front. His face was serious.

"Go on then," she said, and nodded toward the closed door.

Lew Hartman was sitting behind a mahogany desk the size of a dance platform. He nodded at Rowan, but sneered at Nate. "What is it?"

"The town ordinance says you have to swear a sheriff in," Rowan said. "Frank Connor turned the office over to Nate, so we need to make it official."

"I'm not sure this man is right for the job," the mayor said. "I think I should appoint—"

The door burst open and Stacy came in, her blond prettiness filling the room. She had half a dozen shopping bags in her hands. "I am exhausted!" She sounded happy. "I bought four new outfits, including shoes, and I found the perfect gift for you to give Mom for your anniversary. It's a necklace with a single pearl and—" She became aware of the silence in the room, then turned to see Rowan. "Hello. I haven't seen you in a long time."

"I feel like I'm seeing you for the first time." Rowan's voice was *not* that of an FBI agent on official business. "You grew up quite well."

"That's not what you thought in DC."

"Touché." Rowan's eyes were sparkling.

If she noticed, she didn't show it. "I guess you're here because of…"

"The car." Rowan stepped aside so she saw Nate.

"Oh," Stacy said. "You."

All Nate could do was nod.

Lew Hartman stepped forward. "I don't think I should do this. This man is not what we want for our town."

Rowan's face lost its flirty look and grew hard. "Sir! Do you realize that there is a murder investigation going on? Nathaniel Taggert is more than qualified to be the sheriff. He—"

"Like hell he is!" Lew yelled. "He broke my daughter's heart."

"Oh for heaven's sake," Stacy said. "My heart is *not* broken. I'm much more upset over losing the Stanton house than I am about my fiancé. No offense, Nate."

"None taken." His eyebrows were raised.

"You know what's come out of all this?" Stacy said. "Nate opened my eyes to some awful things going on in this town. Things I never thought about. Dad, do you remember years ago when Terri attacked those boys in high school and she was suspended?"

"Yes. Hector's back has never been the same, but what does that have to do with anything?"

"Everything," Stacy said. "When I was a teenager I was like everyone else and took the side of those boys. I saw them as victims. As an adult, I see it all differently." She looked at Nate. "They went after Terri, didn't they? And she defended herself."

"Yes," Nate said.

"And we all blamed *her*. I think it was because of what

we believed Terri's mother had done. But now we know her mother was innocent. That poor woman. It has *all* come down onto Terri. What she's been through because of us, I can't imagine. Father! You are going to help Nate with whatever he needs."

"I—" Lew looked at his daughter. "All right." He turned to Nate and Rowan. "What do you need? My time and whatever I can do to help is yours."

After Nate had been sworn in, he and Rowan were walking back to the sheriff's office.

"I like her," Rowan said.

"I feel bad about what I did to her," Nate said. "I think I was mad at your dad and—"

"No," Rowan said, "I mean I really, *really* like her. Are you sure it's over between you two?"

Nate was beginning to smile. "Absolutely over."

Rowan stopped. "Listen, I, uh… They'll call me when forensics finds anything, so I'm going back. I have, uh, some questions I'd like to ask her." Turning, he started walking backward. "From what I've seen, you need to hire some new deputies. How much is your salary and what's the town's budget for your department?"

"How would I know? I'm not the sheriff."

"You've been sworn in now, so you are until someone else takes over. I—" Rowan's phone buzzed and he looked at it. "It's Dad. I'll meet you later." He put the phone to his ear and turned back to the courthouse, but Nate could hear him. "Yeah, Dad, I met her. Yes! I like her. What about the forensics? Yes, I think she's quite spunky. Is that a word today? What about the case?"

Smiling, Nate went back to the sheriff's office. *His* office.

Chapter 23

The sun was barely rising and Rowan was already at Terri's house. "I'll be honest with you," he said. "I don't know how we're going to investigate this. The time is overwhelming."

"Our one lead was based on Della's snooping," Nate said. "We—" He broke off as his phone buzzed and he looked at it. "It's one of my—" he swallowed "—deputies." He declined the call and looked back at Terri. "My guess is that it was caused by something that happened in a single moment. Maybe your mother saw a robbery or a—"

"Or a murder," Rowan said. "We're running everything through a database to see what went on in this area at that time."

"He made her write a note?" Terri was skeptical, disbelieving.

"Maybe," Nate said. "She could have— Holy hell." His phone had started ringing, then buzzing. Two texts, three emails and a call came through. At the same time, the doorbell rang.

"That will be food and a plea for info," Terri said. "You two better go or you'll never get out."

"You can't stay here alone," Nate said. "Your dad—"

"Is a mess," Terri said. Her phone started ringing, then Rowan's. Nate's had never stopped. "Go! Now. Out the back, around the side."

Nate gave Terri a quick kiss, then left the house, Rowan right behind him. She took a deep breath and went to the door to let in the first of the visitors. As she knew they would, they carried containers of food. She couldn't help but think that the dishes were like a movie ticket. They were paying for a show. In this case it was information about the car found in the lake. And the people who'd been there for years wanted to know about Billy. And Stacy. *Was it true that Terri and Billy were back together? Had Nate really dropped sweet Stacy flat? Good for Terri to dump him and go back to Billy.*

More than one person admitted he/she was torn about Nate. "He fished our son/daughter/dog out of the water" was said many times. But they also said, "Stacy has always been so *nice* to us. I hate to see her hurt."

Terri did her best to be gracious and thank them for yet another casserole—and she listened to all the gossip they told her. The only surprise was when they said that Billy Thorndyke was now a minister. "And he's taking over St. Anne's Church."

"I can't believe he didn't tell you!" They waited for Terri to make a comment but she didn't.

She called Nate three times to see how he was doing, but it went to voice mail. She figured he was as overwhelmed as she was and couldn't answer the phone.

After lunch—eaten cold and quickly—she called Elaine and asked about her dad.

"He ranges between depression and relief. His beloved wife did *not* leave him, but she *was* murdered. He's been talking about her all day. I'm taking good care of him."

Terri wanted to hug Elaine. Most women would have been jealous, but not her. "Thank you," she whispered as she choked up.

"Anytime, honey."

Her talk with Elaine gave her new energy and she greeted the next batch of well-wishers with a smile.

At three, Nate called.

"You can't believe how busy it is here," she said. "I—"

"Terri! Where is the Chinese bowl?"

"It's—" She looked at her coffee table. It wasn't where she'd left it. "I don't know. The guys gave it to me and I'm sure I put it on the table. It was still in that tote bag."

"Could you have put it somewhere else and don't remember?"

In other circumstances, she would have snapped at him that she was far from being senile. But the urgency in Nate's voice kept her from replying.

With the phone in her hand, she ran through the house, throwing open doors to closets, the laundry room, bathrooms. "I don't see it and there has been no time to tuck it away somewhere. Do you think it was stolen?" She remembered that Nate said it was valuable.

"Who has been there today?"

"Half the lake."

"I need their names."

"I'll make a list and send it to you."

"No!" Nate said. "Now. Tell me. I'll write them down."

Terri didn't waste time asking why he needed it. She heard his tone. She thought back from the morning and gave him names. She opened the refrigerator and looked inside. The casserole dishes had the names of the owners taped on them. She read them off to Nate, and if she remembered, she gave him the cabin number.

When the doorbell rang, she ignored it. "Can I ask what this is about?" she asked.

"Not yet. I want you to go to one of the empty cabins and stay there. I want you to hide. Understand me?"

"Yes." She tried to sound calm. "Nate, please don't do anything dumb."

"Change my entire personality in an instant?"

She didn't smile at his joke as her heart was pounding in her throat.

"I love you," he said, then clicked off.

"Back at you," she said to the silent phone as she began running. She threw clothes in a bag with her cell charger, locked the house, then got into her boat.

She knew ways to move about the lake so no one could see her. Even binoculars couldn't follow her as she ducked between trees and under plants that needed pruning.

At last she hid her little boat and made her way up stone steps to a cabin she'd only visited twice before. It wasn't one she usually took care of so no one would know she'd be there. But she knew it was empty, the owners wouldn't be back for weeks and she knew where the key was hidden.

She didn't turn on the lights. Instead, she sat down in front of the glass window, phone at her side, and watched the lake. There wasn't much activity and she thought that fear had taken over everyone. For all that her mother had been locked in a trunk long ago, the discovery was new. The fear was new.

At eleven she dozed off and woke at one with a jolt. Since ten she'd had no calls, but several texts and emails.

None of them were from Nate or Rowan, Elaine or her father, so she ignored them.

She wanted to call Nate but she didn't want to wake him. At least she hoped he was sleeping somewhere.

As she fumbled her way to bed, she wondered what was going on. Had one of the visitors to her house stolen the Chinese bowl? What made Nate ask about it? Was it related to her mother's murder?

She didn't sleep well and woke early. She managed to occupy herself until 10:00 a.m., then she left. She docked her boat at her house and went up the stairs. Right away she saw that Nate hadn't been there.

She called him and got a message that his voice mailbox was full.

It took some doing but she made herself calm down. She ate a portion of one of the casseroles and tried to think about what to do. If these were normal circumstances, she'd call Frank. But he wasn't here. She couldn't call her dad. He was under enough stress without her adding to it.

She drove to the sheriff's office. *Calm*, she told herself. *Don't panic, don't cause anyone else to panic.* Nate had probably slept in one of the jail cells. He's probably just fine—and he'd bawl her out for showing up.

She hoped that was what would happen!

The office was busy—and Della was running it. She was barking orders at one of the young deputies. When she saw Terri, she said, "Where is he?"

Terri put on her best fake smile. "At home reading Uncle Frank's files. He won't be in until later. He sent me here to get something." She tried to look exasperated. "But he didn't tell me what it was. You have any idea what he needs?"

Della stared at Terri for a full ten seconds before responding. "I gave him a package from his mother. It was a book."

"Other than that," Terri said. How did she pull this off without upsetting anyone? Should she say, *I think Nate is missing? I think he found something and went after it?* Would gossipy Della tell the press? The headlines would be Chain Saw Killer on the Loose. "What else?"

Della wasn't one to let go of the topic. "He was really, really interested in the book. He went outside to make a call. He didn't tell me who it was or what it was about but I saw that it was a Connecticut area code. Then he called you and asked who all the people were who went to your house."

Terri's fists clenched so hard her nails bit into the palms. Della the snoop. Della the spy. "Where's the book?"

Della had it on her desk. It was a thick volume about Chinese antiques.

Terri tried to keep her eyes from widening. "This is probably what he wants. Thanks." She started out the door but turned back. Della was staring at her, calculating. "You'd better not say anything about—"

Della cut her off. "I'm a deputy now. The days of this town getting free information out of me are *over*!"

That's one way to look at it, Terri thought but didn't say. She just nodded in agreement and hurried out of the office, the big book tucked under her arm. She drove down the road, then pulled to the side before she opened the book.

It took only minutes to find what Nate had seen. There was a full-page photo of her Chinese bowl. Not one like it but *hers*. The dent in the base was clearly visible.

Under the photo, the caption explained that the bowl was old, rare and valuable.

What interested Terri was that in the margin was a

handwritten name—Monroe—and a phone number. She guessed that the area code was for Connecticut. Della must have been so busy bossing the poor deputies around that she'd missed seeing the notation.

Terri called and asked for a person by that name. Monroe turned out to be the curator of a small museum.

He told her she was the second person to call him that day to ask about the bowl. Yes, it was a man who'd called, said he was the sheriff of a town in Virginia. The bowl had been stolen and Mr. Monroe gave her the date. Terri thanked him and hung up.

She sat there looking out the windshield. The bowl had been stolen two years before her mother arrived at Lake Kissel. Is that theft what caused her mother's death? She was killed over a piece of silver? Was she the one who stole it? Did she run away to escape being caught? Or did someone else steal it and give it to her mother? Whatever happened, the silver bowl had ended up in her mother's possession—and had passed to her father.

After his wife ran off—or so Brody thought—he couldn't bear to look at anything that had belonged to her. He'd taken everything she'd owned to a Goodwill store. It wasn't until years later, when his sister moved out, that they discovered that she had saved the bowl. They found it shoved to the back of a top shelf of a closet. Brody had wanted to set fire to it and melt it, but Terri wouldn't let him. She put it back where they'd found it and didn't bring it out until her guilt about Stacy was eating at her. After all, she'd been living with Stacy's fiancé. The least she could do was help her with her booth.

Terri looked down at the picture. Based on Nate's calls to her and the museum curator, Terri was sure that wherever Nate was now had something to do with the silver bowl. And it looked like someone else had found it and taken it.

"I need help," Terri whispered—and she knew who she had to ask. Billy. He owed her.

She didn't know for sure where he was staying but it was probably at the house his family still owned. The house where Stacy had so lovingly made an office for Nate. She'd heard that Stacy had "sold" the furniture she'd chosen for Nate and that he had paid for. She sold each item for pennies. Not even nickels were allowed. The big, expensive desk went for six cents. Stacy had dropped all the copper coins into a little velvet bag and left it on the floor of what would have been Nate's office.

But maybe that was just gossip, Terri thought.

As Terri drove through Summer Hill to Thorndyke House she knew she was postponing dealing with the horror of her mother's death. She wasn't allowing herself to think about what her mother had been through. Didn't want to visualize how she must have been pulled away from her sleeping two-year-old daughter. Was she forced to write a farewell note? Had she begged, pleaded? Had she…?

Terri pulled into the driveway of the house and put her head on the steering wheel. She couldn't allow herself to think about any of that now. If she did, she'd be like her father and collapse.

Right now she needed to find Nate. Or Rowan. Needed to… To DO something. Anything. Just keep going. Don't stop.

When she heard a lawn mower, she looked up to see Billy pushing it. His T-shirt was so sweaty he may as well have been shirtless. *Stayed in shape*, she thought as she put her hand out the window to wave to him.

But he didn't see her because three young women came around the side. One of them was carrying a tray of glasses of lemonade. Another had a basket full of cookies. All of them wore short shorts and tank tops.

Billy was ignoring them but then one of the girls stepped in front of the lawn mower and he had to swerve sideways. He turned the machine off. "Melissa!" he said. "I could have hit you. Go sit on the porch. I—"

When he saw Terri, he looked relieved. She motioned for him to get in the car with her.

As Billy began running, he grabbed two glasses of lemonade, half a dozen cookies, and stuck out his elbow to hook his shirt off a fence post.

Terri flung the car door open. He slid in, handed her a big glass and closed the door.

As Terri backed out of the drive, the girls were glaring at her. "More people who hate me," she muttered.

"And again it's my fault." He handed her a cookie, which she devoured in two bites. "I see you're still always hungry. So where are we going?"

"I'm trying to find Nate."

"From the gossip I heard, you two are conjoined twins. Did you really live together while he was engaged to Stacy?"

"Yes. And the gossip I heard about you is that you're going to be the new preacher at St. Anne's."

"True."

She glanced at him. "I think that profession suits you. You'll…for my mother?"

"Yes," he said solemnly. "I will conduct the service."

For a moment they were silent. "You like this guy, huh?" he asked.

"I do."

"Save it for later."

"What?"

"The 'I do.' Save it for the ceremony that I'll perform for you two."

She gave a little laugh.

"So tell me what's going on. Are we playing detective?"

"Maybe." As quickly as she could, she told him about Nate's call and the missing silver bowl.

"With the FBI here, it could be that they discovered an unrelated robbery."

Her expression told him what she thought of that idea.

"Yeah, I don't believe it either."

Terri pulled into the parking lot by the clubhouse. "I want to know what Anna's heard, then you and I are going to check cabins." She drained the last of her lemonade.

Billy stopped her as she started to open the door. "Terri, I want to tell you that I'm sorry for what happened. I've been talking to people and I've heard what you've been through because of me. I should have contacted you but I was wallowing in self-pity. I was a kid and about to be a father."

"It's okay," she said. "It's over now."

"But it isn't really. This town seems to think I'm a…a…"

"A saint?" she said. "The Great Billy Thorndyke."

He was looking at her as though he was understanding something. "It wouldn't have worked with us, would it?"

"No. I saw that when you were here the other day. We've become different people. But then, I guess we always were. Youth and hormones kept us together."

"You were a challenge to me."

"I was the only girl who didn't run after you."

Billy was silent for a moment. "I hear Nate and you save lives every day."

"Not quite, but Nate reacts well to emergencies. He thinks quickly. He can fix anything. Boat motors and kids' bikes and roofs. And he can cook. And people really like him. And he—" She broke off, her face turning red.

"I'm glad for you. Very happy that you found each other." Billy kissed her cheek, then got out of the car.

"Stacy's not," she said over her shoulder as they went to the clubhouse.

With a laugh, Billy opened the door into the office.

Anna didn't look up. "I don't know anything. Go ask Nate."

"We can't find him," Terri said.

Anna looked up at them in relief.

"Been bad here?" Billy asked.

"Worse than you can imagine. I don't know why people think the FBI reports directly to me. I would close up the office but..." She shrugged.

"I know. People who live here need looking after." Billy sounded reassuring.

"The minute after they found the car it was in the news." Anna pushed aside a stack of papers. "So far, we've had eight people pack up and leave. They said they wouldn't stay where there was a serial killer on the loose."

"This happened years ago!" Terri said.

"I told them that but they wouldn't listen."

Terri was frowning. "Has anything unusual happened? Other than morons being themselves, that is."

"Nothing. I just listen and act like I understand their fear. We had six people call and cancel their reservations. What's this about Nate? I heard he's now the sheriff. Bet Frank loves that!"

"Can you print out a list of who is still here?" Terri asked.

"Sure." Anna turned to her computer. Minutes later, she held out a list. They had a rule that even people who owned a cabin needed to tell the office when they arrived and left. If nothing else, it was for fire safety. "Oh wait. This couple left this morning." She crossed off names.

"That's a lot of empty cabins."

"And all out of fear that a killer might be on the loose," Billy muttered, and they turned to leave.

"Except for the rats," Anna said, and they looked at her. "The tenants in Mr. Owens's cabin said they'd had an invasion of rats during the night. Tore up things and left a mess."

"Sure it wasn't raccoons?" Terri asked.

"Who knows? Whatever it was, the renters were angry and said they wanted their money back. I called Mr. Owens and asked him what he wanted to do. I suggested he double the rent for the cabin and I'd put a reporter on an expense account in there."

"You did what?" Terri asked.

Billy put his hand on her shoulder. "What did Mr. Owens say?"

Anna looked at Billy. "He was very nice, but then he always is. Spends every August here. He said he couldn't stand to hear what was happening at dear Lake Kissel and he said he'd take care of it in person. Wouldn't even let me hire someone to clean it up. I don't know how he got here so fast since he lives in Connecticut. But, if there's food rotting it'll draw even more rats."

Neither Terri nor Billy gave a hint that Connecticut meant anything to them. "We'll take care of it," Terri managed to say before they left the office.

When they got to the car, Billy insisted that he drive.

He'd trust Terri with his life in a boat but not in a car. "Just direct me and we'll go to the cabin."

"It's probably nothing," she said as she got in the passenger seat. "A coincidence."

"I'm sure you're right. So tell me about Mr. Owens."

"I don't know much. He's a handsome, middle-aged man. When he first arrived I was a kid but even I saw the way the women went after him. He wanted nothing to do with them. Dad and I used to laugh about it."

"Who does he socialize with?"

"I have no idea. I don't remember ever seeing him at any of the community get-togethers. One time Dad said if everyone was like Mr. Owens our lives would be a lot easier."

"But he came by your house yesterday?"

"Yes, he did. He brought some pastries from the Summer Hill bakery. I didn't spend any time with him because everyone wanted my attention." She looked at Billy. "He could have stolen the bag with the bowl in it but so could have lots of people."

Billy was quiet for a while. "So this man usually comes only in August?"

"Yes." She looked at him. "But he's here now. Because of rats that frightened his tenants away."

"Rats that appeared just when a car was found in a lake."

"And the newspapers blasted it all over the country." Terri's heart was beginning to pound.

"And as antisocial as he is, he showed up at your house."

"And said nothing to anyone that I saw," Terri said.

For a second, their eyes locked, then Billy looked back at the road that encircled the lake. "Got somewhere we can park where we won't be seen?"

"Yes." She pointed the way to an empty cabin and Billy pulled into the driveway.

"Guess it would be pointless to—" He halted when Terri hopped out of the car. "To stay here," he finished.

Terri knew a back way to get to the Owens cabin. She climbed over a fence. Straddling it, she saw Billy hesitate. "Come on!"

"I'm saying a prayer of forgiveness. I hope my fellow parishioners don't see me."

Terri nodded toward the nearby cabin. "She's a weekend widow. She'll forgive you *anything*."

Billy scurried over the fence so quickly Terri laughed.

"Stacy Hartman is available, you know."

"Not my type. She's too perfect." He smiled in a way that let her know he was thinking of their past.

"Does that mean I'm not perfect?"

Billy was out of breath. "You, dear Terri, are far and away from being perfect."

She snorted at that, then motioned for him to be quiet and follow her. They were near Mr. Owens's cabin.

Since her father and his partner had built many of the houses, she knew the floor plans. The biggest windows looked out to the water, but there were side windows. They'd be able to see in but probably not be seen.

"Wait!" Billy said as they reached the cabin. He leaned against a wall. "Do you know what I had to do to get a position at St. Anne's? Summer Hill is a coveted site. If anyone saw me now I'd be sent to some remote island."

"Where they dance in grass skirts? Stop complaining and let's go. Say nothing."

With a roll of his eyes, he followed her around to the front of the cabin.

They couldn't see all of the big room, but they did see

Nate. He was sitting in a chair, looking quite calm, as though he was on alert about something.

Standing over him was a huge man with a pockmarked and scarred face. He had a flattened, distorted nose like a prizefighter.

"I think his hands are tied," Terri whispered. She tried the knob to the side door just enough to see that it was unlocked. "I'm going in."

Before Billy could stop her, she picked up a rock and threw it through the window.

Inside the house, both men turned to the sound and in the seconds their attention was on the shattered glass, Terri ran through the door. She grabbed a metal ornament off a shelf by the door and drew back to throw it.

But Nate leaped up from the chair and grabbed her wrist.

In the next second, the side door opened and Rowan and two men in FBI jackets burst into the room, guns drawn and aimed at Terri.

"It's okay." Nate took what was a bronze dog out of Terri's hand and put it back on the shelf. Then he enveloped Terri in his arms. "Everything is all right."

She pushed away from him, anger running through her. "Don't you patronize me, you ungrateful bastard. We've been searching for you. You disappeared and we saw you through the window and thought you were being held hostage. We—"

"Is 'we' you and St. Billy?"

"None other," Billy said with a grin. "Hope no one minds but I need to sit down. This has been too much excitement for me. Oh! Hello. I didn't see you there. I'm William Thorndyke, soon to be pastor of St. Anne's. I think. After today I may be thrown out of the country."

He looked at Rowan and the two agents who were sheathing their weapons.

Sitting in a chair was an older woman, slim and elegant. Her eyes were zeroed in on Terri.

Terri jerked away from Nate's grip. Anger was saving her from dissolving into a lump of embarrassment. "You could have called," she said through her teeth. "But you're here having a party."

"Party! I haven't slept in—"

Rowan cleared his throat loudly. "Terri, may I introduce you to your grandmother, Mrs. Carolyn Fornell?"

It was all too much for Terri. Finding her mother's body, dealing with the press, fending off questions, trying to stay strong while everyone she loved seemed to disappear—her father, Frank, Nate—it was more than she could handle.

Her legs went first, then her head seemed to spin round and round. "Grandmother," she whispered.

Nate caught her before she went down.

Chapter 24

When Terri woke, she was in her own bed and it was early morning. It looked like she'd slept through the night.

There was a dent in the pillow beside her. It seemed like Nate had slept there, but he was gone.

She sat up in bed, blinking, rubbing her eyes and trying to remember what had happened in the last few days. What was real and what had she imagined? Her mother found in the trunk of a car. Murdered. She—

The door opened and Nate came in carrying a tray of food. "Thought you'd be awake. Want some bacon and eggs? Or how about some casseroles? I put eight varieties on this one plate. Think you can handle them?"

"I could eat a shark, teeth and all. I'll eat while you talk."

He put the tray across her legs. "That silver bowl—" He halted. "You know what? I think I should let your grandmother tell you."

Terri paused with the fork halfway to her mouth. "I thought maybe I dreamed her."

Nate went to the door and opened it. She must have been waiting outside as Carolyn Fornell came in right away. Nate motioned her to a chair beside the bed.

She and Terri looked at each other in wonder.

"You look like my Leelee," Carolyn whispered.

Terri started to put the tray aside, but Carolyn stopped her.

"Please, go ahead and eat. If you are as active as my daughter, then I'm sure you're starving. She ate huge amounts but never gained an ounce."

"She burns it off," Nate said. "She drives her boat like a maniac and never walks if she can run. She throws rope like a sailor and—"

Both women were staring at him.

"I, uh, I think I'll leave you two alone." He left and closed the door behind him.

"Where do I begin?" Carolyn asked.

Terri picked up her fork. "Why my mother felt she had to run away from her family." There was anger in Terri's voice.

For a moment, Carolyn blinked back tears. "You are as direct as my daughter. She wasn't one for secrets. If she didn't like something or someone, she told them so." Carolyn took a breath. "She was the opposite of her brother, Kenneth."

"Can I take it that we know him as Mr. Owens?"

"Yes." Carolyn got up, went to the window, opened the curtains, then turned back to Terri. "This isn't easy for me. They're both my children and I love them. I really *tried* to be equal. But Leelee was so...so *likable*. She was funny and smart and she was always getting into trouble. When she was fifteen, she cut classes and ran off to New York to see a show. She drove a car when she was fourteen. On and on. But her father and I had trouble punishing her. She came up with such wonderful excuses and told glorious stories about what she'd seen and done. She—" Carolyn waved her hand. "I must get to the facts. That young FBI man has told me I must remember it all."

"Rowan."

"I've met his parents."

"Everyone has," Terri said.

Carolyn sat on the soft chair in the corner. She looked like she'd rather do anything on earth than tell her story. "My son. He was...is... I don't know how to describe him. He never did anything wrong. His room was always tidy and clean. He made straight As in school. He never got into any trouble. But..."

"No one liked him," Terri said. "We have people here like that." She didn't say that Mr. Owens had been one of them. Here year after year but never made any friends.

"Your father told me that you take care of this place almost single-handedly."

"I have help."

Carolyn looked out the window for a moment. "That's just what Leelee would have said. She ran clubs and charities in high school and college but never bragged on herself. She—" Carolyn paused, then looked at Terri. "My late husband and I refused to believe what she told us about the things Kenneth did. I think we knew but we didn't want to. Does that make sense?"

"Yes. Where is he now?"

"In...in prison. Or jail. I don't know. Rowan took him away. There will be a trial and..."

"We'll be with you," Terri said.

Carolyn stood up. "I need to lie down now. Perhaps later we can get to know each other." Before Terri could speak again, she left the room.

Nate entered as soon as she was gone. "Did she tell you what's happened?"

"Not much."

Nate took the tray, set it on the chest of drawers, got into bed beside her and drew her head to his shoulder. "Want me to tell you what I know?"

She nodded against him.

"Kenneth was born two years after Leslie and—"

"Leelee. My grandmother calls her Leelee. I like that."

"All right. Leelee. Seems that Kenneth—never called by any affectionate nickname that I heard—was one of those kids who was obedient and kind to adults but—"

"A monster to his peers."

"Exactly. He more or less tortured his sister, and he was crazy jealous of her. I mean to the point of insanity. When some distant relative died and left his sister an antique Chinese bowl, Kenneth pretty much lost his mind."

"He wasn't left anything?"

"That's just what I asked. Yes, he was. A Ming dynasty vase. But Kenneth wanted the bowl. Mind you, this happened after Leelee had graduated from college. She said she was sick of fighting with him so she anonymously donated the bowl to a local museum."

"And he stole it?"

"That's right. Kenneth took it. Not sure the how of it matters."

"I guess my mother knew it was her brother who took it."

"She did. And she searched his room until she found

it. He told us that. Said she 'stole' it from him, said it was his."

"Let me guess. She gave it away so she lost possession of it, so when he took it back, it was his."

"Clever girl." He kissed her forehead. "The conjecture is that Leelee was so afraid of Kenneth's revenge, of his rage, that she ran. Disappeared. She left home with just one suitcase and got on a bus."

"And stopped in Lake Kissel, Virginia."

"And met your father and that was it."

Terri took a while to let this sink in. "Her brother came after her."

"There was a photo of the ground-breaking ceremony of the planned community and Leelee was in it. The article was picked up by some major newspapers as a feel-good piece and Kenneth saw it."

Nate swiped Terri's hair from her forehead and kissed it. "I haven't heard all the facts. Kenneth is with Rowan now and being interrogated, but I know Kenneth showed up here and went to see his sister."

"And me."

"Yes. Two-year-old you. The bowl was on the coffee table and…" Nate put both arms around Terri. "They fought and he hit her with the bowl. It didn't…" Nate took a breath. "It didn't kill her, just knocked her unconscious. But I guess he knew that when she woke up, she'd turn him in to the police."

"He tied her up and gagged her," Terri whispered.

"He's a big guy and he carried her to her car and dumped her in the trunk. I don't think he knew what to do next. He hadn't really planned it. Anyway, it was storming outside and he drove to the big pier. We think he meant to drive off but the old posts cracked. Maybe that gave him an idea."

"So he stole the underwater chain saw."

"Right. Your dad's office was close by and it was empty."

"Everyone was out taking care of the storm."

"They were. Kenneth stole the saw and the handcuffs and some duct tape, then went back to the car. He opened the trunk and saw that Summer Hill was beginning to wake up. The rain was coming down hard then. He handcuffed her, taped her ankles and—"

"I know," Terri said. The tears were beginning to come. "She struggled while he went underwater and cut the posts."

Nate held her tightly.

She pushed away from him. "He came back and bought a cabin here! He was here every year. He was watching and listening."

"Yes," Nate said. "He was. We think he was trying to find the bowl."

"Dad was so angry that he got rid of all Mom's things. But Aunt Aggie hid the bowl." She looked at Nate. "Was he that greedy? He wanted to sell it? He needed money? After all these years, it wasn't like it was evidence."

"But it was," Nate said. "That's what I found out from the museum curator. The bowl is two parts. The top with the dragon screws off. When Kenneth hit Leelee, he used only the upper half of the bowl. And remember your grandmother said he was tidy? Seems that after he hit her, he screwed the two halves back together."

"Are you saying…?" Her eyes opened wide.

"Inside the bowl are fingerprints and hair and…" He

shrugged. "Other stuff. It contains evidence of what he did to your mother."

Terri flopped back against the bed.

For a while, they sat together, holding each other.

Nate spoke first. "Do you realize that it's over?"

"Over? I think it has just begun. There will be a trial. My grandmother said—" She looked up at him. "I have a grandmother."

"Yes you do and she's a very nice lady. When her son left her house so abruptly, suitcase in hand, she knew something had happened. She searched his computer and found the news about the car being brought up."

"Maybe the reporters did us a favor."

"I wouldn't go that far. Are you ready to greet the world? Thorndyke has already called twice this morning to ask if you're all right."

"And what did you tell him?"

"That you're with me so of course you're the best you can be."

Terri laughed, but she made no move toward getting out of bed. "Everything has changed, hasn't it?"

"More than you know."

"What does that mean?"

"I sort of blackmailed Della. I told her that if she wanted to stay my deputy, she had to change the gossip about you."

"Gossip?" Terri was pushing him to elaborate.

"First of all, your mother running off with another man. She's the one who fanned those flames so *she* had to change it. Turn it all around."

"She agreed?"

Nate swallowed. "Della said… No, I shouldn't tell that."

"What?" Her question was a command.

Nate rolled his eyes. "Della ordered a dozen DNA kits. She said that if anyone ever again said something bad about Leslie Rayburn, she'd collect samples from cups, tissues, whatever, and she'd publicly announce who fathered what kid."

"That's terrible and probably illegal." Terri tried to suppress a laugh but couldn't.

"Remember Ryan Murphy?"

"How could I forget?" Terri said.

"Della found him and she's paying for him and his family to fly here for a three-day vacation at beautiful Lake Kissel with the stipulation that he confess the truth of what he and Hector said to you back in high school. What caused you to strike out."

"He won't like doing that."

"I'm happy to say that you're wrong about that. He is now the father of two little girls and has a better understanding of what happened that day. He said he looks forward to setting the record straight."

When Terri didn't reply, he pulled back to look at her. "You okay?"

She nodded, then whispered, "Billy?"

"He and Kris Lennon are going to tell everyone the truth."

Terry drew in her breath. "He might lose his job. If he isn't the pastor of St. Anne's, people will blame *me*."

"Remember Mr. Cresnor? Seems that he made some calls—and I think some donations. Your yo-yo boy's job is safe. I think the official stance is that only a sinner can truly understand the sins of others."

"Poor Billy. That will hurt him."

Nate kissed her. "That you think of others before yourself is only one of the reasons I love you."

She moved her leg over his.

"Oh no!" he said. "The temptation of your legs is too much for me to resist."

She was kissing his neck.

"Rowan bought Stanton House from the mayor."

"No." Her kisses were moving downward.

"He's hired Stacy to oversee the restoration and to decorate the place. Knowing those two, the whole house will be white."

Terri's face disappeared under the covers. "Anything else?"

"That about covers it. But you need to—" He drew in his breath.

"I guess it won't matter if we're late," he murmured, then closed his eyes.

* * * * *